Reign of Royal

Samantha Barrett

Reign Of Royal

Memento Mori

Book One

Samantha Barrett

Memento

Author Note

This book is set 19 years after the final book in the Murdoch mafia, it is not needed to read the OG's but for better character development and world-building, it is highly recommended that you read Stalemate. It is a novella that will help bridge the gap between both series to help you keep up with the scenes of the past that will occur throughout this book and the next ones.

This book contains violence, explicit sexual acts, and language that may offend. Kidnapping and many other triggers such as torture, death and gruesome scenes.
If those are triggers for you then I recommend closing this book and moving on to another amazing read.
But, if you are down with the get down and want to get fucked hard and have your heart shattered and ripped out of your fucking chest then this is the book for you babes.
Welcome to the *Next Generation* of Murdochs that fuck harder and play dirtier than the OG's.

For my little warrior princess,

My demon, you are my mini me in every sense of the word. I love you more than you will ever comprehend. You are strong, sassy and unapologetically you. I'm so proud of the strength you have shown through these battles that tried to tear you down, you my girl are an inspiration!

Bambo loves you to the moon and beyond my baby.

Memento Mori

(Latin for 'remember that you [have to] die') is ***an artistic or symbolic trope acting as a reminder of the inevitability of death.***

Who Are They?

When the card is dropped, you are marked.
There is no escaping *them*, they come for their prey and will hunt until your blood soaks the ground beneath your cold lifeless body. They are the new generation and they have something to prove. They are hungry to show the OG's that they are ready to lead, except, the crowned heir got tired of waiting and began the new generation under the name of *Memento Mori* for he is the bringer of death.
The King of Clubs belongs to the heir.
The princess owns the Queen of Hearts.
Jack of Spades represents the coming Chaos.
Ace of Diamonds is for the Havoc.

Prologue

ROYAL

Past...

I watch them follow like the fucking sheep they are, the sight disgusts me, when will these simple-minded nobodies realize that they are nothing, no one will remember their names when they are buried under a pile of dirt because they never stood out. They never impacted anyone or this world because they chose to conform and fall into line like the good fucking sheep they are. I'll never conform or be what society tells me to be, I'm not like *them*. I'm the son of the Don and son of the heiress who owns all of Miami. My grandfather made sure my dad wouldn't be able to cut me out, Miami is mine the second I turn twenty-one there isn't a fucking thing Bishop Murdoch can do about it.

"Yo, Tyson just found his card." I turn to where Chaos is pointing and sure enough, Tyson Grundall stands there pale and shaken as he stares down at the King of Clubs he has clutched in his hand. We watch as he turns the card over and visibly shakes when he reads the words written on the back, *Memento Mori*. He darts his gaze around the crowded halls, the moment his dull brown eyes land on us, he jerks back a step shaking his head trying to deny that this is happening.

Dumb fuck, everyone here at UNLV knows *we* are not to be messed with. Tyson thought he could snitch, well, he is about to learn that snitches get stitches and wind up in ditches and there is no one here that can *or* will save him from us.

Students used to call us the four horsemen until Sin nixed that shit, she hates that she is underestimated for not having a cock. Truth is, Chanel is fucking lethal and a dead shot. Uncle Vincent made sure she could hit any target he put in front of her before she was twelve. The girl is fucking crazy and none of us dare to challenge her, she isn't just good with guns the crazy bitch has blades stashed all over her body. Havoc and Chaos are the brutes, they love to use their fists and call Sin and me pussy's for using guns. Havoc says he loves feeling his victim's bones break beneath his fists, they're both fucking out of their minds and I love it.

As for me, I choose to do things slowly, I love to hunt my prey and taunt them. I want them to know I'm coming but never when or where. I love to watch them slowly lose their minds as they try to prepare for my attack. It gets me fucking hard knowing they are scared, Tyson has known this has been coming for weeks, and receiving his card today tells him he has less than five days before I come for him. I smirk as he shoots me one last pleading look, slams his locker closed then races down the hallway away from us.

"He's gonna run." Chaos sing songs from beside me.

"Nah, he's gonna call the cops." Havoc adds from my other side.

I peer over my shoulder when I hear Sin snort, the three of us eye her and wait for the only female we have allowed close to us to speak. She may be blood but, that isn't what earned her a place among us, her fierce loyalty and unwavering trust in us, is what cemented her place at my side as my second. She and I have always been close, in fact, I'm closer to her than the twins.

"The little bitch is going to hold up in his room and call his mommy to come save his ass." I chuckle, she's right. Tyson's mother is the sheriff in the local county and he thinks he is untouchable for that reason, the fucker was so wrong. No one is safe from us, when the card is given there is no one that can save you from the wrath that awaits. My phone begins to vibrate in my pocket drawing my attention, I pull it out and grit my teeth the moment I see it's my father calling. I shoot the other three a look that they all recognize, Sin nods and leads the twins away as I slip into an empty classroom and answer the call.

"Father, what a pleasant surprise." I smirk when I hear him growl.

"Don't fuck with me you little shit." I clench my phone so tight I fear I may just snap it, he still thinks I'm ten years old and can reprimand me like I am child. "Reroute that fucking ship and get it back here, it wasn't just my guns on there, your Aunt Koby's shit is on it as well."

I can't keep the smile off my face, I was wondering how long it would take for him to figure out it was me that rerouted the cargo ship. "Why do you always blame me?" I defend.

"Kiara!" He roars so loud I have to pull the phone away from my ear.

"What is it?" I hear my mom ask.

"Your son is fucking with my business again and I've had enough of his fucking tantrums, he's a pain in my ass–."

"Did you just call my baby boy a *pain in your ass*?" I bite down on my fist to keep myself from laughing, my dad may be the Don and the boss of everything in New York but even he answers to someone higher, I bet he never expected that boss to be his own wife.

"Baby–."

Mom cuts him off before he can finish. "Put the call on speaker now." A second passes before my mom speaks. "Royal, my sweet boy." I smile, my mom is my only weakness in this world. "What did you do to your father, this time?"

"Mom, I didn't do anything–."

"He's full of shit, he sent my cargo ship back to Russia." Dad shouts.

"Did not!" I say.

"Yes, the fuck you did." He snaps.

"Enough." Mom shouts, I clamp my mouth closed. Dad doesn't scare me *but* mom does, the woman can go from zero to a hundred in a nanosecond, she even tried to shoot my dad when I was fourteen. She caught him teaching me how to cut out the tongue of a snitch in the bunker back home and nearly shot him for that. "Royal." I tense at the firm tone of her voice. "Fix whatever it is that you did."

"But–."

She cuts me off. "I said fix it." Gritting my teeth I nod even though she can't see me. "Bishop, fix whatever it is that you did in order for our son to retaliate."

I can picture my dad gaping at my mom and smirk, I love watching him lose a fight with her. "I didn't do shit to him."

"Mommy, he's lying." I say sweetly, he begins to curse loudly in the background, I hear her sigh tiredly and that sound is the only reason I relent. "Fine, I'll have the ship back in the harbor by nightfall."

"Thank you." She says.

"But dad can't stop me from going to grandpas for spring break, he can cancel my cards and cut me off but I'm still going to Miami!" The shocked gasp that sounds through the phone tells me my mom had no idea that my dad forbid me from going to see my grandfather.

"You cut my son off?" She shouts, I startle, beginning to feel slightly bad for my dad right now.

"I had to, he is too young to take over and I don't give a fuck what you or your father say, he's my son too."

Oh shit. I shake my head, dad knows better than anyone not to pull the *my son* card on my mom, she never takes it well.

"He grew inside me, I birthed him and I fed him from my breast." I cringe in disgust not needing to hear that shit. "He is my baby, if he wants to see his grandfather then by fucking God you will let him. If his credit cards are not activated again by the end of the day your dick will pay the price."

"Oh for fuck sakes." I snarl.

"Watch your mouth." I roll my eyes.

"Sorry mom." I mumble thoroughly chastised, even at twenty years old my mother hates me cussing.

"Go to class baby, I'll deal with your father and rest assured I'll arrange with your grandfather for you to join him on spring break–."

Before she can finish dad cuts in, I grit my teeth expecting him to lecture me like he always does. "I know I'm hard on you, I don't mean to be. I just want to keep you safe Royal, I never knew what fear was until you were born, I fear anything that could take you from me and... Fuck, I know I'm not the best dad but I'm trying."

I admit, I'm choked up. My dad never expresses his feelings so hearing him speak freely and openly like this shocks the fuck out of me.

"You are a good dad, we're just not like most fathers and sons." I say honestly.

He scoffs. "Yeah, most sons don't liquidate their father's assets and transfer them to their cousins." I laugh remembering how Sin, me and the twins were pissed at our parents last year so we liquidated one of their big investment companies and gave the money to our other cousins. Dad was pissed.

"I did you a favor, you hated that company." I defend.

"Yeah well, just get the ship back and I'll reactivate your cards."

"I will." I'm about to end the call but he speaks again.

"Royal?"

"Yeah, dad?"

"Everything, and I do mean everything I do is for you and your mother, this will all be yours but not until you are ready."

"Yeah, I know." I say with a sigh.

"I love you, kid."

I smile, it's not often my dad says those words. "Love you too, old man." I quickly end the call before he can yell at me again, dad hates being reminded that he is aging, you best believe I love reminding him about it every chance I get.

Now, it's time for me to hunt Tyson down and show him what *Memento Mori* means.

Chapter One

ROYAL

Present...

I'm so fucking over having to do this school shit, Dad refused to allow us to join the family business and said we all had to go to college!

Why would the heirs to the biggest mafia family in the continental US have to go to college, you ask?

Because our moms told our dads they didn't want us involved in the business and wanted us to be free to choose what we want to do. We may be cousins, but we are close like siblings, well, at least the four of us are as opposed to our others. We all applied to the same college and given who we are, we knew we would get in, if not on merit our parents would have paid our way in.

"Stop fucking pouting, we have six months of school left and then we're out of here." I glare at the asshole as he reclines back on my bed, tosses a football into the air then catches it.

Unlike me, Chaos doesn't want to join the family business, he wants to go pro and get drafted into the NFL.

"Fuck you! None of this shit is gonna matter when I take over." I state in a matter-of-fact tone, it's true what I say. I am the one who is going to take over and lead this family when my dad steps down.

"Calm down Royal, we all know you're the future King of the family and all that shit." I glare at Havoc as he saunters back into the room with a towel wrapped around his waist water dripping everywhere.

"You're leaving footprints on my carpet!" I scold. The asshole comes closer and shakes his hair, flicking water droplets all over me, Chaos laughs at his stupid ass twin, I strike out and punch the asshole in the arm.

"You sound like Aunt Ally; *you boys stop playing ball in the house.*" We all laugh at his impression of our aunt. We haven't been home in a long time, the last time was months ago to celebrate Meela graduating and becoming a doctor, she is crazy fucking smart but due to the age gap between her and the four of us we never really hung out much. Destiny is three years younger than us, she's seventeen. Uncle Gage and Aunt Anya are pushing her to become a lawyer but Dest isn't having any of that and wants to be an MMA fighter, we all know secretly Uncle G is thrilled at the idea. Nytress and Unique are fifteen and sixteen and only care about cheerleading, Uncle Rook is trying to convince them that they don't need college and to stay home with him. Honestly, my poor cousins are going to rebel so hard when they finally get their freedom from their dad.

The door to my dorm bursts open and Chanel rushes in with a panicked look in her eyes, Havoc, Chaos, and I are on her in seconds.

"What happened?"

"Who did it?"

"Are you hurt?" We all ask at the same time, she shakes her head and pushes through us and rushes to my bedside table, grabs the remote and flicks the TV on turning it straight to the news.

"Chanel—."

She cuts me off. "Shut up and listen Royal." She turns the volume up and the three of them creep in closer to see what has her panties in a twist.

"Just in, the plane that alleged mafia boss, Bishop Murdoch and his brothers, King, Knight, Rook, Gage, and his brother-in-law Vincent Murelo were traveling on from Miami to New York has gone down." My heart stops. *"Police and fire were first to the scene and sources say the bodies of the six passengers have not been located leaving the other four crew members injured and in critical care. The captain and co-captain didn't make it, now over to Jenny who has the local police chief with her, Jenny."* The camera switches over to another woman who stands with the wrecked plane at her back and a man in a police uniform beside her.

"Thank you, Kelly, I'm here with police chief Lawrance. What can you tell us about the missing passengers?"

"We've found five sets of tire tracks that come in one way and out another. We believe that the six passengers have been taken and that this isn't some random crash, we believe this flight was targeted—. My cell ringing pulls me away from the TV, when I see my mom's name, I quickly answer it.

"Mom, what the hell is going on?" I snap instead of a greeting.

"Royal, it's your father–." My mom is one of the toughest people I know and she isn't scared of shit, she can make my father bend to her will with one look. Hearing the fear in her voice has me clutching the phone so tight I fear I'll snap it. When the others crowd around me, I put it on speakerphone. "The plane went down and they–,"

"I know, we just saw it on the news," I say, cutting her off.

"You and your cousins need to get on the next flight out of Utah and come home." The four of us exchanged a loaded look before I ask.

"What the hell is going on mom? Tell me the truth." My voice is cold and emotionless, whenever I panic or worry, I'm somehow able to shut all my emotions off and feel nothing, it's a blessing for me and it will be a curse for the fuckers that took my father, I'll kill them all.

"I just received a video, your father and uncles have been taken by a cousin of mine I didn't even know existed."

"I thought Grandpa killed all your family?"

"We did as well son, apparently he missed one on *his* side and now he has come after us." Hearing her sniffle and the fact she is crying kills me to not be there with her.

"We'll kill the son of a bitch for thinking he could ever fuck with our family." Chaos snarls and the rest of us hum our agreement.

"That's all well and good, except the bastard is the Governor of Miami!" I shoot each of my cousins a look asking if they are ready for what is about to happen, each of them nod.

"We'll be on the next flight out." I growl.

"Royal?"

"Yeah, mom?"

"I won't survive losing him." She sobs, my mom loves my dad with every beat of her heart, their love makes me never want to settle for anything less. They have set the bar so high that I fear no woman will ever reach it which is why I have never tried to settle down.

"You won't have to, I'm my father's son and I swear to you, I'll burn the fucking city to the ground until I find the bastard who dared to fuck with us. We are Murdoch's and we never fucking give up!"

The four of us have barely spoken the whole way home, unlike the three of them I don't allow my emotions to control me, I use those feelings as fuel to anchor me. Some crumble under the pressure of grief but not me, my focus sharpens and everything else becomes white noise as I focus on my target and exact my revenge. Only then do I come out of my haze and focus again.

The car comes to a stop out front of my mom and dad's house, none of us move as we gaze up at the family home we all grew up in.

My aunts and uncles all have their own houses just down the hill, Dad wanted his siblings close so he built each of them houses here near his own and built a fence around the land to keep us all safe from his enemies. A lot of good that fence did when his enemy still managed to get his hands on him.

"If we don't go in, your mom will come get us." Chaos says from his seat across from me, sighing, I nod and get out knowing he's not wrong. The air is crisp and has a chill to it, the sun is out but not even that ball of fire can chase away the cold in the air. It feels like an omen, a warning if you will that death is in the air and knows our Don has fallen. I shake away that thought and clench my fists at my sides, my father hasn't fallen and I'll do everything in my power to make sure I bring him and all my uncles home. Chanel, Chaos and Havoc come to stand beside me.

"Whatever we have to do, wherever we have to go, we are with you always." I turn my head to the side and look down at my cousin, Sin keeps her gaze focused forward as she continues to speak. "We are *Memento Mori*." She looks up at me and the sinister look in her eyes tells me she is out for blood. "My father is the bloodhound, he is the number one assassin in the fucking world and this chump thinks he can take him from me. I am going to burn this mother fucker to the ground."

"No." I say firmly, her eyes narrow but I push on before she can continue. "We are going to dismantle his empire, we are going to take everything from him, break him down slowly, he will never see us coming. When he has nothing left, he will be the first to be delivered the *royal flush*." Her brows raise to her hairline, the twins whistle from beside me. We all agreed when we started leaving calling cards that we would never leave all four cards for someone–the royal flush. "It's time we broke our rule and made an exception for my mother's cousin."

"Agreed."

"Yes."

"Fuck yeah!" The three of them answer in unison. Before we can say anymore the front door opens, Aunt Koby and Aunt Ally step onto the porch, at the sight of their mother's red-rimmed eyes the twins take off and rush to their mom. To the outside world, they are seen as cold, uncaring and self-absorbed but in reality, they feel deeper than any of us. Being loved by Havoc and Chaos is for life, once they deem you loveable, they will never stop.

"I need to see my mom, she won't be taking this well." I nod as Sin heads toward the house, I take a final breath before following her. I've always wanted to lead this family and prove to my father that I am ready and good enough to take over from him but, I never wanted the power handed to me this way.

I say a quick hello to Aunt Ally who looks utterly distraught, her blue eyes are dull and filled with pain, out of all my aunts she is the most emotional, I look to Aunt Koby and decide to leave her with her boys as I go in search of my mom and the others. The moment I enter the living room I freeze, my mom is a wreck on the couch embracing my Aunt Carlina while Aunt Clare and Aunt Anya stand off to the side trying to keep themselves together. Nytress, Destiny and Unique are perched on the couch opposite my mom. Sin slides up next to me, no words need be spoken between us. We can read the room, we know our family is falling apart and it is going to take all of us to fix it.

My mom's gaze lifts to me and the moment she realizes I am actually here and she isn't imagining it, a sob claws its way out of her as she pulls away from my aunt and rushing across the room to me, I wrap my arms around her and hold her tightly as she breaks down in my hold. Sin squeezes my mom's shoulder as she walks past to be with her own mother. Mom's tears begin to soak through my shirt but I make no complaint as I hold her and be the anchor, she needs me to be, it's taking everything inside me to keep my anger in check and not lash out at everyone.

I have always wanted to lead this family but this was not the way I wanted that honor to be bestowed upon me, I wanted to earn it and make it known that it wasn't just handed to me.

"Kiara?" I look up to see Luka standing in the entryway of the kitchen with a grave look on his face, my mother pulls back and uses me as a shield so she can wipe her tears away and pull herself together before facing my father's chief of staff. Luka may be considered family but he isn't blood, my mom needs to get it together and show no weakness.

In this life, if weakness is even hinted at then wolves from all over will come and try to take over what isn't theirs to take, I'll die before I ever let any of these washed up cunts try to take this empire my father built for us. Mom pats me on the chest and tries to smile reassuringly but it doesn't reach her eyes.

"What is it?" She asks as she moves to stand beside me, Luka fails at keeping the pitying look from his face as he stares at her.

"Rumors are already circulating, we need to reinforce each of the territories before a war breaks out." Fuck, dad hasn't even been out of the game for a day and already they are trying to steal from us, each of the low level crews around New York will be trying to take over each of my uncles places before coming for my dad's.

"Okay, uh... we need to—." She isn't in her right mind so I step in and give my mother the out she needs.

"Split the men, station extra soldiers at each of the territories. Make sure Manhattan and Brooklyn are secured, they will try to take those two first." Luka stares at me intently, I stand tall and hold his gaze waiting for him to question me but instead he just smiles and nods.

"You got it, *boss*." My brows raise on their own accord hearing him utter that one word. "I'll shift the men now and have the captains each of your uncles selected step up to take over the day to day operations. Vincent had a meeting in Long Beach tonight with a potential informant, what do you want me to do about that?"

"A meet with who?" Sin asks as comes to stand on my other side.

Luka doesn't take his eyes off me as he answers. "He thought he found a mole and was trying to flip them to get information on the Vargas cartel." I look at Sin who is frowning, the moment our gazes clash I know what she wants and it's exactly what I was hoping she would want.

"Keep the meet, I'll run point with Sin taking Overwatch and the twins watching my six."

"Royal, no–." I spin to face my mom, she can't question me, not even in front of Luka.

"My father is the Don of this family which makes me the heir to Murdoch mafia, this is my birthright and I will honor it." Her bottom lip trembles, I refuse to allow Luka to see her break so I dismiss him with the promise of finding him soon to go over the plan of what the fuck we do next.

"I can't lose you too." She sobs, fuck, I pull her to me and hold her close allowing her to break again in my arms. All my aunts are now crowded around with my cousins looking shaken, Havoc and Chaos stand beside Sin nodding their heads, I knew without a doubt they would always stand with me.

"Aunt Clare, did you want to take the girls to the game room?" I ask, I can tell she wants to argue and be a part of the conversation that will take place the moment she leaves but Nytress clasps her mother's hand and begins to lead her out of the room with Unique and Destiny following close behind them.

Chapter Two

ROYAL

My aunts, the twins, Chanel and my mom all sit on the sofas while I stand staring out the floor to ceiling windows at the backyard wondering how my dad let this happen. He is always a step ahead, he never goes into a situation blind and plans everything out making sure no one would ever be able to get the jump on him.

"You need to see the video." I peer over my shoulder at my Aunt Koby, she rises and heads toward the wall mounted TV where she inserts a thumb drive into the back before pressing play.

My fists clench at my sides the moment the camera focuses on my father, he's battered and bruised, blood trickles down the side of his temple and his arms are bound behind his back but seeing this man that has always wielded power like a second skin looking like this and be on his knees in front of the cocksucker with his back to me. Anger rides me hard as I watch the strongest man I have ever known kneel before this son of a bitch like a weak little mouse. I'll fucking kill these cunts for doing that to my father. I'm so hungry for their blood, anger courses through me, I latch onto it and use it to keep me grounded as I watch the video.

"You have three minutes to make the demands, you fuck around or do anything stupid, your brother and brother-in-law die."

"Go fuck yourself." Dad spits, the cunt reels his arm back and hits him.

"Motherfucker!" I roar.

"Get his ass up." The cocksucker orders. Two other dead men walking come into view as they grip each of my dads arms and lift him to his feet. His face shows no pain but I can see it in his eyes that he is in agony. The three of them step out of view, my brows jump at the sight of Rook, Knight and King on their knees at the back of the concrete room with guns trained on the backs of each of their heads.

"Royal." The fact my father is addressing me and not Luka or my mother has me standing up straight and inching closer to the TV. *"Miami is gone, Chance Bennett now owns it, pull the men back from the corners and let the soldiers loose from the territories. Everything from the family file is to be turned over to Chance and the Vargas cartel. Don't battle this, it will cause a war. Once the demands have been met, Chance will release us from the Siberian jail and Gage and Vincent will be returned home. Do as Chance and Emilio say, son. Let go, Royal, let it all go and do what you need to do to ensure our family remains safe, Chance will be in contact soon."*

The video ends, everyone begins to start discussing what they just saw, I stand here still and reeling, staring at the black screen of the TV trying to work it all out in my head.

"We need to pull everyone back, get Luka." Aunt Ally says.

"No, if we do that they win." Aunt Anya counters.

"What the fuck do you think they will do to them if we

don't do as Bishop told us?" My moms words are what have me snapping out of it.

"He didn't say it to you, he told me." I mutter as I frown at the blank screen.

"Lay it out for me, Royal, let's piece it together."

"Chanel, he is clearly not thinking straight." Aunt Carlina says but Sin ignores her mother as she comes to stand in front of me.

"Tell me." She demands.

"He told me what he wants in clues, my dad doesn't want to give them a single fucking thing, he wants a war."

"No, he doesn't, he just said it's not worth the battle." Mom grits out.

"Because it will cause a war." Havoc announces, I turn to my cousin and nod.

"Dad wants us to be smart, we can't battle them because they will kill them but if we're smart, we can win the war against them and get them all back."

"How?" Aunt Koby asks.

"We need to pull the men from the corners and let them loose through the entire city, if they think we have abandoned our posts and let each of the territories go they will see it as us obeying their orders," I answer.

"We can't win a war without them, we just can't." Aunt Carlina says. "They each have a skill set that no one else does and that is the reason they have always been able to win every war." The twins smile as they come to stand beside me and Chanel drawing all the women's attention to us.

"They taught us everything we know, we will win this war because everything they have, we do as well." That's when my dad's words finally dawn on me, I break away from the others and rush to his office. I hear them following me but ignore them as I go behind his desk and reach for the bottom drawer where his files are kept but it's locked.

"Here." I look up to see my mom taking off the weirdly shaped heart necklace she always wears and hands it to me. I frown at the thing as it sits in the palm of my hand. "You have always hated that necklace but the reason it is so important and always around my neck is because that is the only key to that drawer." My eyes widen as I look up at my mother, she smiles timidly and nods for me to try it.

To my shock, the fucking thing fits in the little enclave perfectly and the drawer lock clicks open, I pull it open and sift through the files until I spot my name in the back, I yank the file out and place it on the top of his desk and drop into his seat.

"What are you doing?" Chaos asks.

I look to each member of my family as I answer. "My dad has always told me he had a family file stashed in here and if anything was to ever happen to him I was to find the one with my name and everything that I would need to know would be in here. He wants me to let go, what he means is that he wants me to let go of all the anger and rage I feel right now and be the man he knows I can be. My dad wants me to lead and in order to do that, I need to read what's in here."

My mom purses her lips as she looks down at me, she looks me over and without me having to say it out loud she nods. "Come on, we'll give him a minute to go over that while we make something to eat." My aunts begrudgingly follow her out, I look up to my three cousins who each stand in front of the desk with their arms crossed over their chests.

"We aren't going anywhere!" Chaos snarls, I knew they wouldn't leave and that is why I will always respect the fuck out of each of them.

Opening the folder I see a small yellowish envelope with my name on it, I tear it open and dump the contents on the desk. There are three single keys and a...

"Is that a tape recorder?" The shock can be heard in Sin's

voice, I've never seen one of these in real life, only in movies, I push the one that says play and wait. A crackling sound fills the room for a second before my dad's voice can be heard.

"Good work, son. I knew you would remember this. I need you to listen carefully, I know without a doubt you have found a way to get rid of your mother so you can be alone and listen." He snorts before continuing. *"Hello Chanel, Chaos and Havoc."* The four of us exchange a look of confusion.

"When I said you would listen alone I had no doubt those three would be with you. If you four are hearing this tape then that means we have fallen, I never wanted you to be the head of the family this way, Royal. Contrary to what you think everything I have done, said and shown you were all leading you to this moment. If I was hard on you it was because I was teaching you a lesson, everything I have done son is to show you how to lead. Never let a bastard come between you and your birthright, if there is ever a time where I will be held for ransom or some shit like that. You never give in, you keep this family together and make sure no motherfucker takes from you what we all built. Think, son, take the time to plan and make sure you don't act rashly, think like a leader, not a soldier. The four of you are the next generation of Murdochs, do not forget who you are and where you come from.

"Never!" Havoc growls earning grunts of agreement from the rest of us.

"Those keys go to three different safety deposit boxes, one is filled with passports and other documentation like banking shit and all the documents to our accounts. One is to a box filled with all the deeds to the properties and businesses and the last is to the safety deposit box that goes to your mother, give it to her when she is ready and not a moment before. I'm sorry I wasn't the best father, Royal. Believe me though son, I am so fucking proud of the man you are and I know for sure no matter what you do in life you will always take care of your mother and this family. I

love you son, I'm sorry I wasn't able to be there and protect you as a father should."

The four of us remain silent as the recording cuts out, none of us know what to say. Strange feelings swirl inside me, my dad and I have always fought and yes, I've always fucked with him and played stupid pranks on my old man but I never thought this moment would come where he wouldn't be here.

"What the hell are we going to do?" Havoc mutters.

"It sounded like he wants us to fight." Chaos answers.

"Then why did he tell us about the passports, I think he wants us to run." Sin announces.

I shake my head and slowly climb to my feet drawing their attention to me. "No. He wants us to fight and send our families to safety." Their eyes widen. "He left me in charge, I'm not following his rules."

"Royal–." I cut Sin a look that has her shutting her mouth.

"They may be the Murdoch mafia but we are the Memento Mori, we are the bringers of death and we submit to no motherfucker." Each of their eyes blaze with understanding. "We don't run, we fight but this time, we do it in a way that is smarter, we'll win this war by being cunning and taking these cunts down from the inside. Chance wants me to hand everything over to him, fine but there will be contingencies in place. I need you three with me for what I have planned, if you choose to walk out now then I won't hold it against you but, if you come with me, our whole family is going to turn against us. When we get our father's back they will all come for us, can you handle that?"

Havoc holds my gaze as he says. "*Et nos unum sumus.*" (*We are one.)*

"*Et nos unum sumus.*" Sin and Chaos mimic, I smile darkly at each of them.

"Get the decks stacked because we leave the moment I get

the call, the only one who will know is Luka. No one else, am I clear?"

"Yes." The three of them say in unison just as my phone begins to ring, I know without a doubt who the fuck it is and now it's time for me to put all the training I have learned over the years to use.

It's time we showed the world and all these doubters in it that we are the bringers of death and we are the new Murdochs who bow to no motherfucker.

Chapter Three

ERIKA

I sit next to him in this luxurious car, he pulls his phone from his suit pocket and taps the screen a couple of times as if he's debating something. I turn and stare out the window not wanting to engage him in a conversation, one where I am forced to listen and act like I am excited and so happy to be here, when in truth, all I want is to be far, far away from him and this place. This was not a life I ever thought I would live, be pretty, remain seen but never heard. Dress this way, stand this way or make sure your hair is always at this length.

Life was already hard before, but now it is almost unbearable.

"You know darling, once we get home I will make sure to show you just how happy I am that you are here with me." I fight the shiver from breaking free and smile sweetly like I have been trained to do, the lustful look in his eyes has me feeling sick to my stomach. The thought of having his hands on me or allowing him inside my body has a wave of self loathing washing over me.

"The line is secured sir, you're safe to make the call now." The man with the laptop says from the seat in the front.

He unlocks his phone and dials a number then places it on speaker, I pretend to not be paying attention to what he is doing. Men like him think of women like they are nothing but a hole to be filled or someone to cook and clean for them. It's better to act docile and unbothered by anything he says or does or I risk his full attention being on me. His phone connects to the car's Bluetooth system the moment it begins to ring, I force myself to remain still and face out the window as the call is answered.

"The fact you have this number tells me you are more resourceful than my father gave you credit for." His deep baritone voice fills the car, the sound has gooseflesh erupting all over my skin. I spy Chance out of the corner of my eye smirking, I have no idea what he has planned but I know without a doubt that the men from yesterday didn't seem like the type to go down without a fight.

"Royal Murdoch, what a pleasure to finally speak to you." The condescending tone Chance uses doesn't go unnoticed by the man on the other end of the call judging by the growl that comes through the speaker.

"I wish I could say the same but I have no idea who you are." His voice is deep and rich, it's a sound I could listen to for hours.

"Well, let me rectify that for you. My name is Chance Bennett and I am Anthony Bennett's nephew. So, I guess you could say we are related."

"Hmmm." Is the only answer he gives, the tight set of Chance's jaw is indication he doesn't like that reply.

"I assume you have my demands?"

"I do."

Chance's grip on his phone tightens as he grinds his teeth,

this man is toying with him and Chance has no idea how to deal with that.

"You have forty-eight hours to hand everything over or I'll start sending pieces of your father back to you."

I tense waiting for the man to lose his cool and make threats or promises of war.

"I'll have it done in twenty-four hours and I will be on a plane to Miami so I can run you through everything you need to know." My brows bunch in confusion, Chance snaps his gaze to the man in the front with the laptop, he shrugs his shoulders indicating he has no idea what is going on.

"You try to play me and I will kill all of them–."

"Do it, I'll hold no ill feelings toward you for it. If you ask me, they all got what they deserved."

"Is that so?"

"Yes, if Bishop had listened to me from the start and handed over control of the family when I asked he wouldn't be where he is. All of them knew I was the better choice but yet they still chose to remain loyal to their Don. I won't take over, I'll start my own thing." A smile as wide as Miami Beach spreads across Chance's face.

"Well, if that's the case, why not stay out in Miami with me, little cousin and learn from the master who was able to fly under the radar for years and amass an empire without anyone knowing who I am or what I planned." The smugness in his tone tells me he loves his ego being stroked.

"Are you serious?" The man is acting the part perfectly, I give him that.

"I didn't relish the thought of killing my own blood, to begin with, so if you are willing to dismantle your father's business and hand everything over I don't see a reason why I should kill you."

"What about my mom and aunts?"

Chance ponders his question for a minute. "They remain

in New York, they are never to try and bring back the Murdoch name or rise against me and the Vargas cartel when they move into the city then they can remain breathing."

"And what of their husbands?" That question has Chance sitting straight in his chair and suddenly looking serious.

"Prove to me you are worthy of my time and can be trusted and you have my word I will release the six of them back to their wives on conditions of course."

"I would expect nothing less."

"It's settled then."

"I'll see you in a couple of days, cousin." He says before ending the call, Chance tosses his phone to the man in the front.

"Did you get a location?" He asks.

"Yes, he's back in New York at the family residence."

"Keep an eye on him, from what I have heard the kid isn't lying, he really did hate his father." I know a lot of people claim to hate their parents but from the research I have done on the Murdoch family there is nothing to suggest that they are not a united front. There are no pictures of Bishop and Kiara Murdoch's son online, there are none of Knight's twins or their sister Carlina's daughter. There is a reason they aren't in the public eye and if Chance wasn't so worried about inflating his ego, he would see that.

We pull up out front of Chance's ostentatious size mansion, I want to roll my eyes but I remember my training and smile politely as he offers his hand to help me from the car, the moment our skin comes into contact I want to tear my hand back but I grit my teeth and breathe through it. His clammy hand wraps around my small one as he leads me up the large marble stairs, who the hell has marble stairs out the front of their house?

"You are going to love it here, darling, you will of course have a limit on the amount you can spend and I will have Charles set up a weekly allowance for you." I just nod and play the part, when we are mere feet from the door it is opened from the inside by a man dressed like a butler who bows as we walk past. "The bags are in the car, take them to Ms. Martinez's room and make sure everything is in order." He barks as the man who quickly scurries out to the car to do as he is told.

Chance takes me on the tour of the monstrosity he calls home, this man is so full of himself it can be seen in every place you look. Everything is gold and white, and no other colors are displayed. I learned many years ago that to truly know someone all you have to do is watch and listen, people get so caught up in talking about themselves that they never filter the information they leak. For example, Chance has just let slip that without him the oil company that was caught paying their workers under minimum wage and didn't have the right permits was being forced to shut down until he stepped and covered it up.

Of course, he gets a kickback from that. I may play the role of damsel well but make no mistake I am listening to every word he says, information is knowledge and knowledge is power.

"Right, I must attend to business but I expect you to be ready and presentable by eight for dinner." Plastering a smile on my face I nod. "Follow Margaret and she will show you where your room is." He reaches out and cups my cheek in what I am sure he thinks is a tender gesture, my stomach rolls. "Until I can train you correctly, I have others coming by to... ease my craving." Bile rises in my throat, the innuendo isn't lost on me, I keep my face blank so he can't see the relief as I turn and hastily follow after the woman.

I kept my gaze down the entire way, I know nothing of this woman and for all I know she could be reporting my every move back to Chance. I need to keep a low profile and gather as much information as I can about my new home and future husband. Margaret points out that Chance stays on the opposite side of the mansion to me, I force a pout and nod, her eyes crinkle at the corners but she says nothing until we reach *my* room, she opens the door to reveal a room so large that I have to spin in a circle just to see the whole damn thing.

"You have your own private bathroom and your walk-in closet is over there." She points to the side of the room where there are two double doors. "Mr. Bennett took the liberty of buying you a *few* things that he likes and thinks will look good on you." I clasp my hands in front of myself and nod. "If you need anything, there is a buzzer on the bedside table, push that, and one of the staff will be here within minutes." It irks me when she bows and excuses herself from the room, I give it a minute before I rush over and lock it, the moment the lock clicks into place I rest back against the door and bang my head.

Is revenge really worth all of this?

Chapter Four

ROYAL

"What the hell are you talking about?" My mom snaps at me from across the room, I school my features and make sure to keep all emotion from my face.

"The family business is no more, Luka was instructed to pull all men from their posts and allow the Vargas cartel entry into New York. I will fly out tomorrow and meet with Chance–."

"Royal, it's a trap!" Aunt Anya shouts clearly frustrated by my news.

"It's my call to make." I roar, my aunt's jaw unhinges at my blatant disrespect. I have never spoken to any of the women in my family this way but they need to learn that I am in charge and they will do as they are told. "You will obey the orders I have given or your husbands will not be returned to you."

"One of those men happens to be your father." Aunt Carlina growls, Sin steps in closer to me offering me her silent support, I appreciate the gesture but it isn't needed.

"Yeah well, maybe if he had listened to me his ass wouldn't be on the chopping block." My mother gasps and covers her mouth with her hand. "Do as I say and then they will come back, defy me and Chance will kill them."

"Why are you going?" Aunt Ally asks with unshed tears in her eyes.

"Because he is offering me something my father never did."

"What is that?" My mom whispers brokenly.

I hold her stare making sure she can see the seriousness in my blue eyes that match hers. "A chance to lead without being hindered by my last name, I don't need Bishop's name to make something of myself, I'll do it on my own."

I leave before another word can be uttered, Chanel and the twins follow me out ignoring the shouts of mothers and aunts to come back. I hate that I had to hurt her like this but it's the only way to keep them safe, they can never know what we have planned or they will come for us. We all know the risk we are taking but if we don't do it, we will live in their shadows forever and I won't have that. It's our time to lead. The four of us make our way out to the idling car and slip inside, Luka and Kyro sit up front. None of them say a word as we drive off, I refuse to look back knowing my mother will be standing on the steps of my childhood home screaming and begging for me to come back.

All in due time.

"The plane is on standby, the pilot knows to take you into the private airfield. Samson will be there waiting to take you four to your house there." Luka hands me all the paperwork and everything I will need, I hand it off to Sin then reach out and shake his hand.

"Everything you have done cannot be undone, you are loyal and that is something I will make sure he knows." Luka nods his head but I can tell he doesn't agree with my plan but he's smart enough not to question my motives.

"He's gonna kill me for this kid." I reach into the breast pocket of my jacket and pull out a manila envelope and hand it to him, he takes it and eyes it warily before looking back to me.

"Disappear until you hear from me." Without notice, he pulls me in for a hug, I stand here stiff and unsure what the fuck to do until he pulls back and pats me on the side of my arm.

"I've watched you grow up and I'll be real with you, I always knew you would be exactly like him," I say nothing as he and Kyro climb back into the car, we stand here until their tail lights disappear.

"Game time baby Bishop." I turn and glare at Havoc, Chaos laughs at his twin's stupid jibe. I shoulder-check the bastards on my way to the private plane that waits for us on the secluded tarmac. The pilot and his staff greet us as we enter the tiny plane, I have to duck to enter the doorway and make my way to the back of the aircraft and drop down into one of the plush leather chairs, Sin claims the one opposite me and the twins choose to sit next to us, I can tell they are in one of their pranking moods. They always get like this when we have a plan forming and a mission set.

We all remain silent as the cabin crew prepares the plane for take-off, the moment the plane is in the air some of the tension eases from my shoulders but the worry remains. If I fuck this up, they will all pay the price, I'm doing as I'm told and thinking like a leader, planning and thinking carefully without acting on instinct and making a rash choice.

"Are we really doing this?" I tear my gaze away from the window and push all the worry from my mind as I look at Chanel. She eyes me carefully trying to find a chink in my armor, she won't. I'm a fucking master at hiding my emotions, she should know that.

"We *are* doing this." I answer firmly.

"So, no communication the moment we land then?"

I flick my gaze to Havoc and nod. "From there, we don't know each other."

"There will be no more anonymity after this, our faces will be everywhere." Chaos brings up.

I blow out a breath and nod, I knew the moment this plan formulated that this would happen. I know we have always lived in the shadows and ran our small operation that way but now, it's time we came out of the darkness and owned who the fuck we are.

"We are the Memento Mori, it's about fucking time we claimed who we are." The three of them wear matching grins. "But, only when the time is right. We each have a part to play and until the moment I give the word, we remain hidden, do you understand?" I make sure to look at each of them so they know I'm not fucking around.

"We stick to the plan." Havoc says.

"Yeah." Sin agrees.

"We're with you." Chaos growls.

"Then let the fun begin," I say darkly.

The moment we land in Miami, Samson is there waiting like Luka said. Chanel and I climb into the waiting car while the twins go their own way, we have a plan in place and in order for everything to work out the way we need it to, this is how it has to go. The three of us remain silent on the long drive to our new house, no one knows about this place except for the four of us. My grandfather left it to me without my parents knowledge, he said it was a place for me to escape and breathe without the pressure of the name I carry. I've never been there before or ever had the need until this moment.

I chose to fly into Miami tonight under the radar because I know Chance will have every airport marked tomorrow waiting for our entry. At least this way we have the element of surprise and that small advantage is a huge win in a situation like this. Samson comes to a stop out the front of a large wrought iron gate that has a large gold M sitting in the middle of the black gate. He peers over his chair to look back at me, I quirk an impatient brow at him.

"There's a handprint scanner over here and something tells me it won't open with mine." I shoot him a warning glare before getting out of the car and moving briskly to where the scanner stands next to his door, I truthfully don't know if it will open with mine and if it does, how the fuck did grandpa manage to get my hand print?

I lay my hand flat against the scanner and silently hope that this works or we are back to square one, the moment it pings I lift my hand and watch as the gate creaks open. I climb back in the car, Samson drives slowly down the long driveway that is lit up on either side by small motion sensor lights. Sin and I exchange a look, clearly grandpa wasn't as lax in his ways as I thought. Motion sensor lights means no fucker can break in and try to take us out.

There's a long oval fountain with a couple statues on either end that spray water, pot plants circle the fucking thing and judging from how well maintained it is there must be groundskeepers still employed here. More lights shine as we come to a stop in front of the old mediterranean looking home, it reminds me of a Walter DeGarmo house, vines cover the front of the mansion but not in a tacky way, you can see they are maintained to look a certain way and it adds character to the home. The hedges that line the front are all well maintained and evenly shaped.

"I'll get the bags." Samson says as we exit the car, Sin comes to stand beside me as I stare up at the home my grandfather left me. The moment lights turn on inside the house Sin and I both have our guns drawn, I hear the bags drop behind the car and Samson is next to me with his gun drawn in the next second. We see a shadow through the glass door that is covered by some intricate iron design on the outside, as the door opens slowly I brace, ready to take out whoever the fuck it is.

"Don't shoot, Mr Murdoch." The stranger calls out as he slowly steps outside and the front lights turn on to show an elderly man in khaki pants and a white shirt, his hair is short and gray, his eyes are wide at the sight of three guns trained on him.

"Who the hell are you and how do you know my name?" I growl. The man stops keeping at least ten feet between us, he's smart enough to keep his gaze trained on me and not look to the others.

"My name is Cable Barnes and I am the caretaker of this home." I remain silent waiting for him to elaborate and refusing to give him anything until I deem him trustworthy enough not to kill. "Your Grandfather was one of my dearest friends and entrusted me with the job of maintaining this home and its security for you." My gun slowly lowers to my side at his admission.

"How did you know who I was?" He smiles welcomingly at me.

"That gate is programmed to only allow Royal Murdoch to enter and no one else, I took a gamble and it looks like it paid off since I'm still breathing. If you like, I can show you to your rooms and help you get acquainted with the home?" I look at Sin who still has her gun trained on Cable, she flicks her eyes at me and I can see it, she doesn't trust him and wants to put a bullet in his head.

"Put the gun down."

"Royal–,"

I cut her off before she can argue. "If Grandpa trusted him, then that has to mean something."

"He could be lying." She counters.

Shrugging my shoulders I say. "If he is, you can kill him but not until I know for sure." Cable says nothing as he turns and leads the way inside. I thought my parent's house was luxurious but this... this is something else. The sheer size and opulence is almost overwhelming. There is marble flooring throughout the entryway, and there is a grand staircase on either side that leads to an overlook in the middle. The further in we follow Cable, I notice all the personal touches, like the paintings on the walls. I've seen some of them at my Grandpa's house. All throughout there are wood-beamed ceilings and arched windows and doors as well as framed vistas which was a typical DeGarmo trait. I was right, this house is one of the three he designed and built in Miami, these houses are historical here.

Cable takes us on a tour and tells us there is a cabin or guest house if you will out back, the house has a clear view of the Biltmore Hotel and sits on over eight acres of land. The house itself has eight bedrooms, six and a half baths, and over ten thousand feet of living space. Cable tells me there is a basement that my Grandpa had converted but he has never been inside of it as the only person to have access to it is me.

I decided to investigate that shit tomorrow, tonight I need to get shit sorted and ready for the meeting with Chance first up in the morning, that is the most important thing. We need to set up a base of operations here and make sure that we have him under surveillance at all times. I want his every move documented and to be able to do that, I need to make sure that everything is in place and I can move freely around the city.

Cable shows us to our rooms, I leave Sin to get settled while I begin preparations for tomorrow, thanks to the amazing view this place provides, I now know exactly where the meet will be set for tomorrow. It's now time to set the plan into motion and get Chance ready for what's about to come.

Chapter Five

ERIKA

The sound of shouting wakes me from my dreamless sleep, I sit up in bed and listen intently. There are a lot of voices but the one I zone in on is Chance's, he sounds worried and slightly unhinged which piques my interest. Slipping out of bed, I grab my silk robe and quickly pull it on as I quietly exit my room and tiptoe down the hall. I come to a stop near the Library nook as he called it, he stands there with five other men and the maid from last night. I find it peculiar that a maid would be privy to such a conversation like this, I run my gaze over her and find nothing extraordinary about the woman until Chance looks to her for... approval.

Got you!

Now, I know why the woman is here and who she really is. That information is going to come in handy considering he has gone through great lengths to conceal her and have her acting as someone of unimportance.

"I want security doubled. His plane lands today, someone is here sending a message already and I won't have some low life piece of shit try to scare me!" I fight the snort from breaking free, Chance is no man, he's a meek mouse. He already has a security detail that follows him everywhere he goes but yet, he still feels unsafe because deep down inside, even he knows he's a pussy.

"Sir, it was just a card–." One of the men says but Chance cuts him off before he can continue.

"This isn't just a fucking card!" He shouts. "This is the same card that was left behind when the Vargas heir was taken and never to be seen again. I want whoever the fuck left this at my gate found and brought to me!" Chance dismisses the men and I wait around the corner a minute longer before I play the part of just waking and stumbling in to find him here. The worried look disappears from his face the moment he spots me rounding the corner, he plasters a fake smile on his face and waves me closer. The moment I'm within reach he grabs my waist and pulls me in closer so he can nuzzle the side of my neck, I force a shy smile and play coy knowing that Margaret is still standing beside him watching.

"Will that be all, sir?" She asks. Chance pulls back and shoots me what I'm sure he thinks is a sexy wink before turning to the maid.

"Yes, carry on with your tasks, Margaret." She nods and excuses herself leaving me and the governor of Miami alone. "Now, I have an important meeting today with Royal Murdoch." Nodding, I wait for him to continue. "He is landing sometime today and I plan to make sure he knows who the boss of this fine state is." I give him my best smile and bat my lashes like he is flexing the best pick up lines I have ever heard before. "I want to show you something, I need to know if this looks familiar to you."

He pulls the card out of his pocket and hands it to me, it's the King of Clubs not a Jack of Spades like the last one I saw. I flip it over and sure enough the same words are inscribed on the back, *Memento Mori*. These cards are like none I have ever seen before, the King has a skull face and instead of it being the normal color and instead of the image being mirrored it is just one solid picture of a skull wrapped in red robes, he doesn't hold the King's scepter like normal cards, he holds a dagger. Smoke rises up from the back of the King and the card looks like it's almost charred but it's just the way it is made to look. The back of the card has the words but it also has smoke in the background but you can clearly see a pair of eyes and a mouth, it's a skull face made out of smoke.

I flick my gaze to Chance and nibble on my bottom lip as I shake my head, his eyes narrow but he doesn't say anything as he snatches the card from my hold and shoves it back into his breast pocket. I can tell he is displeased from the tight set of his jaw and the way he is eyeing me shows that he knows I am full of shit but I'm a master at shielding my thoughts and emotions, it's a skill that I have honed and there is no one better at it than me.

"Be ready when I call, you will be accompanying me to meet Royal Murdoch, I'll also be bringing on a new security team whilst he is in town and until the cartel is fully settled into their new territory in New York. You will have a guard with you at all times, he should be here soon."

I spend the day in my room on my laptop researching anything and everything I can about the Memento Mori and what it means, there is a trending hashtag across social media that shows a college in Utah where a lot of heirs of various gangs go as well as many other kids of politicians and famous pop stars.

No one knows who the cards belong to or if they do, the

only people can confirm who it is have disappeared. It's no secret that over the last three years at least a dozen kids have gone missing from UNLV never to be heard from again, no bodies were ever found, only a card. A King of Clubs, Queen of Hearts, Jack of Spades or an Ace of Diamonds. From what I can see online, there has only ever been one card found at each scene.

I google the names of the Murdoch heirs, no images of Chanel, Havoc, Chaos or Royal show up online. None of them have any social media profiles, they are invisible to the world and have been all their lives. So, the question that is burning a hole in my mind now is, why would they give that up? Coming here they have to know that cameras will be wherever Chance is. Something isn't right, Chance can't see it because all he is worried about his fucking ego and having Royal here will inflate it further because he views his cousin as a prize and proof of his victory, a victory he would never have won if it wasn't for the help of Emilio.

My door is thrown open forcing me to lift my gaze from the computer, Margaret stands there with a scornful look on her wrinkled face. "Mr Bennett is waiting for you downstairs." Nodding, I close the lid of my laptop and place it on the side of my bed. I see her beady eyes looking at it, she is welcome to try to take a look but that laptop has a biometric lock and won't unlock unless it's my eye in the camera. I brush past her and don't miss the growl that tumbles from her lips, I roll my lips over my teeth to keep my smile at bay, she just showed me her cards without meaning to.

Just like she said, Chance stands in the foyer in a fresh suit with his hair done and a vicious smile on his face. Something about the look in his eyes has me feeling uneasy, I stop a foot away from him and give him my best smile. His eyes drink in the sight of me, I'm wearing a long Maxi style dress that ties behind my neck and gives you a glimpse of the top of my breasts. The hungry look in his eyes tells me I made the right choice with this outfit, he clears his throat and tears his gaze from my tits to offer me his arm. I link mine through his without hesitation, the front door is opened for us but the moment we step out onto the marble stairs I freeze at the sight of the man that stands beside the waiting limo with the door open.

He wears a three piece suit, his hands clasped in front of him waiting. He's tall, really freaking tall and wears a serious look on his face, his jaw is sharp and his face is clear of facial hair. His black hair is slicked back, his eyes are hidden behind a pair of sunglasses, I have no idea why the fact I can't see his eyes annoys me but it does. As we approach his head shifts slightly and I feel the heat of his gaze on me, suddenly I feel very exposed and the need to duck my head overwhelms me.

Chance pulls us to a stop in front of the man, I peek up at him through my lashes. It's nearly dusk and the fact he still wears glasses is peculiar. "I don't give second chances, don't fuck this up." Chance snaps at him before ushering me into the limo, he slips in beside me as the door is closed. We wait in awkward silence for the driver to take us to our unknown destination, the ride is tense and I fight the urge not pick my nails. I can feel it in the pit of my stomach, something is wrong but that feeling has a strange sense of excitement zapping through me.

Chance spends the whole ride on the phone, I don't mind because it gives me time to check my own. I make sure that he can't see the screen as I unlock it to find three unread messages waiting for me.

EVE

We're in.

EVE

The city has shadows lurking in it, be vigilant.

EVE

Be alert, the family remains but the heirs are gone, report back.

Shit, everything is sent in code in case there was ever a chance of me being compromised. I have no issues giving a daily report on Chance and his dealings but I don't relish the idea of hurting this family, they haven't done anything wrong.

ME

Enroute to meet the prince, the sun is really hot here. I think someone will get burnt quicker than we thought. Catch up when we get home.

I hit send and slip my phone back into my small clutch, Chance peaks over at me and I act like I don't see him spying on me out of the corner of his eye. I know he doesn't trust me and that is something I will earn over time. All I need is to stroke his ego in the right places and make him feel like a man without using my body. Men like him love it when women think they are the strongest and most handsome thing they have ever seen. Truth is, there is nothing attractive about Chance, if anything the man repulses me and makes my skin crawl.

The driver brings the car to a stop in front of the Biltmore Hotel which sits directly beside the Biltmore Golf Course.

This area is very upper class, only people who have their noses in the air and think their shit doesn't stink live around here. I go to reach for the door handle but Chance snaps his arm out and grabs my wrist stopping me, I cut my gaze to him and frown.

"You don't open your own door, you are not in Columbia anymore." His tone is on the verge of mocking and it pisses me off. "You will act like the fiancee of the governor and never forget that, do not embarrass me." His eyes darken as he glares down his nose at me, even when the door on his side is opened he doesn't release me. "This is your only warning, Erika." His grip tightens for a split second before he releases it with a shove, I grit my teeth and take some deep breaths through my nose to try calm my anger.

I follow after him as he exits the car, the man from earlier stands beside the door but doesn't offer me a hand or even spare me a second glance as I follow after Chance, once we are inside the Hotel, a woman leads us through the swanky restaurant, I almost roll my eyes when she takes us down a narrow corridor toward a hidden room. I peek over my shoulder to see the man following us but this time, his glasses are nowhere in sight.

My mouth dries at the sight of his pale blue eyes, they are so pale they almost look white. When his gaze cuts to me I trip over my dress, before I can fall and make a fool of myself he darts his arm out to grip mine and keep me from falling. I stand frozen with his hand still on me staring up at him, a wave of electrical current surges between us.

I open my mouth to speak but quickly snap it shut and yank my arm free of his hold and race to catch up with Chance and the woman, he shoots me a glare before he steps inside the room. Following him I look around and frown, there are no windows and only one door.

"Your guest will be arriving shortly, sir." The woman says.

"Bring us a round of drinks." He bites out as he heads to the table in the center of the room, four chairs surround the circular table, the lighting in here is dim. Chance motions for me to sit in the seat next to him. The position we are in gives us an opportunity to not have our backs to the door, my eyes take on a mind of their own and seek out the man as he comes to stand behind us, a moment later the door opens again to reveal four more men who station themselves in each of the corners of the room. The woman reenters with a tray of drinks, she places a glass of whiskey in front of Chance and two in the middle, I almost laugh when she leaves without offering me one.

I get it, women are lower than men in this world, we are here to be fucked and create the next generation and that's it. I mean godforbid that a woman can actually have a brain and skillset worth a fucking damn, right?

Before my anger can continue to rise the door opens again but this time, it isn't the woman, it's a man dressed in a suit that fits him like a glove. He's taller than Chance and has broader shoulders, reminds me of a football player. His brown hair is a scruffy mess and his green eyes shine with mischief. I expect him to look nervous at the amount of guards in the room but he doesn't, he seems... at ease. He looks to the man behind us and smirks before dropping into one of the seats across from us. He doesn't ask as he reaches out and claims one of the glasses of whiskey, he drinks the contents in one gulp before going for the next one. I study him silently, if this is Bishop Murdoch's son, the heir to the biggest mafia family in the US then I am unimpressed.

He reeks of entitlement, I can see it in his eyes that nothing in this world can make him focus or settle down, he wants to be free and party his life away rather than take on any responsibility.

"Royal Murdoch, what a pleasure to finally meet you,

cousin." Chance says breaking the silence. Royal leans forward and places his elbows on the table smiling as he looks between me and Chance.

"Oh, the pleasure is all mine, cousin." My eyes widen, my brows are practically touching my hairline at the sound of his voice, this man, whoever he is, isn't Royal Murdoch.

Chapter Six

ROYAL

I see her shoulders stiffen and watch for her to say something.

I didn't expect him to bring a woman to this meeting, much less a stunning one like her. She is fucking beautiful, long blonde hair, hazel eyes that stare right into your soul. She looked at me like she knew my secret, something about her intrigues me. I never knew Chance had a woman, she's a curveball I didn't see coming and will need to rectify that immediately.

"I hear you honored our agreement." Chance says as he leans back in his chair and sips his whiskey like a pompous prick.

"I told you I would." The woman's head cocks to the side, does she know that's not really me sitting across from her?

I maintain my position behind her and Chance, and cut a glance to Chaos telling him without words to stay the fuck on track. See, the bonus about no one knowing who you are or what you look like means you could be anyone, like right now. Chance has no idea the new guard he hired to watch over his fiance is *me*, he also has no fucking idea that the man sitting across from him is Chaos. "Now, will you keep your end of the deal?"

Chance laughs but there is zero humor in it. "Oh cousin, I don't even know you or trust you for that matter. If you want your daddy and uncles to be released you need to prove to me that I can trust you in honoring your word to never allow the Murdoch mafia to return." I fight the urge to growl and clench my fists at my side, I knew Chaos would be the perfect person to impersonate me because nothing fazes him, everything is a joke and no matter what Chance says or does it won't get him to snap.

"How do I prove that?" Chaos asks as he slams the other glass of whiskey back and smacks it down on the table. Chance bristles at his blatant display of arrogance, Chaos is a master at getting under peoples skin and acting like he never meant to do it in the first place.

"By showing me the books and helping me take over the dealings your father was doing, in order for your father to truly fall we need to be able to take over all his holdings and make sure there is no way he can ever recover."

Chaos purses his lips and nods, acting like he is thinking about Chance's offer but in truth, he already knows what he is going to do.

"Fine. You need to give me your word that no harm will come to my mom or aunts and my cousins."

"In truth, I expected you to come with your cousins, well, at least Knight and Carlina's kids but I guess I was wrong."

Chaos snorts. "Nah man, as soon as they found out that they could do as they pleased because their daddies weren't around, they booked it the fuck out of town and I haven't heard from any of those pricks." I tune out the remainder of their conversation and watch the girl, she says nothing but I can tell from the subtle way her head will turn or how her shoulders hunch that she is listening to every word they say. Knowledge is power, that's what my grandpa always said to me and something is telling me that is what this woman is doing. She's soaking up every bit of information she can get, for what, I have no fucking idea but I plan to find out.

"Well, I guess that just goes to show you that your family isn't truly loyal." I see Chaos's eyes spark with anger, that is one of the only things that will set him off is calling his twin's loyalty into question, Havoc would die before he ever gave his brother up. Before Chaos can ruin everything and snap at Chance, the woman places her hand on Chance's arm to garner his attention. He scowls at her but she doesn't cower, just raises her brow and then... Holy fuck, she's deaf!

The movements she does with her hands have me captivated and pissed the fuck off. I can't understand what she is saying. Of course, she has been silent this whole time and listened, she can't fucking speak! Chance looks pissed off but not at her.. At himself, can he not sign either?

The moment Chaos wraps his knuckles against the table both Chance and the woman turn to face him, before Chance can utter a word I watch dumbfounded as my cousin begins to sign to Erika, unlike the woman, he speaks aloud as he signs.

"Hi, my name is Royal, it's a pleasure to meet you...?" He lets his sentence trail off, she beams across the table at him and signs. Chaos smiles and nods and then repeats what he did a minute ago. "Nice to meet you, Erika." She smiles and ducks her head when Chance scoffs, it pisses me the fuck off that he embaressed her like that.

"Ignore her, she is here only because of an incident from earlier." I cut Chaos a look and blink twice telling him to hand it over.

"The incident wouldn't have something to do with a card, would it?" Within two point five seconds the four guards around the room have their guns drawn and pointed at Chaos, the fucker just smirks and shakes his head.

"How the hell did you know that?" Chance grits out as he finally drops his facade, I knew he wasn't a ballsy fuck like he pretends to be. The guys cock is only as big as his security detail, this fucker would never go to war with his men he would remain locked inside his panic room.

"Because I got one as well." Chaos taps his breast pocket and cocks a brow at Chance asking without words if he can grab it.

"Lower your guns." He orders as Chaos removes the card from his breast pocket and drops it in the center of the table, unlike Chance's card, Chaos's is an Ace of Diamonds–Havoc's calling card. "When did you get this?"

"This morning when I checked into the hotel, it was waiting on my bed." The mixture of fear and surprise on Chance's face has me fighting back a smirk, the fucker thought he was slick and could use the cards against me to get the cartel to take us out, nah bitch, I'm ten fucking steps ahead of you.

"If you've been given one, then that means..."

"You thought I was the one behind this pathetic card game?" Chaos snorts and shakes his head. "I have better things to do with my time then run around dropping fucking cards at people's places." Chaos is selling this perfectly. "Whoever the fucker is, I'm gonna find him and kill him because no one threatens me."

Hook, line and sinker.

Chance leans forward and smiles wickedly at Chaos, "I think we need to combine our efforts and find this bastard. Do this for me and I will release your father and uncles, fail and they will pay the price."

Chaos stands and brushes his hands down the front of his jacket then looks down at Chance. "In order for me to do this,

I need access to the city. Am I going to be stopped from doing what I need to do?"

It takes the pompous fuck a second to deliberate before he answers. "No. No one in the city will stop you, my guards stay with me." Dumb fuck, he just told us in no certain words that he has no control over the city, the only men he has are with him at all times.

Perfect.

Chance doesn't rise as Chaos leaves the room, how this fucker got the drop on my father I'll never know but after spending this small amount of time with him, it's become clear that he isn't the mastermind behind this plan.

The ride back to the mansion is tense and filled with silence, Chance demands that Dalton, Jovi, Bodhi and I all ride in the back of the limo with Erika. Clearly the fact he thinks Chaos —Royal, got a calling card as well has freaked him the fuck out. This is the part I love, the paranoia, the fear, the constant double checking and the way their eyes accuse everyone without words always fills me with a sick sense of satisfaction. I love watching my prey go mad. Chance won't die anytime soon, it would be too easy and I still need to get the location of my father and uncles from him.

Luka told me Uncle Vin had a tracker on his ring but these fucks have somehow blocked it. I plan to tear him down from the inside, everything he thinks he owns and has built will come crashing down around him, he is going to learn that once you are marked, you're marked until your final breath.

"I want eyes on Royal twenty-four hours a day, I want updates on him every time he makes a move. He doesn't go anywhere in this city without me knowing. Am I clear?"

The four of us guards nod, tonight he is going to learn what the Memento Mori stands for and I, for one, can not fucking wait for that. My eyes stray toward Erika, she sits straight in her chair and acts unbothered by the tension in the car but the way her eyes keep flicking to Chance is the indication I need to know that she is watching just as closely as I am, but why?

The car comes to a stop a while later in front of the monstrosity that he calls home, the prick doesn't move an inch, he waits for one of his staff to open the door for him. He slides out and doesn't offer his girl a helping hand, as she slides out her eyes connect with mine, in the pits of those hazel eyes I see the same hunger in her that I have inside myself. The connection is broken the moment she slips free of the car and follows after Chance, my post is meant to be with her but I stop and turn to Dalton, playing the role of new guard and unsure of where I am meant to be.

"The fuck are you waiting for kid? Follow the future Mrs. Bennett and make sure she stays in her room, Mr Bennett has company coming this evening and the last thing we need is a cat fight." I raise my brows feigning surprise before I quickly rush away after the bride to be. It's no secret Chance likes to fuck hookers, the sick fuck has a kink for hurting and degrading women. We found the police report from when he was seventeen, he abused a young girl, tied her up and whipped her like a dog. Him being a minor meant the records were sealed and the case never made it to court, in short that just means he paid her off.

I studied the layout of this house all night last night, I know exactly where Erika's room is. I pass the pitiful excuse for a library and come to a stop outside her door. I'm to stand here for the next six hours until the guard changes and be back by seven in the morning. Hours go by without incident, I'm bored out of my mind and over hearing the screams coming from the other side of the house, if the dumb fuck thinks any woman comes screaming that loudly, he has clearly never made one come before. Just as I'm about to pull out my phone and fire off a text to Sin to see if she has any updates for me, a sound comes from inside Erika's room. I lean in closer and strain my hearing.

When I hear the noise again but only this time louder, I draw my gun and shove the door open ready to shoot but quickly lower it at the sight in front of me. Erika's back is to me as she balances on the edge of a chair in the corner of the room trying to reach something, I narrow my eyes to get a better look. The second a red dot flashes anger peaks inside me, the fucker is recording her!

"Hmmm." I bite down on my lips to keep from laughing at her pathetic attempt at a growl, she stretches onto her tiptoes again and this time, I notice what she's wearing. Cream silk shorts ride high enough that the bottom of her ass cheeks are on display, the thin strapped camisole she wears is cropped and shows me the tattoo in the center of her back. I quietly inch closer not wanting to spook her so I can get a better look at what the tattoo is. I frown the moment I work out that it's a sugar skull but it wears a broken mask on one side of its face with the words *we aren't what we seem* written below it.

The sound of her phone ringing has her peering over her shoulder, the moment she sees me standing in here a strangled scream leaves her, she loses her balance on the chair. I dart forward and catch her before she can hit the marble floor, her chest rises and falls rapidly as she gazes up at me with wide eyes. Her little body is tucked into my chest and the feeling of her warmth against me and the scent of her perfume has my cock twitching. Both of us push the other away at the same time, I don't say a word as I turn and leave her room with the sound of her phone ringing again following me out.

The moment I close the door behind myself my own

phone begins to vibrate, I pull it out to see it's Havoc calling, I bring it to my ear and answer.

"Yeah?"

"Chaos is on the move, he has two guys tailing him."

"Where is he going?" I keep my tone quiet so no one can overhear.

"Leading them on a goose chase while Sin and I take care of dear old Jovi." I shake my head, I may have only just met Jovi today but I kind of feel sorry for the guy. Knowing Sin and Havoc, he won't die easily.

"I'll be back in an hour, make sure you aren't seen. If they see you, the whole plan is fucked."

"Yes, mom." He snarks before ending the call, if he wasn't my blood I would have killed him a long fucking time ago.

Chapter Seven

ERIKA

I shake away my wayward thoughts and rush to answer my phone before it can ring out again, I'm breathless and sure to look a sight as I answer the incoming FaceTime call. He smiles at me and I return the gesture, signing hello.

"Hello to you as well my dear. How are things going?" I sign everything that happened today and how Chance met with Royal Murdoch, the mention of his name and the events of the meeting sparked his interest. I even tell him about the cards but what I don't disclose is how I suspect that the man claiming to be Royal isn't really him. "I want an update on who the fuck is sending these cards, any information you get I want to know, do you understand." I nod my understanding. "Good girl, I'll be in touch soon."

The moment he ends the call I flop back on the bed and stare up at the ceiling praying for a fucking miracle. He raised me, gave me a home and everything that I needed but in turn, that all comes with a cost. A cost I don't want to pay. My life and body isn't my own, the freedom to choose what you want from life is something I was never afforded.

The sound of a cough from outside my bedroom has me tilting my head to the side staring at the closed doors, I know he is right outside standing guard. I don't know who he is but there is something about that man that draws me to him, the feeling of his hands on me a moment ago had my body blazing and my nipples hardening. Slamming my eyes closed I push all thoughts of that encounter from my mind and focus back on the task at hand. Sitting up I grab my laptop and comb through the files that were sent to me, all four files are practically blank of information.

Who are you really, Royal?

Four folders sit here with only names, dates of birth, last known address and a rough idea of what they could look like. None of the informants have been able to give us any more details than we have, Chanel, Havoc, Chaos and Royal are like, it's almost like they don't exist.

I spend hours combing through the web trying to find any information I can on Royal and his cousins, no matter how hard I look or try to dig deeper nothing comes up. That's when it hits me, I know how they have managed to stay hidden.

Someone is erasing any evidence of them existing!

I wake the next morning feeling like I haven't slept a wink, I startle when I check the time on my phone. I quickly shower and change, choosing to forego makeup, the moment I step back into the room Margaret is standing there ready to take me downstairs where I will meet Chance daily for breakfast, according to him this is a non negotiable rule. I smile and play my part well as I follow her from the room, the second I step outside my door and spot my guard with the pale blue eyes my breathing picks up.

I push thoughts of him away and ignore the fact he follows after us and I can feel his gaze boring into the back of my head. The moment we enter the dining area, Chance is already seated reading the morning paper. I want to snort at the irony of it but refrain. All he needs is a pipe in his mouth and then he would look picture perfect. Margaret pulls the chair out at Chance's right side for me, once I'm settled I look to him for an indication of what happens next but he ignores me and continues to read his paper so I help myself to the spread of food that is already laid out on the table.

I'm halfway through my breakfast when the front door crashes open, my guard has his gun drawn and aims to where Bodhi and Dalton are and rushes through the dining room, Chance is on his feet and taking two steps backward... is he trying to run?

"Sir, there's a situation at the gate." Bodhi rasps out.

Chance seems to relax slightly, he was going to run. "What is it?" He snaps, the two men exchange a loaded look before looking back to their boss.

"Jovi is dead sir." Dalton solemnly says, Chance stiffens.

"How?"

Bodhi is the one to answer this time. "Part of him was returned this morning, sir."

Chance's brows raise. "Part?"

Dalton gulps loudly and nods. "Yes sir, he was returned in pieces with a King of Clubs nailed to his forehead." I cut a glance to my guard in the corner, his face is blank of emotion as he stands stoically in the corner as if this conversation doesn't bother him at all.

"Fuck!" Chance roars as he swipes all the food off the table, it crashes to the ground shattering into tiny pieces as the porcelain plates and dishes shatter. I push back from the table to avoid having juice spilled on my lap. "Find the cunt who is doing this, I want his fucking head, am I clear?"

Both men nod but I can tell from the way they begin to fidget on the spot that there is more they aren't saying. "Uh, there is something else sir." Chance grinds his teeth and prompts Bodhi with a look to spit it out. "There was a note attached to… Uh, there was some ah…"

Dalton cuts in and saves Bodhi from rambling more. "Jovi's cock was cut off and shoved up his ass, a note was nailed to his ass that read, *you have been marked.*"

Chance's whole face slackens and he pales slightly, I watch my guard for any indication this situation is affecting him. "I want this bastard found and I want a fucking update on Royal Murdoch! If that cocksucker is behind this I'm going to murder the little cunt in front of his whore of a mother and then make her watch as I drag her worthless sack of shit husband back from Dallas and slit his throat in front of her."

There!

If I wasn't paying such close attention to him I would never have noticed the slight twitch of his lip when Bishop Murdoch's whereabouts was mentioned. Chance and the other two storm out of the room leaving me standing here staring at my guard, his gaze bores right into mine. His eyes are cold, there's no emotion in the depths of them almost as if he's soulless. Who the hell is this guy?

"Erika." I jolt out of my staring match with the unnamed guard and rush out of the dining room to find Chance pacing the foyer. "Tomlin will take you to a hotel in the city, pack a bag and wait for me there." Before I can lift my hands to sign a single word he darts his gaze above my head. "Take her to the city, keep her there and make sure no one follows you. I'll meet you there as soon as we sort out this situation."

"Yes sir," The gravelly tone of his voice sends a shiver

down my spine and that's when it hits me, I drop my gaze to the floor and race up the stairs so Chance can't see the look on my face. I don't wait for *Tomlin*, I snort to myself at the ridiculous name he has chosen. I knew there was something about him and I was right. I make quick work of packing my bag making sure to grab my laptop and any chargers I will need.

Tomlin leads me from the room, he tries to grab my bag from me but I twist and glare at him, his eyes narrow but he says nothing as he leads the way down to the garage where a G-class wagon sits. I climb into the passenger seat without complaint, the fact he didn't open or close my door is a dead giveaway that my hunch is right. The moment the engine starts and he puts the car in drive, the tension ramps up inside the vehicle. Not a single word is spoken as he drives us out of Chance's little estate, in fact he says nothing even as we hit the interstate.

I can't help but squirm in my seat, my gut is screaming at me that I'm right and need to get the fuck out of this car but how the hell do I do that when he's driving so freaking fast. My phone begins to ring but I ignore it. I know he's calling because my tracker would have alerted him that I've left the compound without Chance. Both our phones are bugged, the difference between us though is that I know about them and he doesn't.

"Not gonna answer that, Erika?" I tense in my seat, it's posed as a casual question but I'm no fool I can detect the undercurrent of a threat in his tone.

He knows, I know.

I expect him to veer off the highway and find an abandoned road somewhere and try to kill me, *try* being the operative word here. He won't take me down easily and I sure as fuck won't go down without a fight. My heartbeat is erratic, I know he's carrying a gun and I curse myself for not putting my own in the waistband of my jeans instead of shoving it in my bag. I know better than that!

I just need to pray that he doesn't try to kill me until the car stops so I have a chance to shoot him first.

We pull up out front of a hotel that seems just as swanky as the one we ate at yesterday. Tomlin tries to grab my bag again as I exit the car but I smack his hand away. The dark look in his eyes and the way his jaw locks up tells me he isn't used to that type of reaction, he snarls down at me then turns and storms inside the lobby with me following after him.

He gives the woman at reception my name and it takes her barely a minute before she is handing the keys over and telling us to enjoy our stay. He boldly places his hand on my lower back causing me to gasp at the contact, he says nothing as he uses his hold on me to steer me toward the elevators. The doors open instantly when he presses the button, he shoves me forward causing me to stumble a bit. I spin around and glare at the asshole but he has his back to me and waves his card in front of some scanner that sets the letter P alight on the keypad. The ride to the penthouse is tense, I subtly place my free hand inside my bag and grip my gun making sure to keep my hand there as the doors open.

"Move." He growls, the tone of his voice and the cold harsh look in his eyes tells me that his pretense is over. I do as I'm told and step out of the lift and make my way inside the lavish suite not taking in any of the details, I round a corner and come to a halt at the edge of a living room. Sitting on the couch is a woman who I must admit is stunning, standing behind her are...twins. It's not the fact they are identical that has me stumped, it's the fact that one of them was the imposter pretending to be Royal Murdoch.

"Hello, love." One of the twins says, before I can do anything the real Royal is in front of me and has his hand wrapped around my throat and a gun in his other hand pointed at my forehead.

"Give me one good reason why I shouldn't fucking kill you?" I'm no stranger to having a gun in my face so I keep my cool and decide to play along for a while longer.

Chapter Eight

ROYAL

Most women would scream, beg and plead for their life or at the least do what they fucking do best and turn on the water works but not this one. She stands here before me with a defiant look in her eyes, my upper lip pulls back in a snarl.

"Answer me!" I yell, I've barely got the words out before her bag drops to the floor and I feel something pressed into my stomach, I flick my gaze down to see a nine millimeter pressed firmly against me. Looking back at the little witch I narrow my eyes. "Do it, I fucking dare you." I push.

"Royal, killing her will ruin everything." Sin warns from behind me.

"Why the fuck is she even here with you?" Havoc asks.

I keep my eyes on her as I answer them. "This little snake pieced it together, she knew Chaos wasn't me yesterday, the second I spoke to Chance today I saw it in the way her body coiled that she knew exactly who I was, didn't you Rika?" At the twist I played on her name it seems to spark some anger inside her, she tries to yank free of my hold but I tighten it until she gasps. She never tries to force me to loosen it or even moves her gun away; she just stands there gasping for air.

"Royal." Chaos warns as he comes to stand beside me. "She can't understand you." He defends.

I release my grip on her slightly, just enough so she is able to breathe a bit easier. "She understands every fucking word I'm saying, she just can't speak. She's a fucking mute." I growl.

"How did she know Chaos wasn't you?" Sin asks as she comes to stand on my other side, I eye Erika and try to get a read on her but she's a closed fucking book. Don't get me wrong, the sight of her has my cock twitching but the fact she is fucking Chance makes me sick, I'd never bury my cock inside her gaped ass cunt.

"She's fucking mute, how the fuck am I supposed to know that?" I grit out, the dirty little whore shoves her gun harder into stomach.

"You pull that trigger and I promise you that your brain will decorate that wall behind you." Chaos threatens, she flicks her gaze to him for a split second and scoffs.

"Answer the fucking question you little whore or I'll kill you and act like we got ambushed, either way I still win." I snarl, her eyes flick between mine for a moment debating on if she should trust me enough to heed my warning and drop her gun so she can use her hands to communicate. Turns out, Chaos learned how to sign in high school so he is our only point of contact with her.

She slowly lowers her gun and tucks it into the waistband of her pants, I refuse to let go of her throat, she is a liability that I won't risk getting free. The only reason I brought her here to this hotel is because Havoc and Chaos holed up here the moment they landed. The woman at reception has been paid off to not ask questions, which is why I gave her Erika's name and not my own.

She raises her hands and begins to sign as Chaos translates

for us. "She wants to know why she should tell you anything when you are the one who lied."

"How the fuck did you know who I am?" I growl and cock the trigger back on my gun, if she doesn't answer this question I'm going to blow her fucking brains out and skip to plan B instead of carrying on with the current plan we have.

Her nostrils flare as her hands start to move a mile a minute while Chaos speaks. "She said she heard you on the phone to Chance a couple nights ago, when she met me yesterday she realized that my voice wasn't the same as the one on the phone. When she heard you speak today she knew then you were Royal– what the fuck?" Chaos snaps, I turn to him waiting for him to explain why she has a grin on her face and he looks like he wants to resume my position of strangling her.

"What the fuck is she saying?" Chanel shouts at him.

The bastard glowers at the girl as he speaks. "The bitch says from the moment she met me she knew there was no way I could be the heir of Bishop and Kiara Murdoch because I look like a guy who would rather fuck my way through college then actually earn a degree." Yep, I have no choice but to bite the corner of my lip to keep from laughing, Sin and Havoc on the other hand have no qualms about laughing at Chaos' expense. "Shut the fuck up assholes!"

"Why didn't you rat me out?" Sin and Havoc both shut their mouths at my question. She flicks her gaze toward the large windows that overlook the beach below, she doesn't look at me as she answers.

"She says it's because she wants what you want."

"And what exactly do I want, little girl?" I force out through clenched teeth, she slowly turns back to face me but this time, there is no anger in her eyes, just understanding. She makes a gesture with her hands and I look to Chaos to translate but his eyes are narrowed on her as if he's trying to work out what the fuck she is thinking.

"Revenge." He mutters.

"For what?" I ask her.

"For my family and yours." I keep my gaze on her as Chaos continues to translate. "She was sold to him, she didn't choose to marry him. She wants her freedom from this life and if we help her she will help us take Chance down."

In the small amount of time I have spent watching her I could tell she doesn't want to be with him, her face may not give it away but her body language did. I choose to ignore her and storm out of the room heading for the office Chaos has set up in the back of the penthouse. I waste no time pulling my phone from my pocket and dialing Luka's number, he answers on the third ring.

"Royal." He says in greeting.

"They're in Dallas, the bastard lied. He never sent them to Siberia."

Luka whistles. "Are you sure?"

"He let it drop in a panic this morning, send a team to Dallas to scout it out. I'll send Chanel to start tracking and get the twins to hack into his records for any information on what the fuck is out there."

"This could be a trap." He interjects.

"I know."

"She can't go to Dallas, Royal. If they find out what you are doing they will use her against you, I'll go in her place." I grit my teeth in annoyance knowing he's right.

"They're going to come after you for helping me." I warn.

He sighs tiredly. "Yeah I know, at least they will be home though. Just make sure you shut this shit down, kid." I end the call not bothering to respond, if he can get my dad and the others back safely then that means our plans can move quicker and we can take the bastard out. I just need to find what links him to the Vargas Cartel and how the bastard is actually related to my mom. Leaving the office I head back to where the others are, my cousins stand to one side of the room watching Erika gaze out of the window.

"Has she said anything more?" I ask low enough for only them to hear.

"No." Havoc answers.

"You fucked up bringing her here, Royal. She knows our faces now, she can't be trusted." Chanel's words ring true but that still doesn't change that she already figured it out.

"The folder we got from your dad's informant, was there anything in there?" Sin looks at me and shakes her head.

"We ran checks on the names listed, Emilio Vargas had one son who we know is dead. He had a brother, sister-in-law and niece but they were killed years ago. He is the last living Vargas."

"Then why the fuck is he with Chance? He has to have something on the Cartel, if we find out what that is we can flip them." Havoc and Chaos nod their heads in agreement, I know they both feel like shit and blame themselves for this happening but it can't be helped and there is no point in blaming anyone, we're here now and just need to fix this shit.

"What if it isn't something huge and it's just something mundane." Sin announces, the three of us turn to her and wait for her to finish her thought. "What if, it's just about cleaning money and expanding into Miami. Chance pushing out your dad and taking this away from you means he owns Miami. The cartel can work here and have their money cleaned, Chance can make that happen."

That's it!

"Sin, find me a link to the cartel and follow it. Havoc, you need to start shaking down doors and find out who is dealing with the Cartel. Chaos, you're with me, it's time Royal started playing his part and helping his cousin." I tell them.

"What about her?" Chaos asks as he flicks his head toward

Erika, I study her for a moment still unsure of what the fuck she gains out of all of this.

"Sin, find me everything you can on Erika Martinez."

"You got it. I'm heading back to your house, I'll check in later." She says as she gathers her things and heads out.

I leave the twins to it as I stalk over to Erika, I step up behind her leaving a couple inches of space between our bodies, she's fucking tiny. The top of her head just reaches my chest, her long pale blonde hair looks like silk, it's an odd color for a woman of her origins. The fact she has blue eyes as well just adds to my suspicions. I smirk when I see gooseflesh dot the back of her neck, she can try and act like she has no idea I'm behind her but her body betrays her.

Chapter Nine

ERIKA

The hairs on the back of my neck stand up at his close proximity, his scent overwhelms me, mint, cedar and *him*. I've never been one to notice the scent of others but with him, it's hard not to. I knew from the moment I first saw him that there was more to him, he didn't stand or walk like the guards I've known. He carries an air of dominance with him, it's not forced or faked it's just natural. The man is handsome, there is no denying that but the fact he is a Murdoch, makes my attraction to him unacceptable.

"You gonna rat me out to your fiancé, Rika?" His breath teases the back of my neck sending a shiver down my spine, I slowly turn around and face him. His eyes hold a coldness in their depths, like he feels nothing, no pain, no love, just anger.

I dart my tongue out to moisten my lips and don't miss how his eyes track the movement. I shake my head in answer, his gaze flicks between mine and for a second I forget to breathe when he leans down so we are eye level. The tips of our noses brush and I have to bite the inside of my cheek to keep from panting. I have been around a lot of men and never in all my life have any of them ever sparked a feeling inside me like Royal does. I don't know if it's the dominance or the air of danger that clings to him that has me wanting to shroud myself in his shadow but something tells me, Royal Murdoch has never cared for anyone who he doesn't share blood with.

"You keep your mouth shut, you live. You snitch or do anything that risks me or my family, I'll slit your fucking throat myself." My eyes widened, he isn't like most men who deliver hidden threats, he says them as they are. He lifts his hand and brushes his knuckles along my cheek causing me to tense at the tender touch. "Don't worry though, I'll be at the church in the back row getting a blow job while you lay lifeless in your coffin up at the front." I smack his hand away ready to escape his imposing ass. Before I can even drop my hand back to my side his other one is around my throat and then I'm shoved against the glass window. The back of my head throbs from smacking against the glass but I bite my tongue to keep from crying out.

I claw at his arm which does nothing so, I snap my arm out the moment he leans down and slap him across his face. My eyes widen the second the sound of the *thawk* sounds out around the room, I hear the other hiss from across the room but ignore them and keep my focus on Royal. He slowly turns back to face me, a red hand print glares back at me, his eyes blaze with loathing. The grip he has on my throat tightens as he lifts me off my feet, my legs dangle and thrash about as I gasp for air.

"You stupid little girl, I'm going to fucking ruin you for that." He grits out through clenched teeth, my vision grows hazy from lack of oxygen and black spots dance in my vision. I don't bother to look to his cousins for help, I know they won't give it even if I begged, Royal is their leader and they will do as he commands. "Fuck with me again, Erika and I'll fucking kill you." The hatred that laces each of his words can be felt, he releases his hold on me and I drop to the floor gasping for air on my hands and knees, tears trail down my cheeks.

"You need to move now, GPS tracker says he's heading to the city." One of the twins says but I can't focus on anything else aside from dragging in lungful after lungful of air.

"Get the fuck up." I can't move, my arms and legs refuse to budge, I open my mouth to tell him that but no words come out. He grips my ponytail and uses that to hoist me up, I cry out but it doesn't deter him. He gets right in my face the moment I'm standing.

"You remain silent, you live. You do anything to draw attention to me or my family and I'll make sure you suffer." My nostrils flare as I glare at the son of a bitch, his cold soulless eyes dare me to defy him but I'm smarter than that. I answer by nodding my understanding, he grips my arm and drags me toward the elevators, snagging my bag off the floor on our way. "I'll be in touch." He calls out as we step inside the lift, I yank my arm free and move as far away from him as I can.

How can someone so beautiful be so fucking cruel?

He doesn't say a single word to me the entire time we travel to the hotel where Chance expects me to be waiting for him. The moment he opens the penthouse door for me I stalk inside and go in search of a room where I can lock myself inside and not have to see him until I must. How fucking dare he lay his hands on me like that! No man back home would have ever dared touch me in such a way yet, this man thinks he has the right. Disgusting is what he is. I find a room on the second floor and slam the door closed behind me. I want to scream or break something but I do none of that because that would draw attention to myself.

Instead, I decide to make use of the adjoining bathroom. I strip my clothes off and dump them in the corner as I step inside the large stall and turn the faucet on, I jump out of the way so the cold spray doesn't hit me. I hate the cold, I've never liked it even as a child. Give me a warm sunny summer day and I will be smiling wide and living my best life. Once the water has warmed up I step under the spray and relish in the feeling of the water cascading down my body, I needed this. I bend down to use some of the pump soap in here but the second I feel a cool draft on my backside, I spin around and drop down into a crouch with one leg bent at the knee and the other extended to my side ready to strike out at whoever the fuck is in here.

I flick my gaze up to see a smug looking blue eyed monster standing there, my upper lip pulls back in a snarl. "Want to tell me who the fuck you really are?" He says in a casual tone but the slight edge to it tells me he has been digging into my past. I make no move to answer him and slowly climb to my feet, uncaring that I'm naked and dripping wet in front of this man. I see the struggle on his face, he tries really freaking hard to keep his eyes on my face but curiosity wins out after a minute. His gaze travels the length of my body, heat spreads throughout my entire being when a small groan tumbles from his lips. Reaching out he turns the faucet off and then steps into the stall with me, what I thought was a sizable shower a minute ago no longer feels that way with his hulking form in here.

I tense in preparation of him attacking me again when he reaches out, except this time his fingers trace the tattoo's on either side of my hips. He traces the guns I have tattooed there taking his time like he has every right to touch me.

"You have a skull tattoo on your back." I frown not liking that he has seen so much of my secrets, these are the only tattoos I have and they are marked on my body for a reason. They are a reminder of what I have lost. "Two Pit Vipers tattooed on either of your hips, you're an oddity." His gaze is still glued to the gun on my left hip that he continues to trace sending shivers down my spine. In one swift move he has his hand clenched around my hip and the other locked on the back of my neck. I don't fight him as he pulls my wet body against his own, I know for a fact his clothing will be soaked but he doesn't seem to care.

His thumb absentmindedly strokes the back of my neck causing goosebumps to erupt all over my heated body. His eyes hold me captive, my mouth parts on a gasp the moment I feel the hard bulge against my stomach. My eyes widen as his become hooded, what the fuck is happening? How did we go from hating each other a second ago to me wanting to feel him move inside me?

Fuck!

I feel myself getting wet at the thought of this beast throwing me around the bedroom as he fucks me like a savage. That mental picture has a small moan tumbling from my lips and my eyes closing for a moment as I try to gather myself. I should be pushing him away and fighting against... whatever the hell is happening right now but the truth is, this is the most alive I have felt in years and he has barely touched me.

"I'll ruin you." He whispers, my eyes flutter open only to be met with a heated look from him. He wants me and he hates that, if sleeping with him is the price I need to pay to take Chance down and earn my freedom then so be it. I mean, it wouldn't exactly be torture having a God like him between my legs. "You want me to, don't you?" He rasps out as he bends down and ghosts his lips over mine. God, I want him to kiss me so bad. "I'd fuck you, right here, right now and not give a fuck if your fiance walked in the door and heard you screaming."

His words have me trembling and my thighs shaking, my pussy begins to throb. "Except, I don't fuck dirty ass liars." He growls, before he can stalk out of here thinking he won some type of debate I decide to get the upper hand. I smash my lips against his, his mouth opens in shock and I use that to my advantage, I slip my tongue inside his mouth and mewl at the taste of him. When he tries to deepen the kiss, I clamp my teeth down on his bottom lip hard, he growls and tears it free releasing me as he takes a step back.

We both stand here panting and glaring at each other, the look on his face tells me he knows I won't take his shit lying down, I'll fight him if I need to. He says nothing as he turns and storms out of here slamming the bedroom door closed behind him. I crumple to the floor in a heap reeling about what just happened, this day can fuck right off.

Chance arrived an hour after my encounter with Royal, he came and found me the moment he arrived and demanded I follow him into the living room. This is why I am now seated on the sofa while he sits in front of me on the small table. I want to fidget under the scrutiny of his gaze but I don't. I can feel Royal's penetrating stare boring into the side of my head, Chance looks me up and down for what feels like the hundredth time.

"Another message was delivered before I left the house." I purse my lips and wait for him to continue. "This one had your name on it." My eyes widen as his narrow. "Another one of my men was delivered to my gate in pieces, this one had a Queen of Hearts nailed to him." I shake my head not understanding how this has anything to do with me. "Along with that fucking card, there was a photo of you along with it." I reel back into the couch and shake my head denying what he is implying.

These bastards are trying to pin the deaths of his men on me!

Chapter Ten

ROYAL

He's going to hit her!

I can see it in the way he tenses and has one of his arms slightly drawn back, choking her is different to fucking laying hands. If he fucking lays one finger on her I won't be able to stand back and watch it. I know he is becoming unhinged, this is only the second body and already he's running scared like the little bitch he is.

"Fucking tell me who is doing this!" He screams in her face, she shrinks back into the couch clearly scared of the fucker. I look around and see eight other men in here, each of them avert their gazes, motherfuckers. They all know what he's about to do to her and they choose to turn a blind eye to it.

Chance draws his arm back and then smacks her across the face sending her sideways on the sofa, I step forward ready to intervene and put the fucker down for laying hands on a woman but when he grabs her by her hair and pulls her to her feet, she shocks the fuck out of me when she throat punches him! He drops his hold on her and stumbles backward hitting the table before falling to his ass and gasping for air.

Erika stands there breathing hard with her hands clenched into fists at her side, an angry red handprint on her face. Chance uses the table to help him back to his feet, I tense in anticipation of what is to come. He charges her, tackling her tiny frame to the ground. She thrashes beneath him, I move to step in but she flicks her gaze to me and shakes her head.

What the fuck?

I stand here like a little bitch with my gaze locked on hers as the cunt hits her, she cries out when he straddles her legs and begins to punch her, after the fourth hit I can't take it. I tear him off her and throw the cunt back, he lands on his ass. At the sight of me towering above him, his entire body goes rigid.

"Royal Murdoch is here, sir." One of the men said from behind me. Chance smiles and pushes to his feet, he pats me on the shoulder, and confusion wars inside me.

"Thanks for stopping me, I don't need my little cousin seeing me lose my cool. Take her to her room, I'll deal with the bitch later." I grind my teeth so fucking hard I think I hear one of them crack. When he steps away from me, I spin around to find Erika curled into a ball on the ground sobbing.

"Fuck." I growl beneath my breath, I bend down and slip my arms under her, she cries out when I lift her. She buries her face in my chest as I take her back to her bedroom. Once inside, I kick the door shut behind us and gently lay her on her bed. She groans in pain and guilt swims inside me when her big hazel eyes look up at me with tears. "Why did you stop me?" I grit out, a sad smile tugs at her lips but it vanishes just as quickly. "Who the fuck are you, Erika?" I whisper. A shadow falls over her features, she shifts on the bed and cringes in pain, I drop down beside her and gently push her backward until she is laying flat again. The need to touch her overcomes me, I reach out and gently brush my knuckles down her uninjured cheek. "You did it so I wouldn't blow my cover," I whisper, it's not a question but she nods anyway. "You stupid girl, no man has the right to ever lay his hands on a woman."

The deadpan look she gives me has a small laugh escaping me. "I'm different, you enjoyed my hands on you." A spark enters her eyes at my words and my cock twitches in my pants. Shouting can be heard from downstairs, I leap to my feet and look down at her, she may be injured and upset but that's my blood down there so I leave her without thought and head downstairs to see what the fuck is going on. I slam to a stop at the sight of Chaos with his gun drawn and pointed at Chance, the eight men around the room all have their guns aimed and ready to fire at my cousin.

"I didn't have anything to fucking do with that shit, I was at the Biltmore Hotel last night with a chick named Shandy or some shit, check their fucking cameras!" Chaos snarls, Chance looks to Dalton and nods, he drops his gun and pulls out his phone while everyone stands here in a Mexican standoff waiting for Dalton's confirmation.

"His story checks out, he stayed the night in room 601 with a woman." Fucking idiots, It wasn't even Chaos that was there it was Havoc and Chanel, joys of having a twin I guess.

"We good now, *cousin*?" Chaos snarks, Chance nods his head stiffly. Chaos doesn't drop his gun until the others do, he knows never to lower his weapon until last.

"Sorry. I'm on edge, I had another card delivered this morning." Chaos plays the part well and frowns acting taken back by the news. Chance tells him about the body of Bodhi being found at the front gate this morning, I want to puff my chest out and take ownership for the gruesome sight he describes. I was the one to dismember Bodhi and end the pussy's life, Chance is going to get the royal flush and he has no fucking idea.

"You can't stay here."

"Why the hell not?" Chance snaps at Chaos.

"It's too open, too many people coming and going." Good man, keep freaking the cunt out Chaos, he'll be putty in our hands soon.

"Where the fuck do you suggest I go?"

"Come stay with me, I rented a house near Biltmore golf course. It's gated and has a full security system. Let me help you and prove my loyalty, cousin." Chance ponders Chaos' offer for a minute, I can see he wants to decline it so I decide to cut in and push him.

"He isn't wrong, there are too many access points here and being on the top floor, all they would need to do is bomb the lobby and we're all dead." Chance's eyes widen in fear, he turns to Dalton and says.

"Get the men and move everything we need to Royal's house, I want the meeting with Emilio brought forward." At the mention of his name I perk up. "If I'm being targeted because of this deal with him, the least he can do is send men out here to help me." Chaos shoots me a wink and I give him a subtle nod, these fuckers are walking right into the trap we set. We knew from the moment we started taking out his guards that he would run scared to Emilio, it was the only way we could get him back to Miami and out of New York.

I ride in the back of the Limo with Chance, Erika and Dalton, he's forgotten about her for the time being but I know without a doubt when we drop the next three bodies tomorrow morning he is going to go after her. This time, it isn't his men, it's his crooked coworkers. Havoc will be gathering them tonight for their… treatment. My phone vibrates in my pocket, I pull it out to see a message from Sin.

SIN

Erika Martinez doesn't exist! The bitch is a liar and a liability, Royal, take her out.

I flick my gaze to the woman in question, she stares out the window looking at the passing landscape.

ME

Find out who the fuck she is. She is with him for a reason and I want to know what the fuck that reason is.

SIN

On it.

I bring up my message thread with Luka and type out a message to him.

ME

Any updates?

His reply comes a minute later.

LUKA

They're here, all six of them. We need a plan, if we bust them out he will know it's us.

ME

We don't have a choice, shit is moving fast here.

LUKA

I can have them out and back in New York in two days.

ME

Do it. My father can't know where I am, I need the intel to bring the Vargas cartel and Chance down, keep him out of Miami.

I pocket my phone as we come to a stop behind Chaos's car, I had his, Havoc and Chanel's handprints added to the gate scanner. The moment the gate opens and we begin to roll forward, Chance sits up taller in his seat and flicks his gaze between me and Dalton.

"I want the entire property surrounded, Royal may think he is running the show but the boy is mistaken." I keep my expression neutral and nod. "I have a meeting tonight with the new investors, Dalton. I want you and six others with me, Tomlin, you will remain here with two others to keep an eye on my bride-to-be."

Both Dalton and I nod our agreement just as the car comes to a stop out the front of my house, I fake awe as we step outside and gaze up at the house. Chaos motions for Cable to show Erika to her room, the man looks her over and frowns at the sight of the bruise on her face but says nothing.

Dalton orders us men to do a perimeter check, I happily oblige and tell them I'll check the back of the house. Once at the back I look around to make sure no one is around. I input the code to the basement Grandpa had made for me and quickly slip inside. I couldn't help myself and checked it out the first night I arrived. The whole basement is fitted out with computers, guns, blueprints and everything you need to know about the powerful people in Miami. There are hundreds of folders, I had Samson stationed down here to go through them all. He currently sits behind a desk with a stack of files on either side of him, he looks up and nods.

"Got anything?"

He flips the file around and points to a picture. "That

right there is Chance's father." I frown, the man is clearly not Italian.

"He said he was related through Grandpa, how the fuck is that guy related exactly?"

Samson shakes his head. "He isn't. He is Chance's biological father, his mother married your grandfather's cousin, not brother!" My brows raise as a victorious smile splits across my face.

"He's not blood."

Samson shakes his head. "No. His whole campaign was run on the story that his family has been here for generations and all that shit but in fact, his father is from Ohio."

"How the fuck does he link in with the Vargas cartel though?" He grabs another folder from the stack and opens it up to show me bank statements and old ass emails.

"Chance's father owed a debt to the cartel, when he died Chance and his mother inherited the debt."

"And..." I prompt him to continue.

"Chance struck a deal with Emilio, he would work off the debt and the moment he became governor he would launder their money through his businesses."

"So, this is just about money then?"

"It appears so, yeah." I mull over everything he just said, if this was just about money then taking Chance out would be easy.

But why did he go after my family?

That's the one thought that stays with me as I leave Samson and head inside to resume my post of guarding Erika. I make my way upstairs and grind my teeth as I pass by the master bedroom–my room, seeing Chance in there pisses me off. Chaos gave him my room so he would seem like a gracious host, I keep moving until I reach the other end of the hall where Erika is. Her door is slightly ajar so I peek inside and find her sitting cross legged on her bed with her laptop in front of her.

Her brows are drawn in as she frowns down at the screen, she nibbles on her lip absentmindedly, her long blonde hair is out and falls over her shoulders. The sight of her has my cock twitching in my pants, I hear Chance barking orders for his men to be ready to leave in forty minutes. Smiling to myself I decide to wait till her fiance is out of the house before I go after her fine ass, the sight of her naked and wet in the shower has been playing on repeat in my mind all fucking day. Just thinking about that shit has my cock growing hard, ready or not Rika, I'm coming for you.

Chapter Eleven

ERIKA

I reread the email over and over again, I updated him and passed on the information that someone is clearing their digital footprint. No one can stay hidden in this day and age so that only means Royal and his cousins have someone constantly erasing any evidence of them ever existing.

I look over the email again, there is no way he could mean this. He is asking me to switch it up and move on to the next victim, I can't do it.

Can I?

I dart my head at the sound of my door opening, my eyes widen at the sight of Royal standing there in a pair of jeans and a plain black shirt, his hair still wet from the shower he must have taken. I've never seen him in anything aside from his suit. The sight of him in a suit had me hot for him but him dressed casually like this, has my mouth watering and my pussy clenching on air. The man is sex personified, the raw sex appeal oozes off him in waves. If you couple that with the dark cloud that lingers like a second skin and the dominance that radiates around him, you have a lethal fucking mix. He keeps his gaze on me as he reaches back and flicks the lock, I close the lid of my laptop and wait to see what he does next.

The fact he's in my room right now, shows me he gives zero fucks about being caught.

He slowly moves toward me, I track his every movement with my eyes. My mind is screaming at me to run but my body refuses. I haven't felt this way in a long time, I've never wanted to feel a man's touch as much as I want to feel his. It might be the fact I know this will end just as quickly as it started or maybe it's the fact sleeping with him will be my silent revenge. He stops at the edge of the bed forcing me to crane my neck back in order to maintain eye contact. I dart my tongue out to wet my lips, his eyes darken at the sight and a shiver works its way down my spine. He reaches out, grips my legs and turns me so I am facing him with my legs either side. My face is practically inline with his cock, he runs the tips of his fingertips along my cheek tenderly.

"Does it hurt?" It takes a second for me to register what he's asking, I grip his wrist and shake my head. The heated look in his eyes has my nipples hardening against my silk sleep shirt, a satisfied growl tumbles from his luscious lips at the sight of them. "You gonna fight me?" Biting my bottom lip as I stare up at him I shake my head. I release his wrist, he trails his fingertips along my throat and down the center of my chest, my breathing becomes shallow as he glides the tips of his finger along the top of my breast. He grazes his fingers over my pert nipple earning a gasp from me, my pussy pulses as he cups my tits in his large hands and flicks his thumbs over my nipples. I throw my head back and moan, he uses my position to his advantage and leans down to lick a trail from my neck to my ear, a wanton moan escapes me and I quickly clamp my mouth closed so no one hears.

"Make as much noise as you want, *Sirena*." He whispers in

my ear then scrapes his teeth along my lobe, unable to remain still. I reach out and grip his shirt not sure if I want to pull him closer or push him away. I know I should be doing the latter but I don't, the moment his lips mesh against mine my body decides for me, I pull him closer to deepen the kiss, his hands tangle in my hair yanking on the strands as he positions my face where he wants it. He pushes forward until I'm flat on my back and hovers above me.

He keeps his eyes locked on mine as grinds into me, a moan slips free when I feel his hard cock press against my needy pussy. I'm so wet for him I can feel it dripping out of me. Isn't it amazing that you can spend years with someone and never feel a certain way about them but one day you meet a random stranger and suddenly, you crave them, need them to touch you and own you even if it's just for one night? All so you can put your mind at ease and never have to wonder, what if.

He pushes the thin straps of my sleep top down my arms exposing my tits. "Fuck, they are perfect." He growls out before lowering his head to capture one of my nipples in his hot mouth, a cry comes from me as my back arches off the bed. I pull my arms free of my shirt so I can grip the back of his head and hold him there, the way his tongue flicks and swirls around the taut bud has me panting. He switches sides, this time when I cry out he bites down and a strangled sound comes from me, fuck that feels so good.

He shifts slightly and rests one of his arms beside me to hold his weight while he uses the other to push inside my sleep shorts. My breathing is heavy as anticipation gnaws away inside me, his fingertips graze the top of my greedy cunt and I'm powerless to stop my hips from bucking upward. He releases my nipple with a wet pop, he stares down at me as he runs a single finger through my slick folds. His eyes widen when he circles my entrance and feels the wetness gathered there.

"This all for me?" He growls, I whimper when he begins to circle my clit. "Answer me, Sirena." I nod feeling a certain way about him giving me a pet name, praying that's enough of answer for him because I need this, I need him to fuck me so hard I forget about everything else except for how he makes me feel. I need to forget who I am for a short time, just a short while is all I need to clear my head then I can focus again.

That's what I tell myself but the truth is, I don't know if I want this to be a one time thing.

He slips a finger inside me and my back arches off the bed as a moan tears out of me, he smashes his lips to mine to quieten my cries as he continues to finger fuck me at a brutal pace, he swallows my cries. I feel my orgasm cresting, my stomach begins to coil in preparation, I lock my arms around his neck and anchor myself to him. His thumb presses flat against my clit and that's all it takes for me to scream my release into his mouth, he doesn't bring me down gently. He yanks his hand free and leaps off the bed, he pulls his shirt over his head as I lay here in a blissed out state and marvel at him.

Sweet baby fucking Jesus!

The man has a body sculpted by the fucking Gods, his abs stand out without him flexing and the grooves, you know the ones that form that V? He has it. My mouth waters at the sight. He pops the button on his jeans and pushes them down his legs exposing his thick cock that slaps proudly against his abdomen. I've never seen a dick that big before, my eyes widen when I see he has a Prince Albert piercing!

"Clothes off, now!" He growls in a husky tone that has me shuffling off the bed and standing on shaky legs to obey him. I slip my shirt over my head and push my shorts down my legs and stand before him naked. I've never felt beautiful in my own skin until today. Earlier when he saw me in the shower he didn't see any of the imperfections that I do, even now as he drinks in the sight of me I see nothing but raw hunger for... me. "Get on the bed." I do as he says but he grips my ankles and yanks me to the edge where my ass tethers on the edge. He pushes forward to use his body to keep me there, he grips his cock and pumps it twice groaning, the sight of him doing that has me wanting to touch my own pussy.

"Hmmm." A whimper escapes me, his gaze snaps to mine and the dark look in his eyes has me gulping.

"You're a greedy girl, aren't you?" I clamp my teeth into my bottom lip and nod, what's the point in lying he already knows I want him. Gripping his cock he runs it through my slick folds drawing a moan from me, he circles the tip at my entrance, teasing me. Just as I ready myself to beg and plead he pushes inside forcing a strangled cry to tear from me.

I thought he would ease inside me but no, I should have known better. He has given me no sign of being a soft, caring lover, he's shown me today that he is rough and takes what he wants without permission. He groans when he's ball deep inside my pussy, a cold sweat breaks out over my body as I breath hard trying to calm myself enough to adjust to his size, my pussy is burning and sore from the sudden intrusion. He reaches down and grips my throat, this time he doesn't squeeze it hard, he applies enough pressure to add that slight fear that he could kill me if he wanted to. That feeling and the fact he's inside me has a mixture of emotions erupting inside me. He draws his hips back until the tip of his cock is all that remains inside me before he thrusts forward, my back arches off the bed as I scream out.

The pain bleeds way to pleasure as he continues to move inside me, fuck, his piercing rubs perfectly against my sweet spot, my body begins to heat as I feel myself starting to prepare for another orgasm. My breathing shallows as I realize I'm about to come from just sex, I've never come during sex, the thought that this beast could bring me to the peak of pleasure with just his dick has me locking my legs around his waist to hold him in place as I push his hand off my neck and reach up to pull him down to me.

His face hovers above mine for a second before I cover his mouth with mine, the moment my tongue slips inside his mouth something changes, his thrust begins to slow as he kisses me back. He's not trying to fuck and run now, he's taking his time to enjoy this, to enjoy me. I drag my nails down his back as he deepens the kiss, the growl that comes from him when I dig my nails into his back has my pussy clenching down on his cock, he breaks the kiss holding my gaze he grips one of my legs and lifts it over his shoulder. He feels so much deeper at this angle.

"You gonna come all over my cock, Sirena?" My only answer is a sharp cry when he bottoms out inside me, fuck, I can't think straight as he picks up his pace and forces me to feel everything he is inflicting on my body. "Come." He demands, like a slave obeying its master, I do as he says. I shatter beneath him crying out my release for all to hear and not giving a fuck. If Chance were to walk in right now and see us, I would happily take whatever punishment he dished out because it would be fucking worth it to feel what I'm feeling right now.

Aftershocks continue to wrack my body as he pulls out of me and pulls me off the bed so I'm kneeling in front of him. With his cock in one hand and the other tangled in my hair to keep in place he pumps himself four times before his head is thrown back roaring out his release as jets of his cum spurt all over my face, hair and chest. His breathing is ragged as he stares down at me, his face is blank, his eyes back to being cold and calculating. How he can go from blissed out and wanting me to cold and closed off in a split second befounds me.

He removes his hand from my hair to smear his cum all

over my face, chest and hair. I remain motionless allowing him to defile me like this because fuck, I never knew feeling this dirty could feel so fucking good.

"You look better with my cum on you." My mouth opens in shock. "You open those legs for him and I'll kill you, the only one fucking you from now on is me, defy me and I'll ruin you." I just stare at him in disbelief as he dresses, how can he stand there and think he can make a demand like that, I'm not his to control, I'll do as I fucking please! Once he's dressed he turns back to me and grins, that look has me tensing. "Until you can tell me with words that you don't want this, I'll keep fucking you whenever and wherever I please." My jaw unhinges, the fucker laughs as he turns and leaves my room while I remain still and angry as fuck I could let such a piece of shit fuck me.

Chapter Twelve

ROYAL

I wait for the cover of nightfall before I loop the camera feed around the property, Chance and his gang of douche canoes are still out and from the conversation I heard between the two dickbags he left behind with me, he won't be back until late. I use that time to my advantage, Chaos is out in the city playing the part of trying to track down the person leaving these cards. Havoc and Sin are in the basement with Samson, I do a quick check to make sure Phil is guarding Erika's door, she hasn't come out since I left her hours ago. Yes, I crossed a line and fucked her, I know she's lying, she knows I know she is full of shit. So, until I can find the proof why not use this shitty situation to my advantage and get my cock wet.

Fuck, just the memory of the way her pussy fit me like a glove and the sounds that came out of her as I fucked her have my cock getting hard. I push thoughts of her fucking delicious cunt and perfect body out of my head as I head to the foyer to see Don patrolling the down stairs.

"I'm gonna go check the perimeter." I say as I walk out the

front door, the fact none of these fuckers have pulled me up or used their rank to pull me into line and tell me what to do just shows how under qualified for the job they really are. The background checks we ran on them show that none of them have military training, most of them have only done security for offices or nightclubs. I make my way to the back of the house and double check to make sure I'm not followed before punching in the code and heading inside. Sin is seated at the computers, Samson still sits at the same desk as earlier. I look around the corner to find Havoc securing our guests to their chairs. The three of them snap their gazes to me, Congressman Jack Ives, Congresswoman Helen Barton and Congressman Kevin Monarc all sit there with tape across their mouths, hands cuffed behind them and their legs cuffed to the legs of the chairs.

"How the fuck did you get them all here undetected?" I ask, Havoc spins around and smiles proudly.

"Dude, easy as fuck. Sin looped the feed as we came in through the back entrance."

I scrunch my face. "What back entrance?"

"Through the golf course there is a gate, we figured the pin code would be the same as this one so we tried it and it worked." Sin says from across the room.

"Seal that entrance off, too many entrances are bad." I growl, pissed that I had no idea about that gate, anyone could use it to get to us so I want it gone.

"What's the plan?" I look at each of our guests documenting their faces to my memory, if I'm going to kill them the least I could do is remember their faces and names. Havoc comes up beside me keeping his back to the three guests and speaks low enough so only I can hear. "I can do it, you don't need to."

I flick my gaze to him and shake my head. This, him offering this and Chaos pretending to be me while Sin scrubs any trace of us from every camera around the city is why we work. The four of us are a unit, no one comes between us, no matter it's the four of us till the fucking end.

"Nah, I want this. He fucked with my family, I'm going to make him watch this shit." Havoc's eyes shine with lust, the fucker always gets off on the sight of people dying, it's weird as fuck but that's just him. I make my way over to the three members of congress, the woman in the middle has tears trailing down her cheeks and it fills me with fucking joy to see the bitch scared out of her mind. The men on either side of her quiver and shake, Jesus, they could at least fake that they aren't sitting there shitting themselves, they're piss weak.

Havoc has the table set up against the wall with all the devices I'll need to tear each of these bastards apart, they thought they got away with fucking with my family. I'm about to show them what happens to fuckers that come after my family, they thought because I disbanded the family business that they were free, think again fuckers. I grab the bolt cutters and sling them over my shoulder as I turn back to my new toys and smile, I take three steps toward them, Jack and Jevin shrink back into their seats while Helen shakes uncontrollably as sobs wrack her body.

"Get the camera ready." I bark at Havoc, I stand in front of Helen and wait for her to slowly lift her gaze to mine, the fear in her shit colored eyes spurs the monster inside me to life. I thrive off the fear of my victims. "Helen, I don't believe we have ever formally been introduced." Her brows slant in the middle of her face. "I believe you know my parents though." She shakes her head, I tsk her. "Don't lie to me Helen." She tries to speak but it just comes out a jumbled mess because of the tape. "Let me jog your memory, you helped the governor and the cartel kingpin bring down a private jet carrying my father and uncles." Her eyes widen as the reality of who I'm talking about sinks in. "Yes Helen, my father is Bishop

Murdoch, Don to the Murdoch Mafia. You and your two wingmen here thought you could get away with helping those cunts take my family out, well I'm here to remind you that we never forget or forgive. You and the two congressmen here are going to pay with your lives for what you did."

The three of them try to fight against their restraints but it's futile, they won't get free no matter how hard they fight. I peer over my shoulder to see Havoc has the camera set up on the tripod, I look to Sin and Samson to see they both have their skull masks on. We had these masks custom made to match the skulls on the backs of our cards, with Chaos not being able to be here we needed Samson to stand in for him, it's time we let the world know who the fuck we are. Havoc, Sin and Samson come to stand behind the three traitors, I look between the three of them in disgust.

"You will die tonight but before you do, I want you all to know who the fuck is about to end your miserable lives. I am Royal Murdoch, heir to the Murdoch and Bennett Mafia, Don to the Memento Mori and I'm here to serve each of you with my card so you know who is calling you to death." I drop the cutters in front of Helen as I move to join the others at the back of them and snag my mask from Sin. I give Havoc a nod, he pushes record on the camera as I hit the button on the voice distorter in my mask. I place my hands on the top of Helen's shoulders and love the shudder of fear that rolls through her disgusting body.

"Governor Bennett," I say as I address the camera. "As you race through the city looking for me and calling in favors from your crooked friends to protect you from me, I've already got you. You think you can hide, run and flee the safety of your home but just know, every move you make is the move I forced you to. You thought you could take what wasn't yours and strike a deal with the cartel to keep you safe from repercussions? Think again, when the card is dropped, you are marked.

There is no escaping *us*, we come for our prey and will hunt you down until your blood soaks the ground beneath your cold lifeless body. We are the *Memento Mori,* we are the bringers of death and your time is now. The King of Clubs belongs to the heir. The princess owns the Queen of Hearts. The Jack of Spades represents the coming Chaos and the Ace of Diamonds is for the Havoc we will wreck."

I leave the camera recording as I get to work on Jack, Havoc holds him still as I take the cutters and take each of his fingers off one by one, I only made it to the third before he passed out. The other two try to scream and break free, Kevin manages to flip his chair but Samson just lifts him up and turns him to face us, holding his head still so he has no choice. Once the fingers are gone, I start on the toes, he remains passed out through the rest of it. Havoc grabs the tourniquet and wraps it just above his knee as Sin grabs the skilsaw, she nudges me out of the way so she can do the honors. Jack screams the moment she cuts him, I tear the tape from his mouth wanting them to hear everything when they watch the video. He can scream as loud as he likes, this basement is soundproofed, no one will hear their cries.

This is nothing new to us, we have done this before to the fuckers that tried to fuck with us at UNLV. We have never gone public and confirmed that the calling cards are real or that the Memento Mori really exist but tonight I changed that. I want Chance Bennett to know we are coming for him, he may not know directly who we really are but that doesn't matter, in the end he will know and that's all that matters. The four of us learned enough from Amelia without her realizing that the questions we were asking her about medical advice would be for torture, we know how to inflict the maximum amount of pain without killing someone. We leave Jack once his arms and legs are nubs, I cut his ears off as Sin wraps a rope around his torso so he doesn't fall, I want him to watch as

Kevin is dealt with next. Each of these fuckers helped Chance track the plane and made sure that local authorities were placed elsewhere so they wouldn't reach my father and uncles until Chance could get them out of there.

Anyone who had anything to do with helping in the abduction of my family will pay with their lives. The three of us get to work relieving Kevin of all his limbs and then I take his eyes before I move to Helen. I saved this bitch for last because I know she has been fucking Chance and he has an attachment to the cunt. I rip the tape from her mouth and stare at the woman, unlike the men I want to hear her beg and plead for her life from the start. I grab my chisel and hammer, so I can dig it beneath her nails and remove them one by one but she speaks, halting my movements.

"I can tell you where they are." I cut a look to Havoc, he fishes the remote from his pocket and pauses the recording.

"I already know they are in Dallas." She shakes her head rapidly.

"N-no, they aren't." I lift my mask so she can see me without any obstructions.

"You're a terrible liar, Helen." Her face pales the second I yank my mask down and Havoc begins the recording again, Sin holds her head in place as I go for her tongue first. She screams as I use the pliers Havoc handed me to hold her tongue and slice through it with a blunt knife. Yes, I am that fucking sick I like to use blunt knives so they hurt more. The moment her tongue is severed, I shove it back in her mouth and tape it closed. I remove each of her nails, she doesn't pass out until I remove the toenail.

Unlike the guys, I only remove her hands and feet, while the three of them are still alive I step behind them and look at the camera as I say.

"The three of your co-conspirators will go to hell deaf, dumb and blind. Each of these deaths are on your hands. You have been served the King, The Queen and now you have just been served the Ace." Havoc pulls his card from his pocket and drops it on Helen's lap. "When the Jack comes for you, it will be your last chance to escape because the next one will be the royal flush." Havoc, Sin and I all draw our guns and put a hole in their heads.

Havoc ends the recording and we all remove our masks, I'm covered head to toe in blood and so are they, Samson stands off to the side staring at the bodies of the fuckers that tried to ruin my family.

"How did you know she was lying?" He asks, I remove the gloves I wear and run a hand through my hair as I answer him.

"Because Luka is already in Dallas, they aren't in Siberia like Chance said. They are being held in one of the Vargas cunt's border houses. They can stay as close to the border as they want, if I have to send an army of men down there to get my father then I will, the Mexican cartel won't do shit unless we cross the border."

"Chance has no idea that Uncle Vin did some work for the kingpin of the Mexican Cartel years ago so they have an understanding, Carlo won't rise against our family as long as we don't head into their territory." Havoc adds, it's true, Chance thinks keeping that close to the border will stop us from going after them because we risk a war with the Mexicans, dumb cunt should have researched my family better.

"What do you want done with them?" Samson asks, nodding toward the three bodies.

"Drop the two congressmen at Chance's office in the city, return Helen back to her husband with the USB attached. I want him to know what a trifling whore his wife was, it may also help that he's the police chief and hates Chance. I want to tear this asshole's empire down before I finally end his pathetic life. By the time I'm done with him he is going to beg me to end it."

"And what about his bride to be?" Sin asks from behind me. I slowly turn to face her, I know she's pissed because I haven't killed Erika.

"She poses no threat right now." Her eyes narrow and her jaw stiffens.

"You fucked her?" It's posed as a question but it really isn't, she scoffs and shakes her head. "Don't start thinking with your cock, Royal. You are better than that, *we* are better than some bitch with a tight pussy." Anger courses through me.

"Who I fuck doesn't concern you—."

"It does when that bitch is part of the reason my dad is missing!" She yells. I stand firm, her father isn't the only one missing, we're all wound tight right now and under pressure but I won't take her shit.

"What pisses you off more, Sin? The fact I wouldn't kill her when you said to or the fact I fucked her without you knowing?" Sin and I have always been on the same page, if she hated a bitch I wouldn't touch her much less fuck her but Erika is... different. I don't know what it is but the girl got under my fucking skin and I couldn't stop myself, I needed to do it just once to get her out of my system but now, all I can think about is cleaning off so I can go fuck her again.

Chanel steps up to me keeping a foot of space between us, she looks me up and down scoffing in disgust. "You think I'm wrong but I'm not. There is something off about her, Royal. She is going to fuck you over, there is no way she is some random bitch with no record. She is a *someone*, mark my words cousin she is going to play you and I pray to fucking God you aren't dumb enough to fall in love for the first time with that lying bitch."

Chapter Thirteen

ERIKA

I startle awake when a hand is placed over my mouth, I dart my arm out and grab the dagger I stashed under the pillow ready to stab whoever the fuck this is but then my wrist is gripped and placed beside my head. I buck my hips trying to fight whoever it is off me, the fight flees me when his lips brush against my ear as he whispers.

"Keep fighting Sirena, it only makes me harder." My eyes widen as my tummy begins to coil with need, I push those feelings away and remind myself that he left me here earlier on my knees and mocked me. I don't take kindly to being mocked about not being able to voice my thoughts or feelings. I try to latch onto that anger as he trails open mouthed kisses down my neck and grinds into me, a gasp flees me when his cock pushes against my clit. I feel him smirk against my neck when I shudder, I may be angry at him but my body doesn't get the memo and my legs open wider to accommodate his size. He nips at the tender flesh between my neck and shoulder as one of his hands skates down my side forcing me to tremble in his wake.

He releases my hand and without thought I reach up and grip him by the back of his head and use my hold on his wet hair to move him until his mouth is mine. This kiss isn't like the one from earlier, this one is more forceful, he fights for dominance when there is no fight to be had. I want him to lead and take control but clearly something has provoked him into thinking he needs to show me without words that he is the master and he is the one who calls the shots. He pulls back and rests back on his haunches scowling down at me.

"You mean nothing to me, this is just me needing to fuck and you being the only pussy available, got it?" The only lighting is from the moon high in the sky, the tight lines that mar his face tell me his angry tone has nothing to do with me so I decide to be reckless for once in my life. I sit up so we are chest to chest, grip the hem of his shirt and pull it up, he helps me. Given the height difference between us there is no way I could do it on my own. He chucks his shirt to the side as I grip my own and yank it over my head, his gaze drops to my lips and a growl of appreciation comes from him, the moment he cups my breasts in his hands my head lolls back and a moan tumbles free.

He pushes me backward so I'm flat on my back and then captures one of my nipples in his mouth, just as a cry begins to break free he clamps his hand over my mouth to keep me quiet. He leaves his hand there as he switches sides and pays my other nipple the same amount of attention. I can feel I have already soaked through my thong and he has barely touched me. He licks a trail down my stomach only stopping when he reaches my belly button, he swirls his tongue inside it and I gasp. I quickly place my own hand over my mouth as he peels my sleep shorts down my legs but leaves my thong in place.

I jolt when he runs his nose along my pussy inhaling. "Fuck, your cunt smells so good, Rika." I moan into my hand. "I need to taste you, I want to see if you taste as good as you look." A whimper escapes me when he pushes the thin material to the side and blows his hot breath across my heated core, my pussy clenches on air in anticipation knowing how good he can make me feel. He darts his tongue out and licks from my clit all the way to my opening where he plunges his tongue inside me.

"Fuck, you taste so sweet." He rasps out as he swirls his tongue around my clit forcing me to bite down on the side of my hand to quiet my moans. I pinch my nipple between my fingers and slam my eyes closed, you know the feeling of when you're on the verge of coming but want to prolong it as long as you can so you can live in this blissful heightened state? I feel like that right now and fuck me it feels amazing. Royal pushes two fingers inside my tight wet hole as he sucks my clit into his mouth, I shatter. An orgasm so strong tears through me without mercy, white spots sparkle behind my closed lids as I bite down harder into my hand.

Just like earlier, he doesn't bring me down slowly, he just pulls back and pushes his pants down enough to free his cock, his piercing gleams in the moonlight and my mouth waters wanting to taste him and feel that metal in my mouth.

"Turn over." He orders, I shuffle around to do as he says and press my face into the pillow so it will mute my cries, he runs his hands over the globes of my ass and hums out his approval. When he lands a hard slap to my ass I jolt forward, he grips my hip to hold me in place as he does it again but this time, I moan into the pillow. My pussy clenches on air, do I like being spanked?

He runs his hand over my stinging ass and massages the ache away, he spreads my cheeks and I tense when I feel his spit dripping down my crack. The head of his cock prods my entrance while his thumb begins to circle my asshole, in unison he pushes his thumb and cock inside both my holes at the same time. A cold sweat breaks out over my body as I groan into my pillow, my ass burns but it slowly begins to fade as he works his cock and thumb in and out of my holes I start to realize that it feels fucking amazing. I've never had anyone touch me there or ever try to fuck my ass but now I find myself wanting to try it, with him.

"Fuck, I love it when your pussy clenches my cock, Sirena." All I can do is moan into the pillow and grip the sheets to try to remain on my knees, his thrusts are hard and punishing but fuck it feels amazing. If this is how he fucks to work out his frustrations, I wonder what he would be like if he actually loved you and wanted you to feel that through his actons. The thought flees me when he grips the back of my neck and forces me into the pillow further, he uses that grip to hold me in place as he slams into me so fucking hard the bed slides.

My pussy quivers as he continues to fuck me like a savage, the second his cock hits that sweet spot I detonate, screaming into my pillow which does nothing at all to mute my sounds. His grip on my neck tightens to the point of pain as he chases his own release, the pain mixed with the pleasure only heightens the feeling. I've barely calmed from the first orgasm before I feel another building, his cock swells inside me and I know he's going to cum while I remain on edge.

"Come with me, Rika." He reaches around and pinches my clit between his fingers, my greedy cunt clamps down onto his cock for the second time in mere minutes as I cry out my release with his name on the tip of my tongue but I manage to swallow it before it slips free. He growls low in his throat as he cums deep inside me, shudders roll through me as I ride out the high of my climax. When he releases my neck, I turn my head to the side so I can drag in lungfuls of air. "I'm gonna pull out." I nod, unable to do anything else I'm boneless and spent after the three life altering orgasms he just gave me.

I flinch as he slips free, it stings a bit telling me we were rough but it was so worth it. He slips off the bed and I drop flat on my stomach ready to pass out, I hear him shuffle around the room as I close my eyes, I expect him to leave but when he taps lightly on my ass, I startle and flip over to him standing there fully dressed with a washcloth in his hand. I look from him to the cloth confused until he pries my legs apart and begins to... Oh my God, he's cleaning me. I remain still as he goes about his business, when he's finished he heads back into the adjoining bathroom and tosses the cloth in the hamper. He heads for the door and a pang of longing hits me but I shove that feeling away, I don't want him to cuddle me, this is just sex!

He grips the handle but turns to look over his shoulder at me, suddenly feeling exposed. I grip the covers and pull them over my body. He chuckles but it's a dark sound with no humor. "Cover up as much as you want, Sirena but I still know what lurks beneath those sheets and fuck me if I don't enjoy the taste of it." My brows raise slightly taken back by his declaration. I sit here and watch him leave utterly perplexed by the fact he just came in here and fucked me like he had every right then, cleaned me and kind of gave me a compliment as he left, what the fuck changed in the past six hours for him to be... sort of nice to me?

Waking up the next morning I smile to myself when I stretch and feel how sore I am between my legs. I revel in the pain because it's a reminder that it did happen. In my own way that was my little fuck you to him. The smile vanishes from my face when my phone dings with an incoming message. I debate on ignoring it but think better of it since I ignored the four from yesterday. I take a deep breath and then grab my phone.

EVE

Update?

EVE

I've tried to call twice, do not make me wait.

EVE

My patiences is thinning....

EVE

Now I'm fucking pissed off and will be there in a few days.

My eyes widen as I sit up in bed and reread the message again, I read the newest one and all hope of getting out of this flees my body.

EVE

I land in four days, you will marry him then and secure this for our family or I'll snap your neck.

Tears prick the backs of my eyes, why is he doing this to me, I've always done everything he asked of me. Days ago he wanted me to switch from one man to the next and now he is telling me I have to marry the first. I can't do this, I won't. Yeah right, I don't have a choice. If marrying him is what gets me my revenge then I will do it, I may have crossed a line yesterday but it's just sex, nothing more. I keep repeating that line in my head until I believe it because there is no way Royal Murdoch can be anything more to me than someone who I fuck, when he finds out who I am, he'll hate me as much as I hate his family.

Chapter Fourteen

ROYAL

Chance is a basket case this morning, he's just been notified by his chief of staff that the two bodies were discovered at his office this morning. The fucker is pale and beside himself, if he thinks this is bad wait till he learns of his little fuck buddies death and watches that tape. I can't wait to smell the stench of fear that'll be wafting off him, he continues to pace my lounge room stopping every couple of seconds to look at myself and twelve other guards.

"We need more men." He snaps just as Chaos steps into the room. "Royal, have you found anything out yet?" The hopeful tone of his voice has me wanting to laugh.

Chaos shakes his head. "No, whoever this is, is slick." Chance's face falls. "But, I did find this." He pulls out the Jack of Spades and hands it to Chance. "I don't know if this is for you or me since it was delivered here."

Chance shakes his head. "It's for you, they don't know I'm here." Chaos nods and pockets his card, everyone in this room knows that card is for Chance. "We'll be fine, reinforcements arrive tomorrow and then we will take this sick fuck down. When we catch him, I want him alive so I can fucking kill him myself." When his phone begins to ring he pulls it out of his pocket and checks the caller ID before ordering us out of the room, Chaos and I exchange a knowing look as I pass by him. Chance is about to blow a gasket and shit himself when he hears the news of Helen which I'm sure is being delivered now. Just as I enter the foyer to head upstairs to resume my post of guarding Erika, she comes down the stairs in a pair of jeans and sweater that hangs off one shoulder, her long hair is out and flowing around her.

She lifts her gaze and at the sight of me standing at the bottom of the stairs she freezes, I cock my head to the side when I register the anguish in her gaze. Before I look further she wipes the look off her face and plasters on a fake smile as she descends the remaining way and brushes past me without another look or a sly touch like most women would.

Did she just fucking ignore me?

It takes me a minute to snap out of it before I race after her, she peers over her shoulder at me and her eyes go wide at the sight of me stalking toward her. The dirty little witch darts into the living room where Chance is knowing that I won't do anything in front of him to risk blowing my cover. But, I do follow after her to make sure he keeps his hands off my new toy.

"Fuck!" His outburst has her freezing on the spot, I use it to my advantage and slip past her but make sure to brush against her side as I do so, the gasp that comes from her has a smirk crossing my face. "Get me that fucking drive now!" He shouts then tosses his phone across the room where it smashes to pieces against the wall.

"What happened?" The fake concern in Chaos's tone is award worthy, Chance continues to let expletives free before he finally spins around to face Chaos.

"A USB is being delivered, when it arrives, bring it to me in my office. There's another body, the cunt doesn't know where I am so he dumped the bodies elsewhere."

"But you said reinforcements are coming, we should be fine right?" Chance nods stiffly but doesn't elaborate further as he stalks past Chaos and shouts for Dalton to meet him in his office. Chaos looks at me and I nod, he leaves the room so he can disappear to the basement to listen in on the conversation Chance is about to have. This whole house is bugged except for Erika's room. I was supposed to plant a bug yesterday but I couldn't. I don't want Sin or the others hearing me fuck her. Speaking of, I turn to face the woman herself but she's already rushing from the room.

Fuck her, I got bigger shit to deal with then worry about her moody ass.

An hour later the USB is delivered, Chance orders Dalton, Chaos and Erika to follow him into his office. I attempt to go with them but he refuses me entry and tells me to go watch the gate. It grates on my fucking nerves for this cunt to think he can order me around but I bite my tongue and do as I'm told. Not five minutes after I reach the gate does my phone begin to vibrate, I assume it's Sin or Havoc as I pull it out of my pocket but it isn't, it's Luka, I accept the call and bring it to my ear.

"What happened?" I bark.

"They didn't need rescuing."

"What the fuck do you mean?" I grit out.

"Your father and uncles are on a plane back to New York, Carlo caught wind of the attack on your family and owed Vincent one."

"Fuck." I scrub a hand down my face, my dad being out is going to fuck with my plans. "I need you to keep him busy in New York, I'm so close to ending this shit here and taking Chance and Emilio both out."

"Why do this on your own, your father can help you–."

"Because he needs to fucking see I can do this without him." I hate to admit that shit aloud but it's the truth, as much as I talk a big game the truth is I want Bishop to see I can do this shit and do it better than him.

"He knows you can, just get it done because your mother will tell him where you are. It's been fucking hell keeping those women in place, they have wounded nine men trying to escape and the only reason all nine are alive is because Clare saved them." I snort out a laugh.

"She's a vet."

"I fucking know, Royal. Get this shit done and fast or I'm gonna be the one getting stitched up by my fucking sister while her husband laughs his ass off." He ends the call the second I start to laugh. No sooner have I hung up from him does my phone begin to ring again, when I see it's Sin I accept the call.

"What is it?" I breathe out.

"Get your ass in that fucking house, now!" The worry in her tone has me stiffening.

"Why?"

"They have a gun on Chaos because of your bitch, save him now or I'll kill them all!" I'm already racing toward the house before she can finish speaking. We're not gonna be able to wait four days at this rate. It's time to come clean, I'm about to fuck shit up and kill Chance for touching my cousin and... her. I burst through the front doors and follow the sounds of a commotion, down the right corridor where my office is. The door is open and I rush through to see Chaos on his knees with two guys holding them there with a hand on each of his shoulders and a gun to the back of his head.

"Fucking bitch." Chance screams as he kicks Erika who is in a fetal position on the ground, I see red. I draw my gun ready to put a bullet in Chance's fucking head for touching her, again until his next words have me freezing. "You're a fucking rat! You've been leaking information to them this whole time." Is she a mole for the cartel?

"She can't fucking talk, how is she going to be blabbing to anyone you jackass." Chaos shouts.

"What the fuck is going on?" I roar drawing all their attention to me, Chance points to Erika's quivering frame on the ground as he speaks.

"Lock her fucking ass in her room, I don't want to see her fucking face until we meet Emilio tomorrow." I keep my face blank of all emotion as I ask.

"What about him?" He looks to Chaos and nods to the guards to release him.

"Don't ever intervene when I discipline my fiancée again." Chaos grits his teeth and nods stiffly before storming out of the room and shoulder checking me on his way out. I can't blame him for being pissed, I know this shit needs to end. I gather Erika into my arms and lift her gently, she wraps her arms around my neck and buries her face in the crook of my neck. Chance eyes me warily but I ignore it as I storm out of the room and head upstairs, once we're inside her room I kick her door shut and march over to her bed. I try to put her down but she clings to me tighter, after the second attempt at putting her down I give up and sit on the edge of her bed with her molded to me.

The fact I want to wrap my arms around her and promise to kill that cunt downstairs for touching her tells me I need to put space between us. If I feel this protective over her after only a couple days then I can only imagine how I would feel after a few weeks or months with her by my side. I force myself to drop my hold on her, Chanel's right. Erika Martinez doesn't exist which means this girl that is occupying too much fucking time in my head is a liar. Last night after I left her, I texted Havoc to dig deeper and find out whatever the fuck he could on her. She has to have a file, everyone does.

With that thought in mind I reach up and untangle her arms from around my neck ready to push her off me but when a pained hiss escapes her I stop, instead of pushing her away like I should have, I find myself shuffling up the bed until my back rests against the headboard while she nestled against my chest and holds me tighter, Jesus Christ.

Chanel needs to kill her or Havoc needs to prove her innocence because this girl is becoming a distraction I can't afford.

I don't know how long I sit here holding her against me but when I look down at her I see she has fallen asleep, it's midafternoon and I know without a doubt that Chaos and the others will still be waiting for me in the basement. I gently move her off me not wanting to wake her, I slip off the bed and pull the covers over her tiny frame, I can see a hand print bruise on her arm and where her shirt rides up on her stomach I see bruising already forming were he fucking kicked her. I grind my teeth as I cover her and slip out of the room quietly, I task Jackson with guarding her and making sure she stays in her room under the pretense I need a break. As I make my way outside to head to the hidden basement I notice more guards patrolling the grounds.

"Shit." I grit out when I notice guys patrolling the back half of the property, there is no way I can make it in there undetected so I do the next best thing, I act like I'm patrolling the grounds as I pull my phone out and call Sin, she answers on the fourth ring.

"Finally come up for air, did ya?" The angry bite to her

tone isn't lost on me but I choose to ignore it given I did leave them waiting for hours.

"I can't get in."

"We know, more guards arrived over two hours ago. You would have known that if you weren't balls deep inside that bitch." My grip on my phone tightens.

"I wasn't fucking her, Chanel."

"Oh, were you cuddling while we worked our asses off to figure out a way to end this cunt so we can go home?" I take several deep breaths to try to temper the rage brewing inside me, her and I have bickered in the past but not like this. Sin is just pissed she can't get her hands dirty and wants in on the action instead of being holed up in the basement.

"Cut the fucking shit, Chanel. Did you find anything or not?"

"We're not done with this conversation, Royal, the bitch needs to go and you need to remember why the fuck we are here, just in case you forgot, it isn't for her. She isn't our problem, she's his and you need to keep your fucking nose—."

"Remember who the fuck you are talking to Chanel, I'm not the fucking twins. I'm the one who runs this fucking shit not you, don't ever forget that." Silence, that's what I'm met with for a long ass time. I hate I had to throw that shit in her face but she needed to be reminded, I am the fucking heir to the throne, not her!

"The new guards are Emilio's men." Havoc says breaking the tension filled silence. "According to the shit we have managed to dig up, he lands in Miami in two days. Him and his men have caused a shit show in New York, something isn't right either Royal."

"Explain." I growl.

"I've been going over the shit Uncle Vin's rat gave us, I dug deeper into Emilio's brother and his family, turns out they fled Columbia to get away from the cartel. The guy wanted nothing to do with his brother, he was executed and his wife was gang raped in front of his daughter before she was executed, the kid saw the whole thing."

"And?" I prompt.

"Royal, the kid's body was never found, I've hacked every network and there is no trace of Monica Vargas, either they killed her and hid the body or..."

"She's still alive and being hidden." I answer.

"We need to find her, we can use her as leverage against Emilio."

"What makes you think he cares enough about her?"

"If she's in the wind and untraceable that means she is running, we all know the kid would be a loose end, he'll want her back."

"Find the girl, we'll be at the meet with Chance and that's when we'll end this with or without the kid."

Chapter Fifteen

ERIKA

I lift my shirt as I stand in front of the mirror of my adjoining bathroom to inspect the damage, the bruising looks worse than it feels. I'm no stranger to getting my ass beat, that's how I wound up here in the first place. I laugh and flinch in pain, nothing about this situation is funny but either I laugh about it or I'm gonna cry and I'm not the type of girl to sit around and cry over the shitty hand life dealt me.

I turn to the side and sigh at the bruising that mars the side of my body, is this what my life is to become? Is revenge on the men who put me here really worth being married to a piece of shit like Chance? All these questions swirl through my mind as I strip off my clothes and get in the shower, the water cascades over my body giving me the false sense that it's washing away all the bad.

I wrap my arms around myself and just stand here getting lost in my own head, my fingers trace the guns on each of my hips absentmindedly as I recall the minimal memories I have of my parents, we were so happy. I was loved and cherished, we had a great life until those bastards took it from me, they took the only two people in this world I have ever loved from me.

I feel a tear leak from the corner of my eye and brush it away angrily, I refuse to be weak. I lock all these feelings and memories back in the box they belong in, if I allow myself to go down that path then I'll break and I can't do that when I'm so fucking close to ending this. He'll be here in a matter of days and I need to prepare myself for that, he's going to be watching me like a hawk, this thing with Royal needs to end, it was fun while it lasted but it can't be anything more than that.

I finish up in the shower and step out, I wrap the large towel around my body not caring that my wet hair is dripping everywhere as I walk back into my room only to freeze at the sight of Royal standing by the window gazing out at the backyard. At the sound of my approach he turns his head, looks me up and down then dismisses me. That pisses me off! He doesn't get to come in here and fuck me when he feels like it and then act like I mean nothing.

I decide to bait him, I drop the towel and run my fingers through my wet hair, I know he can see me from the corner of his eye, the way his body stiffens and his hands clench at his sides all the indication I need to know that I affect him as much as he does me. I sway my hips as I walk over to the closet, I bite my lip to keep from smiling as I sift through the hangers to find something to wear. I just grip the hanger with my navy blue shirt on it then it's ripped out of my hand. I spin around only for his hand to grab my throat and back me up until I'm flush against the cold floor length mirror.

His eyes are void of every emotion except for anger, it's at the forefront. "You're hiding shit, I'm going to figure out what it is and when I do." I gasp and jump to my tiptoes when he cups my pussy. "This pussy won't be able to save you from what I'll do to you, this is your chance to come clean, Erika."

I hold his gaze as I lift my hands and sign, *ask me who I really am*.

His brows brunch as he tries to figure out what the hell I just said, if he just asks me the right question I'll answer it. I have never wanted to speak more than I do in this moment, I see the war in his eyes. He wants the truth but he also hates himself because even without the truth he still wants me. I reach and cup his cheek, he stiffens but after a second he relaxes into my touch for a brief moment before he leaps away from me like I've burnt him.

"Emilio Vargas will be here for a meet in two days, Chance wants you there." It takes every ounce of power I possess to keep the guilt from showing on my face, I latch onto my anger from earlier. I need to remind myself he's the enemy, he may not have done it directly but his family ruined me. "Why the fuck would he want you there?" The mocking tone of his voice isn't lost on me, I keep my face blank as I raise my hands again and sign.

Ask me the right question and I'll answer you, give me a reason to speak.

He may not be able to understand what I just said but from the way his eyes search mine I know he can feel that what I said was important.

"Emilio's men are here." I nod my understanding. "Unless you want to be free game for them to take turns, stay the fuck in your room." I recoil, he has no idea that his words just hit too close to home. "For your sake, I hope whatever secrets you hide are worth it. If whatever you are hiding impacts my family, I will be the one to deal with you, my face will be the last thing you see."

I watch him leave and stand here thinking, if his face is the last thing I see in this cruel world I'd be okay with that. He's made me feel more in these last couple of days than I have in over ten years.

With Chance being gone for the evening and taking more than half the men with him it leaves me with some freedom to roam the house and go in search of the person I know is his weakness. He thought he was smart hiding her in plain sight, it was a solid plan until shit went down and he kept looking to her for approval. The man clearly has a mommy complex. I enter the kitchen and stop in the entryway watching Margaret move around the space like she has been living here for years, I scuff my foot to announce my presence. Her head snaps my way and for a split second she forgets to mask her feelings and her clear disdain for me shines bright in her eyes.

"Erika, what can I do for you dear?" I fight the eye roll from breaking free at the fake cheeriness in her tone. I lift my hands ready to sign until an arm wraps around my shoulders, I turn to look up at Chaos and narrow my eyes. He beams at Margaret and smiles wide.

"Carry on Maggie, I'll take care of this one." He doesn't wait for a reply as he turns and drags me along with him. I expect him to march me back to my room but he doesn't. He leads me out the back door and motions for me to take a seat on one of the patio chairs, I cross my arms over my chest and shake my head. "Sit the fuck down now!" The grit in his tone is enough to tell me he isn't fucking around and will force me to do as he says, rather than add to my collection of bruises I do as he says.

He claims the seat opposite me, he says nothing as he looks me over trying to dissect what I'm thinking, unlike Royal, Chaos's presence doesn't set me on edge or have my heart racing with what may happen. There is no... electricity between us but with Royal, it feels like I've been shocked and woken from a long slumber. The man brings me to life just by being in the same room as me.

"I may not know exactly who the fuck you are but what I do know is, you know a lot more than you have let on." I remain still and plaster a bored look on my face. "See, if you were innocent and actually who you say you are, you would have ratted on us the second you figured it all out. Thing is, I can't decide who you want to hurt more, is it Chance or is it Royal?" He keeps his voice so only I can hear, the fact Chaos has been able to piece this together shows me I have let my skills slip. I lift my hands and sign.

If you know this, why am I still breathing?

A cruel smirk crosses his face. "You shouldn't be, you should have been the first one we took out except Royal wouldn't allow it." I frown, his brows raise in surprise. "He didn't tell you?" I shake my head. "You will die." He says it in such a matter of fact tone I actually believe him. "Sin has you marked, once she drops her card there is no coming back from that. Not even Royal will be able to save you from her." He stands and peers down at me. "Remember that when you try to fuck us over, they don't call us the bringers of death for nothing, Erika. We've never missed a mark and there is no fucking way we will allow you to be the first."

Waking up the next morning to see rain and lightning feels right, today is going to be a bad day so it's only fair that the weather reflects that. I waited for hours last night to see if Royal would come to me but he didn't, I know it was for the best but I would have loved one last night to get lost in him. My phone begins to buzz but I ignore it knowing it's him telling me he's here. I force myself to shower and change into some casual clothes, I decide to go with a pair of jeans, sneakers, a plain black V neck shirt and a hoodie.

Steeling my spine I open my door and step into the hallway, I'm surprised to see no guards standing around, Royal is nowhere to be seen either. I make my way downstairs only to find it empty, where the fuck is everyone? I check Chance's office and find it vacant, and an eerie feeling washes over me. Something feels off. I move to the front of the house and peer out the windows, the same three SUVs from yesterday are still parked there.

I go to the back thinking they may be congregated out there but the moment I step out onto the back patio and hear voices I relax a little, I'm a nervous mess. I leave the back door open as I go and make myself a coffee. I push on my tiptoes to try to reach the coffee cups in the cupboard but I'm too short. Who the hell puts coffee cups that fucking high up, it's ridiculous. My fingertips just manage to brush the side of the mug, I growl my annoyance ready to give up and go grab a chair but then he presses up behind and reaches over to grab the cup for me. My whole body heats at the contact and my heart begins to pound inside my chest, I don't need to turn around to know it's Royal. I just know it's him from the way my body comes alive and the hairs on the back of my neck stand on end.

"We leave in three hours, be ready." He says as he places the cup on the counter and then walks away leaving me here to try and catch my breath. Three hours, that's all the time I have before everything changes and I can finally rest, this will all be over.

Chapter Sixteen

ROYAL

Dalton, Chaos, Erika, Chance, Elliot, Brock and I all sat in the back of Chance's limo, he arrived back at the house about an hour ago and had everyone loaded into the cars and ready to leave for the meeting. Sin, Havoc and Samson follow behind us in an unmarked SUV, Chaos and I both wear mics so the three of them can hear and know if it's an ambush or not, we just need Sin to get there and set up so we have a sniper on the roof, that crazy bitch is a deadshot.

No one has uttered a word since we left the house, I know Cable is thankful to have everyone out of the house he calls home. The guy did good, he managed to be our ears when we couldn't get close enough, he's shown he's loyal. The tension in the car is thick, Chance keeps tapping away on his phone, Erika sits beside him and stares out the window but I can tell from the look on her face she sees nothing, she's too lost in her own head.

Time seems to stand still as my mind begins to blank of

every feeling, this is the euphoric feeling I crave. Unlike the others I don't allow my emotions to cloud my judgment or hinder my decision making, I just act on instinct. In less than an hour I'll be putting a bullet in Chance and Emilio's heads. I'll take back New York and Miami and may even move into Columbia if I feel inclined to do so. My dad will have no choice but to see that I am ready and capable of doing this without him, the fact he hasn't called me yet does make me feel slightly uneasy but I can't worry about that now, I'll deal with him later.

"I feel like I need to confess." Chance states drawing all our attention to him, he looks at Erika and smiles but it's a vindictive one. "I think it's time the truth comes out." Erika stiffens as she stares at Chance with wide eyes. "I feel like I have been underestimated and even though I am used to being the underdog, I don't relish being laughed at and thought to be a fool." I cut a subtle glance to Chaos, he sits opposite me tense and poised to attack if he should need to. Chance shifts his gaze from Erika to stare at Chaos, "You nearly had me, nearly being the operative word."

"I don't follow." Chaos says.

Chance tsks him and pulls a dagger from his breast pocket, Chaos and I both move to grab our guns but I still when I feel the barrel of a gun pressed into the back of my head. Erika gasps and shifts as if she is about to try to do something but Chance darts his arm out and presses the dagger against her throat. Her eyes widen in fright as she looks at me, I grind my teeth to keep myself in check. I spy Chaos out the corner of my eye with Dalton's gun aimed at his head, Chance laughs and it sounds manic. He uses his free hand to reach out and brush the loose strands of Erika's hair behind her ear, my teeth fucking ache from how hard I'm clenching my jaw.

"She's beautiful isn't she, Royal?" He says as he looks

directly at me, when I say nothing a broad grin splits across his face. "Did you really think I wouldn't figure it out?" I remain silent, I have nothing to say to this piece of shit.

"You must have hit your head–." Chaos snaps his mouth closed when Chance presses the dagger into Erika's skin hard enough to draw blood, she keeps her gaze on me the whole time.

"Does she fuck as good as she looks?" He asks me, my nostrils flare when he leans into her and licks the side of her face, she tries to shift away from him but the cunt digs the dagger in further. "Keep fighting me, I fucking love it when they scream." This motherfucker is going to die. He uses the dagger to force her flush against the seat and trails his other hand down her chest. I remind myself she isn't anything to me, she means nothing but the moment he tries to force his hand inside her jeans I snap.

"Do it and I'll fucking kill you." My tone is cold and deadly, he turns his head and smirks.

"I knew it, I wasn't a hundred percent sure my hunch was right until now. I thought it was odd how much you looked like your father and sure enough, you are his fucking offspring. I knew you had a weak spot for her I just had to exploit it so you would crack." I don't deny it, there's no point I just showed him I did. "You fucked up the moment you saved her from me the first time, I knew then there was no way you were some random guard. All I had to do was play dumb and assign you to her and I knew without a doubt you would fuck her and form an attachment." My face twitches in anger. "It was you, wasn't it?"

"Say what the fuck you mean." I grit out.

"You've been the one committing the murders and planting those fucking cards." Chaos snorts, Dalton pistol whips him across the back of the head, I leap across the car landing a solid punch to the cunts jaw and go for another until the other two fuckers cock their guns but they aren't aimed at me, they're pointed at Chaos and Erika. "Sit the fuck down now, Royal or they die." Gritting my teeth I do as the fucker says, I look to Chaos who rubs the back of his head. The angry look in his eyes promises death, Dalton's fucked if he thinks he's walking away with his life.

"We're five minutes out." Brock announces.

"Here's how this is going to play out, Erika and you will be with me as I meet with Emilio while, I assume he's one of Knight's bastards remains here with Dalton to ensure you behave, disobey me or try anything and Dalton will kill him.

"I thought you two were buddies." Chaos grits out.

"So did I, until I received word that the money I laundered for him was wired to an offshore account that is untraceable and now it's my ass on the chopping block." Sin and Havoc are the ones to thank for that transfer. "Emilio isn't happy so that's where Royal comes in, he's my leverage."

"Go fuck yourself." I snarl.

"How about I fuck her instead while you watch?" The car comes to a stop cutting off my reply, I peer out the window to see we are at some random airfield where a private jet sits on the tarmac. "Let's go." Chance growls, Brock shoves his gun into the back of my head forcing me to move, I shoot Chaos a look telling him I'll do whatever it takes to get us out of this. Dalton and Elliot remain in the car with Chaos while the four of us climb out, the three SUVs that came with us park beside us, the men all exit the cars and spread out around the area as Chance puts the dagger back in his pocket and grabs Erika's hand, interlocking his fingers with hers as he moves toward the hanger where the plane is. Brock is smart enough to keep his gun on me at all times, I dart my eyes around and see no other buildings around, fuck, Chanel is gonna have to improvise and find somewhere to set up.

"Get Chaos first." I say knowing they will hear me through the mic.

"Shut the fuck up." Brock growls. We're halfway to the hanger when everything happens, the sound of guns cocking all around us has everyone slamming to a stop and all the men that came with Chance form a protective circle around him and in turn me and Erika.

"A lot of men for a friendly meet, Governer." As Chance steps forward the men part for him, Standing at the top of the stairs to the plane is Emilio Vargas. The sight of the piece of shit disgusts me, I know that prick has received the cards we sent. Unlike Chance, no bodies have been dumped on his doorstep, he and Chance are the first two people to ever receive all four cards.

"Given the threat you made I thought it wise to come with backup." Chance counters as Emilio slowly makes his way down the stairs, his men come out of the long grass surrounding the tarmac wearing ghillie suits and their rifles trained on us. Unlike Chance's guys you can tell Emilio's men have been trained.

"What do you expect when millions of dollars go missing?" Emilio's tone is firm and lethal, Chance doesn't cower like I thought he would. "I gave you a shot to prove yourself and work off the debt your father owed, you fucked up."

"I did everything you demanded of me!" Chance retorts.

"No, you allowed the new found power to go to your head because I got rid of the Murdoch's." My blood begins to pump in my ears at the mention of my family.

"You benefited out of their demise." Chance is becoming unhinged and it's clear for all to see.

"I gained nothing, I still lost my son!" Emilio roars. "You think taking over their territory and sending them to Siberia is punishment enough?" Chance darts his gaze around looking uneasy suddenly. Something isn't adding up, he's being very wary of what he says. "You look pale, is there something you need to get off your chest?" Emilio taunts as he takes two steps closer toward us.

"No, I have done nothing aside from try to make Miami a better place." Emilio narrows his eyes.

"You lying little prick, it's fuckers like you that ruin great nations. Not only have my men informed me about your bull-shit but I also have a trusted source that has told me you never sent the Murdoch's to Syberia, did you?" He doesn't let Chance answer. "You also failed to mention that you have been meeting with the FBI." My brows jump to my hairline and Chance pales.

He shakes his head trying to deny what Emilio says. "I have no idea what you are talking about, whoever told you this is a liar." Emilio shakes his head and clicks his tongue, toying with Chance. He turns toward Erika and I stiffen, he better not touch her!

"He's calling you a liar, my dear." My blood freezes in my veins as I turn to look at her, she pries her hand from Chance's. He looks just as shocked as I feel, instead of going to Emilio she comes to me and stops a foot away gazing up, I feel nothing for this bitch except for hatred. She's a dirty fucking rat.

She darts her tongue out to moisten her lips and swallows a couple times before she opens her mouth. "All you had to do was ask my name." My face slackens at the sound of her voice, Emilio gasps and stares at her with a stunned expression.

"What good would your name have done?" I force out through clenched teeth.

"No one has ever asked me what my full name is, if you had asked me I would have told you." I wasn't wrong when I called her Sirena, her voice is like a siren's call, the sound of it could become an addiction but like any addiction, I'll kick this fucking habit to curb without a second thought.

"Your name means nothing to me. You mean nothing to me, I made you a promise and I swear to God I will keep it. Run little Sirena because I'll hunt you down like the fucking dog you are." Hurt shines in her eyes but she masks it quickly before taking a step back and shoving her hands in her hoodie pocket.

"For what it's worth, I'm sorry." I spit at her feet, she's going to fucking die for this.

"After twelve years I thought I would be the one you spoke your first word to." Her eyes close as if she prays for patience when Emilio steps up beside her and wraps an arm around her shoulders drawing her into his side as he places a kiss to the top of her head. "You did good, you got him to drop his guard enough to let you in."

"What the fuck is going on here?" Chance shouts, Emilio keeps his beady eyes on me as he answers.

"Royal Murdoch I presume?" I say nothing, the smug fuck already knows who I am thanks to his bitch ass— what the fuck is she to him? "I knew the moment your father and uncles were captured that you would come for Chance, I needed someone on the inside and what better person than my own flesh and blood. I knew there was no way you would hand over your fathers empire, all I needed to do was bide my time until you eventually came out of hiding."

"Who the fuck said I was hiding?" I snarl, Emilio grins.

"She was right, you really are like your father. I'm going to take great joy in what comes next."

"You and me both." Chance says just as the sound of helicopters and sirens can be heard in the distance, everything happens so fast, out of nowhere four helicopters appear and gunshots start popping as men begin to propel down ropes from the choppers, shots come from the hanger roof and I know without a doubt that it's Sin on the roof when Brock's gun disappears from the back of my head when he drops like a sack of shit. Emilio draws his gun and aims it at me, just as he's about to squeeze the trigger, Erika shoves him and throws him off balance, the bullet scrapes the side of my arm leaving a flesh wound. The sound of sirens get closer, Emilio runs for his plane, Erika tries to race after him but a shot rings out and she goes down.

Fuck.

Before I can take a step toward her, four men in black masks and blacked out clothes come toward me with their guns drawn. I pull my gun from my waistband ready to shoot until the one at the front yanks the mask off his head.

I drop my gun to my side. "Dad." I breathe out as he rushes forward and wraps his arms around me for a second before drawing back.

"Get the fuck out of here now, feds are going to be crawling all over this place soon." I nod and spin around to where the limo was parked with Chaos in the back but it's gone.

"Where the fuck is it?" I shout.

"Where's what?" Dad asks as I spin back to face him.

"The limo, Chaos was in the back." The other three men behind my father yank their masks off and I'm not surprised to see it's my uncles, Knight, King and Rook.

"Where the fuck is my son, Royal?" Knight snaps.

"I don't know." I answer honestly, his face turns red with anger. "I think Chance had him moved as leverage."

"Fuck." Knight screams.

"We need to find him." Rook snaps.

"How?" King asks.

"By using his mother." At the sound of her voice I push past my father and shove my uncles aside to find Erika standing there gripping her shoulder. Pity, I thought that was a kill shot. I say nothing as I grip her by the hair on her head and drag her toward the vehicles my father and uncles run toward, Erika Vargas is going to learn the hard way what happens when you fuck with death.

Chapter Seventeen

ERIKA

My shoulder burns, the bullet is still inside and it fucking hurts but I make no sound. From the moment Royal threw me inside the car I've been blindfolded, handcuffed, when we stopped I was dragged from the car by my hair and forced into the chair I currently sit on with my hands cuffed behind my back.

I know what comes next.

I'm ready for it. He told me what would happen if I ever defied him and I knew saving him today meant certain death for me. For a split second I allowed myself to believe that the sins of his father don't reflect on him but I was wrong. Emilio left me behind but I have no doubt he'll come for me, not because he cares but because it makes him look weak that I was captured by the enemy he was supposed to have defeated.

The sound of the rain pelting down on the tin roof jars me from my slumber, I keep dozing in and out of sleep. The pain in my shoulder has reached a new level, shivers tear through my body, I know I have a fever but there isn't a fucking thing I can do about it. My mouth is dry and feels like a ball of cotton, my stomach has finally stopped cramping from lack of sustenance. I've urinated on myself at least half a dozen times and that is the only sign I have that I have been stuck in this spot for at least two days with a blindfold on and my arms still cuffed. I haven't seen anyone or spoken to a single person since Royal brought me here.

A small part of me wishes I did run with Emilio but I know the punishment from him would have been worse, Chance stealing his money is one thing but the Murdoch Mafia getting the jump on him is another level. He hates them for what they did to our family, I share in that hate. I was a fucking fool to think diffrently of Royal, he will always be one of them!

The sound of chain clanking from behind me sets my senses into overdrive, I hear the heavy chain drop to the ground and then a door squeaks as it's opened. I may not be able to see them but I can hear two sets of shoes scuffing along the ground, the moment they come to a stop in front of me my breathing begins to turn shallow in anticipation of what is about to happen. The bag that covers my head is yanked off and I slam my eyes closed against the harsh lighting, it takes me a minute to finally blink them open without tears clouding my vision. I look between the man who I know to be Knight Murdoch and the woman who stands beside him is his wife, Koby Murdoch.

I've heard stories about these two, from what I hear Koby is just as ruthless and cutthroat as her husband, why the two of them are here though, I have no idea.

"I'll give you one chance, *one*, you tell me the truth and I won't hurt you." I keep my gaze on Koby as she speaks knowing she is the one who calls the shots here and not her husband. "Lie to me and I will fucking show you the wrath of a mother who has nothing to lose." I scrunch my face in confusion, I have no idea what being a mother has to do with anything. "Do you understand?" Gritting my teeth I nod. Her eyes darken as she stares down at me trying to decipher if I am going to lie or not. "Where is my son?" I inch back into the metal and hiss when the movement jars my shoulder, I open my mouth to speak but words won't come. Speaking for the first time after a decade was the hardest thing I have ever done but the urge to make Royal understand was too great to ignore and the words flew out of me. Koby doesn't see the struggle I'm facing, she takes a step forward and I shake my head trying to tell her that I can't speak. "I warned you little girl." She says as she grips my shoulder and plunges her thumb inside the hole the bullet left, a scream so loud and foreign rips out of me as my body begins to thrash against it's restraints, I know the seat is bolted to the ground which is the only reason I don't flip over.

"Koby!" Knight tries to reign his wife in but she won't listen, she applies more pressure to my wound and grips my hair in her other hand, yanks my head back and headbutts me. Black spots dance in the corners of my eyes, I welcome it hoping I pass the fuck out so I don't have to feel this pain. "That's enough." He wraps his arms around her and yanks her away from me, my chin hits my chest just as bile rushes up my throat and I vomit all over myself.

"She knows where my son is!" I hear her screaming through the haze that has overtaken me as I dance between the lines of consciousness. "I'll kill her if I have to."

"Kill her and we will never find our son." is the last thing I hear before I finally black out, the escape is a welcome reprieve.

I gasp awake and splutter and cough as water drips down my face, I blink rapidly to clear my vision. It fucking stings but it's not like I can rub away the ache, when my eyes land on Chaos—no, that can't be Chaos it must be his twin, Havoc and Chanel standing before me. Both of them wear looks of disgust as they stare down their noses at me, my chest rises and falls as I look between them both waiting for them to strike.

"People think Chaos is the bad one because he voices how he feels and how he will hurt you or dismember you when he kills you." Havoc's tone is filled with hate and rage as he spits the words at me. "They're all wrong. I may be quiet and hide in the shadows but let me tell you, I'm the one who does the breaking and killing, not Chaos. My brother has never taken a life, I just allow him to take the credit for my handy work." From the way Chanel's brow raises I can tell this is news to her as well.

Again I open my mouth but words fail me, years of not being able to speak a single word has taken a toll on me. Now, when I need my voice the most it fails me.

"Tell me where my brother is and I promise you, I won't make you suffer, I'll end it quickly." You would think a moment like this you would feel every ounce of fear and would be willing to do whatever it takes to guarantee your survival but that isn't the case. Resigned to the fact I am going to die here I stop fighting, I go lax in my chair, close my eyes and nod my head. Not a second later, the first hit comes, my face jerks to the side as pain blooms in my jaw. I cough and spit blood on the ground, when the next hits come there isn't a break, punch after punch land all over my face, chest, stomach and ribs. When Chanel finally stops, I slacken in my chair, my body is dead weight and I haven't the strength to even lift my head. Pain radiates through my entire body, I'm too fucking sore to even cry from the pain. One of my eyes is swollen shut, the other isn't much better but I'm able to see enough that I watch Havoc step behind me with a pair of pliers. I clench my hands into fist but it's futile, he pries them open. Tears do cascade down my cheeks this time, he's going to remove my fingers— I scream so fucking loud my head spins when he rips my fingernail off. By the time he reaches the fourth finger I see black spots again and welcome the feeling of blackness.

"Enough." The sound of his voice has the haze of spots clearing from my vision, when Havoc releases my hand I sag in defeat.

"Don't fucking stop this, it's happening whether or not you are on board." Havoc seethes.

"She knows where Chaos is, Royal." Chanel adds.

"Leave." That one word from him holds so much fucking power I can feel it.

"Royal–."

"I said leave, Chanel, now!" I hear them leave but the grunt that comes from Royal tells me that he was shoulder checked by his cousin. I hear him move closer and no matter how much I know it's going to hurt I can't help but tense. A whimper escapes me but I bite down on my bottom lip to keep quiet as I feel him come up behind me, he grips my wrist, I try to yank it free but he's too strong and I'm way too fucking weak. When I feel the cuff release I almost weep, he frees my other hand and moves to stand in front of me but I can't look at him. I can't even lift my arms, they have had no blood flow for who knows how fucking long so it's going to take a while for them to work.

I hear another set of footsteps enter the shack I'm being held in, even with my arms free I couldn't run if I wanted to. My body is too weak and battered to make it a single step. I see a pair of black combat boots next to Royals Chuck Taylors but I can't lift my head to see who they belong to.

"This won't stop until you tell me what I want to know." All I can manage is a jerk of my head to acknowledge I understand. "Tell me where Chaos is and this will end quickly, you have my word." I dart my tongue out to moisten my lips then flinch, my lip is busted. I use every ounce of strength I have left to lift my head but the moment I see who is standing next to Royal a new wave of anger overcomes me, Bishop Murdoch stands next to his son with his arms crossed over his chest and a scowl on his face. I can feel Royal looking from me to his father not understanding what is happening.

I don't know what it is but it seems Royal being present gives me the courage I need to finally speak. "Tell me where my mother's body is and I might be inclined to help a piece of shit like you." I spit at the bastard that ruined my life and took everything from me, I'm here right now because of him. Bishop frowns at me then looks to his son in confusion, fuck him and fuck his son. I latch onto the anger coursing through me as I use it to channel what little strength I have left to stand to my feet, I sway but I refuse to fall in front of them.

I may be smaller and have to look up at the bastard but if I'm going to die it won't be like some weak submissive bitch strapped to a chair. Bishop stares down at me with a cold callous look in his brown eyes. "I'd rather go through this every single fucking day for years then ever help a rapist like you." Bishop's eyes widened at my declaration. His mouth opens but I lose the fight and I stagger sideways before I feel myself falling toward the ground as I pass out but this time, I pray I don't wake up.

Chapter Eighteen

ROYAL

I slide across the dirt floor and land on one knee as I catch her before she can hit the hard ground, her face is busted and bruised, her shoulder is red and inflamed, fuck she reeks of piss as well. I've watched everything on the cameras that are hooked up all around this shed, after we fled from the fucking feds my dad brought us all back to one his off-grid safehouses in Orlando.

"I never raped nobody!" My dad growls, I look up at him to find his hateful glare pinned on the unconscious girl in my arms. "Get her cleaned the fuck up and treated, I want to know what the fuck that girl thinks she knows." He turns to leave but my words have him turning back to face me.

"What about Chaos?"

"She has no idea where he is, I saw it in her eyes when you asked her. She only alluded to knowing so she could get under my skin." I frown, how did I miss that? "You didn't see it because you're too close to her." I open my mouth to deny him but he just pins me with a bored look. "I may have been inclined to believe your bullshit ass excuse if you didn't just slide across the dirt to catch her."

He leaves me here with her, if she doesn't know where Chaos is then she is of no use to us. I promised Sin she could kill her once we got the information we needed or when she was no longer useful. I war within myself, Chaos is gone because of me. This was all my fucking fault, I should have been a better leader but I let my infatuation with this girl cloud my judgment. I gather her in my arms and stand, a whimper of pain escapes her. Even knowing she is the reason my cousin is missing I can't help but hate myself a little for allowing this shit to happen to her.

I walk the worn path from the shed at the back of the secluded property and head for the guest house rather than the main one. Chanel and Havoc are already pissed off at me and taking her inside would only add fuel to that fire, all our parents are pissed off at us. This was my one chance to prove myself and I fucking blew it over some girl.

I've never been distracted by pussy before, what makes this girl so special?

I shake that thought away and I head straight for the bathroom to clean her, I stand here wracking my brain for how the fuck I'm going to be able to do this.

"I'll run you a bath so you can get in with her." I spin around to find my mom standing in the doorway with a sad smile on her face, she doesn't wait for me to answer as she steps into the room and begins to run the bath. "You're gonna have to clean her in here and then hopefully she'll be awake and able to shower afterward." I nod.

We stand here in awkward silence as the bath fills, once it does mom shuts the water off and turns to me with a raised brow. "What?"

"Well, how are you gonna get her in there?"

"Toss her in?' I deadpan, mom glares at me for a second.

"Bishop!" I balk at her.

"Why the hell are you calling, Dad?" Just as I finish speaking the man himself appears in the doorway looking pissed the fuck off.

"Yeah?" He asks, sounding less than impressed, to be summoned here. Mom turns to him and motions for him to come closer but he ignores her request. "Spit it the hell out, Kiara." He growls, my brows raise as mom places her hands on her hips, idiot. He should know better than to snap at her like that, she may have only just got her husband back but that doesn't mean she will put up with him disrespecting her like that.

"Hold the fucking girl while he gets in the bath." Dad reels back.

"Fuck that, that little bitch called me a rapist!" He roars, Erika stirs in my arms and groans as she tries to blink her eyes open but only one does. The second she sees me she stiffens. "Look at that, the accusor is awake she can wash her fucking self and if she so happens to drown, I'll make sure to tip the gas on her worthless ass before I strike the match." Mom's mouth drops open as Dad stalks out of the guest house slamming the door behind himself.

"Can you stand?" I ask the troublemaker in my arms. I don't wait for a reply as I place her on her feet and grip her waist to keep her steady. I cut a look to my mom over her shoulder, she nods.

"I'll find a doctor or something." She says as she leaves and closes the bathroom door. Erika sways unsteadily, I grip the front of her shirt and tear it down the middle.

"What the fuck?" I toss the ruined shirt to the side, I ignore her as I go for her jeans, she tries to smack my hands but my patience snaps, I wrap my hand around her throat forcing her to stop. Her eye widens as far as it can but unlike the other times I've had her in this position, this time I see a hint of fear in her eye.

"Get your fucking clothes off and get in the bath, you stink and the sight of you disgusts me."

"Fuck you." She seethes.

"Never again will my cock slip inside that nasty ass fuck hole."

"You fuck like a bitch anyway." My nostrils flare in outrage.

"I liked you better when you didn't speak." I snarl as I storm out of there slamming the door so fucking hard that the pictures on the wall rattle. I storm out into the small living room to find my mom sitting on one of the couches, she looks up at me and smiles, I sigh as I drop down beside her. She shuffles over and and rests her head on my shoulder, I haven't had a chance to apologize for being a fucking prick to her since we got here two days ago. "Mom,--."

"Shhhh, you don't need to say anything." I sag into the couch and shift so I can wrap my arm around her shoulders and place a kiss to the top of her head.

"I had no right to speak to you and treat you the way I did but I couldn't risk you coming after me." Guilt has been eating at me for the way I treated her, I've never spoken to my mother like that before. My dad and I may fight all the time and he puts up with my shit but one thing he never allowed was for me to ever disrespect my mom, he would whoop my ass if I did.

"I knew you would grow up to be just like him." I scoff, we are nothing alike. "Deny it all you want but you and your father are the exact same, being like him isn't a bad thing, Royal. He loves with everything he has, he's fiercely loyal and will do anything for the ones he loves."

"I don't want to be Bishop." I breathe out. All my life

everyone has always compared me to my father, I've always tried to find a way to branch out, be someone different, do things differently which is how I came up with the Memento Mori. The calling cards that are unique to each of us, like me, Sin, Havoc and Chaos wanted to be seen as an individual and not as their parents.

"You will never be your father, Bishop is... well, he's just him and you're you. You may be similar but you will never be the same."

"You know he hasn't looked me in the eye since he got back." I mutter as I turn and peer out the window.

"Look at me, Royal." I do as she asks, she shifts so she is facing me with a serious look on her face. "He can't look at you because he's angry with himself, not you."

"Yeah right." I bite out.

"Boy, you are not too grown for me to take my shoe off and smack you up the side of your head with it." Laughter bursts out of me, the serious look on her face vanishes as she tries hard not to laugh along with me.

"Mom, if you can stand and reach my face I'll let you smack me around with your shoe."

Her eyes narrow to slits. "Don't sass me."

"Yes, Ma'am."

"Your dad is angry because him being taken from us meant you had no choice but to step up and run the family. He wanted to be by your side when that time came. The moment he came back home, the first thing he asked me was 'where the fuck was his son?'" I can't keep the suprise from my face, I know he's said he's loved me my whole life but he's never shown it. "When he found out what you were doing, he nearly killed Luka for going along with your plan until Luka made him see, you were doing exactly what he would have done. Take a second to see things through his eyes for a moment, his only child flew across the country to dismantle the empire of the man who abducted him and his brothers, on top of that his son was also going after the biggest cartel in Columbia. Imagine the guilt he is carrying for putting his own son in that position."

I hear everything she is saying but what she doesn't realize is my dad trained me my whole life for that moment, I was to expect the unexpected and always be ready. I did everything he taught me and I still fucked it up, he had to swoop in and save my ass because I thought I could prove myself by handling everything on my own. Even with Uncle Gage and Uncle Vincent still recovering from their wounds, dad managed to get everyone together and pull off a rescue mission. I was pissed when I found out that Samson was the one to leak our location to my father but honestly, without him doing that I probably would have gotten us all killed.

A throat clearing has me and mom turning toward the hallway where Erika leans against the wall with a towel wrapped around her. I push to my feet, mom follows suit but I push her behind me not wanting this rat to see her. Her gunshot wound looks infected, her hand that grips her towel is swollen from losing her nails, she looks like death. The fact she is strong enough to walk out here on her own two feet shows just how tough she really is.

"I'm gonna pass out." She rasps out just as her eyes begin to roll into the back of her head. Fuck. I race across the room and leap over the single chair and manage to catch her just in time before she smacks her head against the hardwood floor.

"Shit, get her something to wear and bring her to the main house. Your aunt is the best doctor we have here." I peer over my shoulder at my mom in outrage.

"Aunt Clare is a vet not a fucking doctor!"

Mom's lips thin. "Watch your mouth." I smile sheepishly, twenty years old and still I can't cuss in front of her. "She's all we got, unless you would like your girlfriend to die?"

I bristle. "She isn't my girlfriend." I grit out.

"Right and I didn't blow your father in the back of the church when King got married." I splutter in disgust, she winks and rushes out of the room like she didn't just give me the worst mental picture of my life.

Chapter Nineteen

ERIKA

I come to with a scream.

I thrash around the wooden table as I try to get free, my eyes snap open and I see many strange faces hovering over me. My arms and legs are being held down as some woman speaks to me but I can't hear a word she is saying over my own screams.

"Royal." The woman yells, a second later the man himself is standing at the top of my head, even upside down he looks fucking beautiful. "Make her stop. I can't remove the bullet while she is moving." The woman shouts again. He reaches out and grips my face in his hands and kneels down above me so he can whisper in my ear.

"Stop fucking screaming." He growls.

"Fuck. You." I grit out through clenched teeth as the woman prods around my wound, I arch off the table trying to get free.

"Royal." The woman shouts as she applies pressure to my shoulder to hold me down.

"Fuck!" I scream so loud my ears ring as she digs some tweezer looking things into my wound, I open my mouth to cuss the bitch out but the words die in my throat the moment Royal presses his lips to mine momentarily shocking me.

I'm doing the Spiderman kiss.

Is the thought that swirls through my mind as he kisses me upside down, I get lost in the kiss as he pushes his tongue inside my mouth, I moan into his mouth lifting my head to try to deepen it. Royal's distraction is forgotten the second the woman pulls the bullet out, I scream into his mouth and accidently bite down on his tongue when I try to quieten myself. He yanks his tongue free and glares down at me, his eyes are dark with anger.

"The fuck did you do that for?" He snarls, I ignore him as I turn my head to the side to see the woman who I now recognize as Clare Murdoch holding a bullet between her thumb and index finger, she smiles kindly at me.

"I'm sorry you had to feel all of that, I wasn't exactly prepared for this so I had no pain killers or sedatives." I nod my head unable to speak, I've realized I have no issues speaking to Royal but when it comes to anyone else I choke up. "I'm gonna clean your wound, will you be okay if I get the others to let you go?" frowning I lift my head and look around me to see, Rook, Anya and Carlina holding my legs. I turn to my other side and cringe at the sight of Royal's mother, Kiara standing there holding my arm down.

She just saw me make out with her son!

"Let her go, she won't move." Royal answers for me as I continue to stare at his mother, she stares right back there is no judgment or loathing in her gaze just... Curiosity. They release their hold on me and step back, it's not lost on me that Chanel, Havoc, Koby, Knight and Bishop aren't here. I know Gage and Vincent were injured so I'm guessing they are both recovering somewhere. I hiss when Clare pours fucking whiskey on my wound, I slam my eyes closed and breathe through my nose trying to focus on something else aside from the pain. On the plus side, I can't feel pain anywhere else at the moment so I take that as a small win.

Clare bandages my wound and gives me some antibiotics, I find it fucking comical how she has antibiotics on hand but has no sedatives. It wouldn't surprise me if she was instructed to not administer it so I could feel every fucking thing she did. Once she's finished I attempt to sit up I'm still so fucking weak, I try again and growl when I flop back against the table. On the third attempt a hand lands on the middle of my back and helps me sit up, my head spins and I begin to sway, before I can topple off the table Royal comes to my side and lifts me into his arm. I'm too wrung out to argue or fight him.

He says nothing as he walks away from the others and heads down a hallway, I expect him to take me back to his shack but the moment he enters an office where I see, Knight, Koby, and Gage Murdoch all sitting on a leather sofa, I dart my gaze past them to see Bishop Murdoch sitting behind a desk with a pissed off look on his face. Royal stops in front of his father's desk and places me on my feet, he grabs my waist to keep me steady but I step out of reach. If I'm going to face this motherfucker I'm going to do it without the aid of his son.

Bishop eyes me with disdain, he looks at me like I am nothing but shit beneath his shoe and you know what? The feeling is mutual. He pushes back from his desk and stands up slowly, the man fucking towers over me but I don't cower under his scornful look I force myself to stand tall and weather his brutal glare. I can see why at this moment he is so feared by many, his name alone can have grown ass men pissing themselves.

"Your wound was tended to so you didn't die." His tone is devoid of all emotion as he speaks. "Do not misinterpret my family helping you for weakness, my son's affection for you means nothing to me. If I order it, he will kill you."

A scoff escapes me, his eyes narrow but fuck it, if I'm going to die here I'm gonna say what I want to. "Seems to me your son has a habit of not doing what he's told, unless I'm mistaken you and your brothers were locked up like animals while he infiltrated Chance Bennett's team and managed to get close enough to him so he could dismantle his shit from the inside." Bishop slams his fist down on his desk, I jolt but remain where I am.

"You know nothing little girl."

"I know more than you think." I snap back.

"Like where the fuck my son is?" I turn to see Koby standing there shooting me the filthiest look, but beneath that I can see the worry and fear. Those feelings aren't for herself but for her son and that's the only reason I answer her because if that was my mother standing there in her position, I wish someone would be honest with her.

"I don't know where your son is." I answer honestly.

"But you have an idea of where he *might* have taken him." Royal grounds out, I keep my gaze on Koby as I answer.

"I overheard Chance and Dalton talking about a new beach house he acquired in the Hamptons, it's only new so it wouldn't be listed as one of his assets. I suspect that would be where he would go to stay off grid and hide your son." Knight is on his feet and looking at Bishop.

"I'm going." He says.

"No." Knight opens his mouth to argue but Bishop pushes on. "We're going."

"No." Both men swing their gazes to Royal. "We are going, we got him into this shit and we are the ones that are going to get him out." As pathetic as it sounds, pride swells inside me that he is owning who he is.

They may be the mafia but Royal and his cousins are the Memento Mori.

"You're not ready and nor are they–."

He cuts Bishop off before he can continue. "I'm not asking permission. He was given the royal flush and there is no fucking way we are going to let him or Emilio go free. We've never let anyone go and we won't start now."

"Chanel, mentioned *she* was given a card." Bishop says as he flicks his gaze to me, it's true, I was given the Queen of Hearts.

Without missing a beat, Royal fires back. "She wasn't given *my* card."

Bishop chuckles but it's dark and mocking. "Oh, let me guess your card is the King?

"Damn fucking right it is, you may be the King of this family but I am the King of mine." Oh shit, the air just got thicker in here with that declaration, Royal just drew a line between him and his father. Bishop rounds the desk slowly, I turn to my side to keep him and Royal both in my sight. I see Kiara, Chanel, Havoc, Rook, Anya and Allison enter the room. Call me crazy but I have spent years researching these people and only ever seen pictures of them, to be in the same room as them is kind of awe inspiring.

"You think you have what it takes?" Bishop says in a low deadly tone, Royal closes the space between him and his dad. Standing chest to chest, Royal is maybe an inch or two taller than his father and uses that to his advantage to look down his nose.

"I know I do, I did all of this without you. I brought Emilio here." Bishop scoffs and shakes his head.

"No, you think you did but the truth is, she brought Emilio here." Bishop turns and looks pointedly at me, Royal slowly follows his father's line of sight and looks at me with disdain. "Didn't you, Miss. Vargas?"

"Don't call me that!" I snap without meaning to, I grind my teeth to keep quiet. I suddenly feel closed in and vulnerable with all of these people surrounding me. I know without a doubt that each and every one of them hate me, I don't blame them for that but they need to know the feeling is reciprocated I hate everything about them and this fucking family!

"You're a Vargas." It's posed as a question but it isn't, he just wants me to confirm what he already knows now. So, I do nothing and stand tall holding Royal's gaze waiting to see what he does next.

"Royal, do it." Chanel says from behind him, he doesn't take his blue eyes off me as he answers his father.

"She's going to be the bait, we'll get Chaos tonight, kill Chance once Havoc and Sin have finished funneling his accounts and dissolving his assets then we go after Emilio." He steps away from his father and comes to me, I have to crane my neck back to hold his gaze as he steps into me. He reaches out, grips the back of my neck and pulls me up until I'm on tiptoes, a whimper of pain escapes me but he ignores it. "I'm going to kill every single bastard that shares your blood while you watch, by the time I'm finished with you, you are going to be begging me to fucking kill you."

"I'll never beg." I whisper. "You can't kill someone who has already been dead inside for years, all you can do is erase the existence of who everyone thinks I am." His gaze flicks between mine trying to gauge what the fuck I am saying, he can beat me, break my body and patch me up to do it again but he will never break my mind.

"Thing is, I've seen who you hid from the world. You showed it to me the night you let me slip between your sheets." The gasp that comes from behind him makes me want to hide, I know that came from his mother. "You're like every other bitch, you'll spread your legs to get what you want."

My features harden. "No. I spread my legs for you because

regardless of everything else that was going on around us, I thought you were different. You're just like every other male, thinking with your cock instead of your head and that is the reason you will fail."

A cruel smirk crosses his handsome face as he bends so his lips ghost over mine. "Luckily for you, my cock isn't hard because the sight of you disgusts me. I'm going to slit your throat in front of him." Before he or anyone else can move, bat an eyelash or say another word I reach out, pull his gun from the waistband of his pants and hold it to the side of his neck.

Chapter Twenty

ROYAL

The barrel of my gun presses into the side of my neck, chaos erupts around us but I ignore as I stare down at her. Guns are drawn and pointed at her, everyone shouts for her to drop the gun but she hears none of it as she continues to stare at me. I see it in her eyes, she isn't going to pull the trigger she wants my attention, stupid girl, she didn't need to hold me at gunpoint to get it.

"You pull that fucking trigger and I swear on my family, I will become your worst fucking nightmare." Sin yells.

"I am begging you, please don't hurt my son. No mother should have to witness this–."

Erika cuts my mother off. "But a child should have to watch both her parents be executed and tortured in front of her?" The tremble in her voice is a dead giveaway that she is talking about herself. The anguish in her hazel eyes has a pang of sadness hitting me in the chest.

"No. No child should have to witness what you did." Dad answers, a shuddering breath escapes her at the sound of my father's voice. The anguish evaporates from her eyes and is replaced by hatred. I may be out of my fucking mind but even though we have slept together and I've tasted her sweet pussy, this moment feels more intimate than when we fucked. She has dropped her walls and let me see the real her, something about her letting me in has a feeling of protectiveness wash over me.

"Then why the fuck did you do it? Why kill my father and force me to watch as you raped my mother and then killed her? Why?" She screams as tears leaks from her eyes, she sways on her feet and without thought I drop my hold to her waist to keep her steady. I could have easily disarmed her and killed her but I... Can't.

"I never touched your mother or father." She spins around in my hold to face my dad with the gun pointed at him, I'm in the perfect position to snap her neck. Chanel and Havoc stare at me, waiting for me to move my hands from her waist to her neck and end this. I told her I'd kill her, promised it even but I can't force my fucking hands to move!

"Bullshit!" She screams, dad lowers his gun to his side. No one else follows his lead, they all keep their guns trained on the woman in my hold.

"Bishop!" Mom shouts but he ignores her as he looks at Erika.

"I never knew who the fuck your father or mother was until about an hour ago, I may be a lot of things but a rapist isn't one of them. If I killed your father, I would have owned that shit. In my family, we don't kill women and children, they are protected above all else." Erika begins to tremble, she can try and deny it but even I hear the truth in my father's words. We have all been raised to never harm a woman or children. Which is why I sent Sin in to deal with Erika, I could never lay my hands on her in that way.

Mom darts out in front of my dad, dad's eyes widen in fear

as he reaches out to try to shove my mom out of harm's way. Without a second thought, I strike out and wrangle the gun from her hold, she doesn't fight me. I place the gun back into my waistband and wrap an arm around her waist gently as she sags into me. My dad has my mom in the position, he may gamble with his own life but he would never do that with my mom's.

"Kill her!"

"Take her out." I ignore Sin and Havoc's pleas.

"Erika?" My mom hedges, silencing everyone else in the room, mom waits for her to finally lift her gaze and smiles kindly. "I am so sorry for what you have lived through. I can't imagine the pain you have been dealing with but let me be the first to reassure you, Bishop has never and I mean *never* forced himself onto me or... anyone else." I roll my lips over my teeth to keep from laughing, my mom hates the fact that my dad has been with other women before they got together.

"H-he." Erika clears her throat and tries again. "He told me it was you." She whispers as she looks at my father. "I never saw their faces, they made me watch as they defiled my mother in front of me and..." A sob claws out of her and her body begins to shake, tears cloud my mother's eyes as I spin Erika around and press her against my chest, holding her close as she breaks down. No one speaks as they all stare at the woman who is currently clinging to me, the only sound in the room is her cries. I shoot Sin and Havoc a look telling them without words to lower their fucking guns, Havoc does as he's told but Chanel, she takes a minute longer.

"Who told you my husband did that to your mother?" My mom asks softly, Erika sniffles and tries to step away from me but I refuse to allow her.

"Emillio told you my dad was the one to execute your family, didn't he?" I ask, she nods against my chest. "Why did you go to Chance?" This time when she pulls back, I allow it. She gazes up at me with tear filled eyes.

"It was planned out months ago." She whispers, I cock my head to the side not following.

"What was?" I push.

She darts her tongue out to moisten her lips, when she sways again I growl and swoop in. I scoop her up bride style and stalk out of the room with everyone's shouts following me but I don't give a fuck. I just showed all of them and Erika herself that I can't fucking kill her much less harm her so why keep fucking around. I head straight for the kitchen, placing her on one of the stools, I make my way to the fridge but just as I grab the handle a dainty little hand I know all too well covers mine. I turn to look down at my mom, she smiles knowingly and wiggles her brows.

"Sit down with her and talk, I'll get her something to eat and drink and then we can hatch a plan to get your cousin back before your aunt and uncle burn Miami down to find their boy." I smile my thanks and do as she said, I slide on the stool beside her and wait. I won't push her to speak but I also need the information she has. Clearly torturing her didn't get her to spit it out. She watches my mom gather all the ingredients out of the fridge for a sandwich as she speaks.

"Chance has always worked with Emillio, he had to work off his father's debt so he struck a deal to launder money for Emilio and gain him access to all the docks in Miami. Columbia is hot for feds and police at the moment so we needed to get out but still needed to have somewhere shipments could arrive without problems. We had no issues with your family, Emillio had led me to believe that there would be no issues with your family because we would take you out and then take over Miami and New York." I grit my teeth in anger, did he really think it would be that easy to get rid of us? "Chance promised to give us all access to the docks but then, he called Emillio and told him that he knew who had killed my cousin."

"How did Chance know?" Comes from Havoc as he enters the room with Sin, Dad, Vincent, Gage, King and Ally. She keeps her gaze on my mom as she answers him.

"He never said. Emillio just thought it was because of us wanting to enter the states but I knew better." She slowly lifts her gaze to face Havoc, a loaded look passes between the two of them. He stiffens, his nostrils flare the longer he looks at Erika as he can read her thoughts.

"How do you know?" She smiles and shrugs but winces from the pain in her shoulder, I feel like a fucking prick now.

"Every great war always starts over the love of a woman, it wasn't too hard to figure out." Frowning I look between the two of them not following.

"You had no idea who the fuck we were, so how did you know it was over Rico marrying Lailani?" Mom places a glass of chocolate milk and the sandwich in front of Erika who smiles her thanks and downs the glass of milk in one go, she coughs a few times but I'm frightened to tap her back in case I cause her more pain.

Once she gets herself under control she answers. "It didn't take a genius to work it out, Rico had told me he didn't like some guys from UNLV. He even told his father he wanted to marry Lailani, Rico never wanted to settle down so it was easy to put it together that he did it out of spite." I cut a glance to Sin to find she is studying Erika, no one else knew about this, shit Sin and I didn't even figure it out until it was too late and the war had started because of the twins.

"That answers why Emillio is here but that doesn't answer why the fuck you are here." Chanel clips out.

She takes a bite of her sandwich and then turns to face me, I make sure I give nothing away as she looks at me. "I knew you would come out of hiding if your father was taken." I can't hide the shock from my face.

"It was your idea to take the plane down?" Uncle King asks, she keeps her gaze on me as she nods.

"Why?" That one word out of my mouth holds so much fucking weight, she started all of this. Everything that has happened is because of her.

"I wanted you to feel half of the pain I felt when my parents were murdered in front of me. I made Emillio see that forcing Bishop's son to step up and try to fill the shoes of his father would hurt him more than just killing him."

"Why were you with Chance?" I grit out.

"To get to you." My brows raise to my hairline, I feel Chanel close in on us.

"Start telling the whole fucking story bitch or this time I won't fucking miss because of a helicopter!" Sin snarls.

"I knew you would find a way to go after Chance, the only way to get a man on the inside was if Emillio promised to wipe Chance's debt to him by marrying me."

"You agreed to that shit?" I seethe.

"Yes. I wanted revenge for the deaths of my parents, I would have done anything to get it even if it meant marrying that piece of shit. Chance had no idea why I was there, Emillio wanted me to marry him to secure his alliance with Chance. I agreed but I had a plan of my own."

"Which was?" Dad presses.

"To find you." She says as she continues to stare at me. "I planned to capture you, take you to your father and force him to watch as I killed his only child in front of him. Emillio figured out that I wanted something different, which is why I managed to convince him to keep your father and uncles alive." I reel back.

"I knew it." She looks over my shoulder at Vincent. "He wanted to kill us at the tarmac, you stopped it." She nods.

"You signed something to me that day, what was it?" She swivels around on her stool to face my father who leans against the far wall with my mom tucked into his side. Erika signs something to my father and his eyes narrow. "What does it mean?"

"See you at the close." Dad's brows draw in, he looks confused as fuck so I say it for her.

"It means she will see you when it's time for you to die." Erika bites her bottom lip then cringes, her face is fucking bruised and swollen as hell. Mom's features harden as she glares at Erika. "Why didn't you rat me out when you realized Chaos wasn't me? Your main mission was to kill me while he watched, why didn't you do it?" I press drawing her attention back to me.

"I was twelve when my parents were murdered. When Emillio found me in that house two days later I couldn't utter a single word, I haven't been able to for over a decade until I met you." I cock my head to the side, unsure of what the fuck she is trying to say. "When I first met you..." She pushes her tongue into her cheek as a slight blush begins to coat her cheeks. "I felt something other than self loathing, I don't know how or why but I have never wanted to say a word for years but you were so frustrating and made me so angry I wanted to yell or scream just so you would know how pissed off and angry you made me." That has me smirking.

"He has that effect on people." I hear my dad mutter, I shoot him a scathing look before focusing back on Erika who is smiling.

"My revenge suddenly didn't seem like it was worth the cost." The honesty in her words rings out around the room.

Chapter Twenty-One

ERIKA

After our little conversation in the kitchen, I thought I would be sent back to that fucking shack, I was surprised as fuck when Royal led me from the kitchen to the second floor of this old plantation style home and showed me to a room. I thought it was a guest room or something until I saw his clothes thrown over the chair in the corner. He gave me a pair of his sweats and a shirt and told me to get cleaned up while he formed a plan with the others to get Chaos back. Which is how I have now found myself standing in front of his bathroom mirror staring at myself in *his* shirt. He must have dressed me after I passed out in the guest house. I struggle to pull the shirt over my head and cry out when I feel the stitches in my shoulder pull. I drop the shirt to the floor and fall forward gripping the counter so I don't fall to the floor in a heap, the door behind me bursts open to reveal a pissed off looking Royal.

I meet his gaze in the mirror for a second before his drops to the reflection of my tits in the mirror. Even though I'm in agony and hurt all over, my body doesn't get the memo and begins to heat all over from the lustful look in his eyes. He stalks into the bathroom kicking the door closed behind him, I keep my eyes on him the entire time as he comes to stand flush against my naked back. He places his hands on each side of mine on the counter and bends down so his chin rests on my shoulder.

"You're the first girl to ever wear my clothes and I can't say I'm mad about it." The husky tone of his voice has me wanting to clench my thighs but I fight against the urge.

"Your mood swings are giving me whiplash, your royal highness."

He scoffs. "The last person who thought it was a good idea to try to mock me about my name ended up buried alive, want to be the next?"

"Isn't that what this is?" He frowns. "Aren't you here to remind me I'm on borrowed time and when you finally kill my uncle, I'll be in the hole next to him?" Anger flashes in his blue eyes.

"Is that what you want? You want me to drop your corpse in a hole next to the cunt who lied to you your whole life?"

"Just do me one favor, when our deaths become public knowledge because they will. He's the kingpin of the cartel and Chance is the governor, don't let them splash pictures of my body all over the news. Burn me to a crisp first, I don't want my parents' names dragged through the mud because I trusted the wrong fucking person."

"Answer me one question Erika, is that even your real name?" A whoosh of air escapes me as I shake my head. "Are you Monica Vargas?" I haven't heard my real name in over ten years, hearing it come from his mouth sounds so strange. I became Erika after the deaths of my parents, being called Monica was just too painful.

"Yes, but I haven't been Monica in over a decade."

"Why?"

"Because Monica died the night her parents did."

His eyes shine with understanding which baffles me, how the hell could he understand my meaning when both his parents are still breathing? "If you had known from the start that it wasn't my father that did that to your parents, what would you have done?"

The answer blurts out of me before I can stop. "I would have killed Emillio the first night he dragged me back to Columbia."

"Why?"

"Because my father and mother fled Columbia to get away from him, they never wanted to be a part of this life and wanted something different for me."

"Then ask yourself this, what cartel do you know of let's their family members go free unless they are in a box?" He shifts one of hands to trail the tips of his fingers up my arm causing gooseflesh to erupt all over my naked body. "Don't tell me you haven't thought about the possibility." He whispers as he peppers kisses along the side of my neck drawing a sharp gasp from me.

I try to string a coherent thought together but I can't, the way he is kissing my skin and touching me has all rational thoughts fleeing my body. Jesus, he is the best type of distraction. I don't know what this thing is between us but it's consuming me, his touch is becoming an addiction. Today when shit got hard to deal with, I found comfort in him. I haven't had anyone to comfort me since my parents were taken from me but today, he did. They say you can't hack the heat of the sun and have to admire its beauty from afar. Royal is the opposite, I can see his beauty up close, touch him, feel him, taste him but loving him would be like being burnt from the heat of the sun.

I close off all my rational thought as I turn around and

face him, he cages me against the counter, his scent overwhelms me. He leans in and brushes his lips against the shell of my ear as he whispers. "Fuck me like it's the last time you ever will." I refuse to deny myself this, I need the distraction only he can give me so I give into him. The moment he draws back to rest his forehead against mine, I seal my lips to his and fuck his mouth with my tongue. He growls his approval as he slides his hands down my back and grips the globes of my ass in his strong hold. A whimper escapes me, he jumps away from me like I've burnt him. We're both breathless and panting as we stare at each other. "I didn't mean to hurt you."

My face slackens at the genuine regret I hear in his tone. "You didn't hurt me."

He runs a hand through his hair in frustration. "We shouldn't be doing this, shower and then meet me downstairs." He doesn't give me a chance to argue, he turns and stalks out of here slamming the door behind himself. I stare at the closed door baffled, I needed him to fuck me and get me out of my own head but no, he had to go and ruin it. I felt how hard his cock was for me, I know he wanted me as much as I wanted him. Now, I'm left standing here with an ache between my legs he caused. Fuck it. If he refuses to fuck me then I'll do it myself, Royal Murdoch can kiss my ass.

No matter how hard I tried to make myself come, I couldn't. I'm on edge and moody as hell, I've never had a problem before when I got myself off but now, all I want is for him to do it and that makes me more angry because he denied me! I yank the bathroom door open so I can grab the clothes he left out for me on the bed but freeze at the sight of him sitting there shirtless with his jeans open and his hard cock in his hand. My mouth waters at the sight, his gaze snaps up to mine.

"You sounded frustrated in there?" My mouth drops open, mother fucker was listening to me!

"Seems like I'm not the only one who can't come." I sass back as I walk over to the bed where the clothes he laid out for me lay next to him. At the last second he snakes his arms out and grips my waist directing me to stand between his legs. Even sitting down on the bed we aren't eye level, the height difference is really unfair.

"I need inside your pussy but you're in no state for how I fuck." Feeling reckless with nothing to lose I grip the knot and yank it open, his eyes drink in the sight of my nakedness, I smirk triumphantly when a groan comes from him.

"Then let me fuck *you*." His eyes are back on mine in a split second.

"You can ride me but make no mistake baby, I'm the one that's in control and driving this shit, got it?" I don't answer, instead I push him until he is laying on his back, I crawl up his body ignoring the pain in my body. I need this, I need to feel him inside me one last time. I straddle him and rub my pussy along the length of his cock, he growls clearly not liking how I'm edging him. "Erika, put me inside that pussy now!" Rising to my knees, I grip his cock in one hand and rub it along my slit loving the torture I'm putting us both through because this time, I know I'm getting the happy ending.

Lining his cock up with my entrance, I slide down on it slowly relishing in the burn of his cock stretching me out. I keep my eye on him the whole time, I love this look on him. No masks, no hate, in these moments, he isn't the heir of the mafia and I'm not the niece of the family he hates. We are just two people allowing bodies to do the talking for us. Once he is fully sheathed inside me, we both moan.

"Fuck, your pussy was made for me." He rasps out, I rock my hips loving this feeling of being connected to him. God, he doesn't even have to touch me and already I feel myself growing wetter by the second. The only sounds that can be heard are our moans and the squelching of my wet pussy sliding up and down on his cock. I want to fuck him harder but the pain is too much to bear and I hate knowing that he won't be enjoying this, he must see the look on my face. "Don't stop, you're doing amazing."

I whimper when he gently thrusts his hips up, "I need you to touch me, Royal." He sits forward until we are face to face and scoots to the edge of the bed and plants his feet on the ground and spreads his legs open forcing me to do the same. He brings two fingers to my mouth and presses them against my lips.

"Suck." I open for him without delay, he forces his fingers so far into my mouth I gag and split my lip open again. He pulls them free and then licks the trickle of blood from my lip. I'm so distracted by him tasting my blood I don't realize what he's doing with his fingers until he circles my tight hole.

"Royal–."

"Do you want to come?"

"Yes."

His eyes darken. "Then shut the fuck up and take what I give you, I told you I'm the one in control, not you." I tense as he begins to stretch my ass with his fingers, it burns. I try to escape the pain and push forward but he uses his other hand to tangle in my hair and hold me in place. His gaze drills into mine, my mouth drops open as a silent gasp escapes me as he breaches through my muscle wall. "Take it." He growls as he tightens his hold on my hair forcing me to sink back onto his fingers, my pussy clamps down on his cock. "Ride me."

Those two words have me obeying his command, I fuck him in sync with him fingering my ass. He captures one of my nipples in his mouth, a shudder rolls through me as I feel my orgasm cresting on the horizon, my moans grow louder. He releases my nipple with a wet pop and yanks my face to his forcing me to hold his stare as I continue to chase my release. Fuck, looking directly into his eyes and seeing the lust in the depths of his is what pushes me over the edge, I open my mouth to scream out my release but he covers my mouth with his swallowing my cries. He thrusts inside me chasing his own high as I break the kiss and sag into him, I feel his cock swelling inside me.

He bites down on the soft flesh between my neck and shoulder to keep quiet as he cums deep inside me, I shiver loving the feeling of having him inside me. I've never fucked anyone without a condom before but with him, I never want a barrier between us. I want to feel everything he has to give. Once our breathing calms, he slowly pulls his fingers out of my ass then gently helps me off him. His touch is tender as he grips my hand and slowly leads me back into the bathroom and into the shower, I wait as he adjusts the water temperature. He reaches for me and I go willingly, He positions me under the spray and then to shock me further he leans down and kisses me, this kiss is nothing like all the others.

This one has feelings mixed with it, I can feel what he feels for me without him saying it. I can feel his confusion over the way he feels about me, the loathing he feels for allowing me to get under his skin. I understand his feelings because it's the same for me, we are meant to hate each other and want nothing more than to see the others bloodline erased completely and yet here we stand, entwined in each other and not knowing how to break whatever spell we are under to do what needs to be done.

Emillio lied to me, I know that now but that also doesn't change what has happened. I tried to destroy him and his family, I have to answer for that and he and I both know it. What I did can't go unpunished. I may have been misled but he wasn't, I won't allow him to go down for this. I'll make sure he and his family win this war and put an end to the Vargas name.

Chapter Twenty-Two

ROYAL

I ride shotgun as Havoc drives, Sin sits in the back with Erika who hasn't said a word since we left the house. I had Luka send the family plane to an airfield here so we could beat my dad and the others to Chance. All three of our phones have been ringing non stop, dad and the others thought they could call the shots and tell us to stay put while they went and rescued Chaos. They are out of their fucking minds, now that I've had a taste of leading and running things, I can never go back to taking orders from my dad, I'm my own man now and I have my own family to run.

"What's the plan?" Sin asks.

"We get to the Hamptons, scope out the joint and work out where they have Chaos before we go in." I answer.

"We don't have the manpower, dude." Havoc grits out.

"You won't need it." I peer over my shoulder to look at Erika who is gazing out the window, Sin glares across at her.

"And why is that, you filthy little rat?" I grind my teeth to keep from snapping at Chanel. Erika tears her gaze from the window and looks over at Chanel.

"Because we are going to make a pit stop at Royal's house and pick Chance's mom up and use the bitch as leverage." My eyes widened.

"What?" The shock is evident in my own voice.

"I tied her ass up and locked her in the attic the day we left, let's hope she's still alive."

"Why the fuck would you do that?" Havoc asks.

"I had a feeling the meet wasn't going to go as planned." she answers.

"Yeah, it sure as fuck didn't because you're still breathing."

"Chanel." I warn but she ignores me as she continues to scowl at Erika.

"You hate me." Sin snorts. "Good, because the feeling is mutual. I may be a bitch but I had to become that in order to survive the cartel life, what's your excuse?" Havoc is the first to break and laugh, I follow after earning a glare from our cousin. Everyone knows Sin is a royal cunt, it's her default setting but no one has ever called her on it.

"You don't fucking know me–."

"I don't need to know you to know you're angry and pissed off all the time because you got your heart broken." The words are barely out of Erika's mouth before Sin has her gun drawn and pressed against Erika's forehead.

"Chanel, put the fucking gun down!" I roar, they both ignore me as they continue to glare at each other.

"You think you get a free pass because you're fucking him?" She doesn't give Erika a chance to answer. "Newsflash bitch, you are just one of many pussies he's fucked. Whores will come and go but I will always remain because I'm blood. You know nothing about me or my family, when this is all over, it will be me ending you not *him*." That thought has anger brewing inside me, the card may have been dropped but

I can't let it happen. We have never denied each other their kill when we've marked them, I won't let Chanel do it, I can't.

"Who I fuck has nothing to do with you." A growl tears out of me at the thought of someone else touching what's mine, yeah that's right, Erika is *mine*. "Like who you fuck has nothing to with, Royal. Whoever he was that hurt you, was it worth letting him go if it meant being angry all the time?"

"Sin's never loved anyone." Havoc says with laughter in his tone, we have never seen Sin with a guy before. I look at my cousin waiting for her to deny what Erika claims but when she slowly lowers her gun I realize she was right, someone did hurt Sin and she didn't kill him.

"I'm going to enjoy killing you but until that time, I have questions."

"Ask me what you want to know." I shake my head, these fucking women confuse me, how they can go from wanting to shed blood to talking in under a minute is something I will never fucking understand.

"Why didn't Chance know who you were and why did you change your name?" I turn around and act uninterested but in truth, I'm hanging onto every fucking word.

"Chance was a means to an end, I told my uncle it was better Chance didn't know so he would let his guard down and we could see if he was loyal or not. I had always planned to kill him. Martinez is my mother's maiden name."

"Why did Emillio tell you it was my uncle who killed your parents?" I hear her exhale as she tries to gather her thoughts to put them into words.

"I have a hunch but I need to prove it first." Anger laces her tone.

"How are you gonna do that?"

"I'm gonna ask the bastard before I kill him, when I get my answer then you can kill me, I won't fight you or run, I swear."

"You'd let me kill you, just like that?"

"Yes, because only in madness do you find a beautiful death."

"Glad you see it that way because you've been marked and no one escapes that, not even you."

Like fuck will you be dying on my watch, Sirena.

As we near the house Grandpa left me a feeling of belonging washes over me, I don't know what it is about this house but it feels like home. I know without a doubt that I won't be returning to New York or UNLV, I've finally found where I belong and I don't plan on leaving. I just hope Sin and the twins feel the same. Havoc places his hand on the scanner to open the gates, the lights are on inside the house, the three of us draw our guns as we creep up the long drive. When we come to a stop I turn and look over at Erika, her gaze is already on me.

"Stay in the car, don't try and run." The second she nods I slip out of the car and close the door quietly, I motion to Sin and Havoc with my hands for him to go around back and her to scout the property to make sure Chance's guy's aren't lurking around. When I texted Cable to tell him we were on our way back he said the house was empty but you can't be too careful. Plus, the sensor lights would have given us away, I keep my gun in my hand as I make my way to the front door, before I can even touch the handle it's opened from the inside, I lift my gun and aim ready to shoot until I see Cable standing there with a smile on his face.

"Master Royal, a pleasure to see you again." Lowering my gun I smile at the old man.

"Stop with that Master shit." The old fool just chuckles, I

wave out for Erika to come to me. I wait for her to exit the car and come to my side before walking inside. Cable eyes Erika with concern as he looks her over, when he flicks his gaze back to me I see anger in his eyes. "Say whatever it is that is on your mind." I demand.

The old man squares his shoulders and looks at me with disappointment. "I gave your grandfather my word that I would stand by you and help you navigate your way through this transition but one I cannot do is work with a man that harms a woman, I can not and will not standby—."

I cut off his tirade. "I never laid a hand on her." I grit out through clenched teeth. Cable frowns and looks between me and Erika, the woman in question shifts into my side and smiles.

"He didn't, I swear." At her declaration he seems to relax, he tries to apologize but I wave him off. He has no need to be sorry, I respect his morals and appreciate that he spoke his mind and said it directly to my face. Cable leads Erika into the kitchen to get her some meds and offers to change the dressing on her shoulder.

I pull out my phone and text both Sin and Havoc to get in here, I walk aimlessly through the house. I stand in front of an oil painting of him in the living room and smile. Tony Bennett was a fearsome Don, he led with an iron fist but he was also fair. Grandpa spent most of his life hunting for my mom and trying to bring her home except, when he did find her she refused to leave my dad. Mom told me that Grandpa and Dad wanted to murder each other all the time but because they both loved her so much, they knew hurting the other would just cause her pain and they couldn't do that to her.

"I heard stories about him." Erika says as she comes to stand by my side, I keep my eyes on the painting of the man I idolized.

"Stories don't do him justice, he was better than any story you would have heard." I say solemnly.

"I have no doubt." She whispers, I reach out and skate my fingertips down his face.

"I miss you old man." Erika places her hand on my back drawing my attention to her.

"Life asked Death, why do people love me but hate you?' Death responded 'Because you are a beautiful lie and I am the painful truth.' Death is not something to be feared Royal, it is inevitable. That is why life is the greatest gift because you only get one life on Earth but eternity in the afterlife with your loved ones." I gently cup her cheek and smirk when she nestles into my hold.

"I don't fear death, Sirena, I am death and relish in the power it gives me when I'm the one making the decision on who lives and dies." I expect to see disgust or some form of fear in her gaze but all I see is understanding.

"That's why you call yourselves the Memento Mori, you four are the bringers of death."

"Yes."

"You're only twenty years old and have already taken more lives than men double your age." I drop my hold on her when I hear the others enter the room.

"And I will continue to take more. This is the life I chose to live, make no mistake, Erika. I am going to kill your fiance and your uncle and feel nothing aside from the need to bury my cock inside your sweet pussy to celebrate my victory." Longing and lust shines in her eyes, fuck, this girl was made for my dark soul.

"We doing this or what?" Sin snaps from the doorway, I keep my gaze on Erika as I answer.

"Show me where you hid your soon-to-be-dead fiance's mother." The little devil smirks and leads the way. The three of us trail after her as she takes us to the attic, I didn't even know this house had one. The moment she opens the door that leads to the attic I cover my nose, it reeks of shit and piss. Unlike me and my cousins Erika doesn't cover her nose as she climbs the stairs, she flicks a switch and then the bright light illuminates the room. Sitting there on an old worn chair with her hands, legs and waist tied up is Chance's mother, Margaret. Erika saunters over to her and tears the duct tape from her mouth, not only did she tape her mouth she also shoved a... she pulls out a fucking sock from her mouth.

"Just in case the tape came off." She says as she drops the sock to the floor, I can't stop staring at her in wonder. This fucking woman is not what I expected her to be that's for fucking sure!

"My son is... going to kill you." The old hag spits out, Erika grips her chin in a punishing hold that has the woman wincing as she forces her face to hers.

"He's going to die and it's your fault." The woman splutters but Erika doesn't give her a chance to speak. "You raised a sorry ass excuse of a man, if you had raised him right we wouldn't be taking you with us to watch him die." Margaret tries to argue but Erika just continues to taunt her, Havoc leans in close and speaks in a hushed tone so only Sin and I can hear.

"Either you fucked the devil into her or she was always this fucked up." A dark chuckle escapes me.

"Nah, I just fed the dormant monster inside her that thirsts for blood like I do."

Chapter Twenty-Three

ERIKA

Margaret squealed when I tied her up and locked her in the lavatory of the private plane Royal had waiting for us, I've never been to the Hamptons so I'm actually excited to go. For years I have felt trapped and caged, forced to be a puppet and live my life by someone's rules. I'm twenty-two years old and this is the first time I have felt like I'm actually living. I never want this feeling to end but I know it will and I'm okay with that but I don't want her to be the one to end it, I want it to be him. It seems fitting, he woke me from a decade long slumber and breathed life back into me. I want his face to be the last thing I see before I join my parents in the afterlife.

Royal stands from his seat across the aisle and moves to the back of the plane where there is a bedroom and full bath. If his cousins weren't here I may have been tempted to follow after him and join the mile high club.

"I can see the crazy in your eyes." I look across from me to see Havoc studying me.

"And I can see the same in yours except unlike you, I don't hide from mine." I taunt, his eyes crinkle at the corners.

"Want to know something I worked out that you didn't?" I quirk a brow enticing him to continue. "You only speak when Royal is around, if he isn't near you turn back to being mute." My brows bunch as I mull over his words.

"I... I mean..."

"Stop talking to the bitch." Chanel snaps from her seat across the aisle near where Royal sat.

"This is an A and B conversation so C your way out of it before D jumps over E and fucks you up like a G." I choke on air, Havoc shoots me a wink while Chanel mutters about how both he and Royal are out of their minds for acknowledging me. I tune her out and focus back on Havoc, I see it in the way he carries himself. He's used to being the twin everyone passes over, he lives in his brother's shadow not by choice but because it's easier than dealing with his brother's annoyance.

For the next hour until we land Havoc and I spend it talking about the most mundane crap, it feels weird to talk so much but also freeing. I think I enjoyed not being able to communicate so my uncle couldn't use me more than he already did. Once we touch down in the Hamptons Royal comes to stand beside my seat and offers me his hand, I take it with my good hand, The other still fucking burns from having my nails ripped off. I should hate Havoc and Chanel for what they did but honestly, I don't. If I was in their position I would have done the same thing to protect my family.

Two blacked out SUVs idle on the tarmac for us with six men dressed in tactical gear standing there, Chanel orders two of them to go and retrieve Margaret from the plane. Havoc, Royal, Chanel and I all climb into the SUV at the front with one of the men jumping in to drive. Chanel rides shotgun while I sit in the middle of the two hulking men, when the car takes off I hiss as we hit a pothole and Havoc knocks my shoulder. Every turn or bump in the road I find myself flinching or trying to maneuver myself so he stops knocking my wound. As we round another corner he slams into me and I whimper, unable to hold it back.

"For fuck sakes, Havoc." Royal growls as he grabs me and hauls me onto his lap.

"I can't help it!" Havoc defends, I turn to him and try to smile comfortingly.

"It's okay, I'm sorry." I say.

"The one fucking time I miss the shot." I hear Chanel mutter from the front, I am getting real fucking tired of her shit and sooner or later I am about to tear into her. Royal wraps his arms around my waist gently and draws me back against him, I nestle into him and soak up his warmth. I curl up on his lap and trace a pattern with my finger on the side of his neck smiling to myself when he shivers, the big brute is ticklish.

"Get some sleep, we got a three hour drive." He whispers, I say nothing as I lean forward and place a kiss to his neck. A shiver rolls through me when he growls and his hold on me tightens, his eye bore into mine when I pull back. "Do that shit again and we'll be making a pit stop." I can't stop the laughter that bubbles out of me, he subtly jerks his hips and my eyes widen when I feel his hard cock.

"Sin, swap seats with me I don't want to see them fuck." Havoc whines, I bite the inside of my cheek to keep from laughing.

"Get fucked. I don't want to see her herpes ridden snatch." I balk at Chanel's comment.

"Herpes or not, her pussy tastes fucking amazing and fits me like a glove, so perfect and tight." My mouth drops open and my brows hit my hairline at Royal's comment, he just defended me against his bitch of a cousin. Chanel shoots him a glare but says nothing further, I tuck into Royal and close my eyes smiling, maybe in a different life he and I could have been more than this.

I wake to the feeling of lips on mine, I snap my eyes open and melt into him, he pulls back and smirks down at me. Fuck, this man is going to be the death of all my panties. Even wearing his clothes, no makeup and my hair in a messy bun he doesn't seem put off by my appearance and that warms my heart.

"We gotta move Sirena." Nodding, I slowly sit up and shuffle off his lap, he climbs out of the car and offers me a hand to help me out. I look around us and see we are parked in front of a beach style home. It even has the wrap around porch, the waves of the ocean can be heard crashing against the shore. Royal's hold on my good hand tightens as he leads me inside the home, it's very rustic and decorated in bright colors. He leads me into a tiny kitchen where a woman in a teal pantsuit sits on one of the stools, she stands when she sees us and smiles.

"Erika meet Amelia, she is going to tend to your wounds." I look up at him in surprise. "Amelia is a doctor and my cousin." The warning in his tone is clear, don't fuck with her or try anything. I look the woman over, she's stunning. Brown hair with hints of blonde that frames her slender face, her green eyes hold a hint of disdain but it isn't directed at me. "Meelz–."

"Don't, Royal." She snaps cutting him off. "The next time you have one of your henchmen drag me out of my room in the middle of the night I'll stab the bastard. I told you, I want no part of this life and I'm not at your beck and call to tend to the wounds of your conquests." I jerk backward at the venom in her tone.

"She isn't some conquest." The protective tone of his voice has Amelia eyeing skeptically. "Help her and when we get back from getting Chaos, you're free to go." Her eyes widen.

"Where the hell is Chaos?" Royal gives her the cliff notes version of what happened.

"Mom told me her and dad were flying to Miami to help your dad but she never said anything about Chaos, I'm sorry."

"You should have been in Miami." He forces out in an even tone.

"Don't judge me, I love my father more than you know but there are also a lot of things you don't know, Royal. I have my reasons for staying away from my dad." He ignores her as he turns to me and cups my face gently between his hands, before I can react he places a chaste kiss to my lips then my forehead.

"Stay here, don't run, Sirena. If I'm forced to chase you down you won't like the man I'll become." Reaching up I grip his forearms and hold his gaze.

"I promise I'll be here when you get back." He stares at me for a minute longer then nods and steps back and walks away, I watch him transfixed until he disappears out the front door. Immediately my stomach begins to knot with worry, what if something happens to him? Before I think better of it I race after him and out the door, the moment he hears me call his name he turns away from the waiting SUV and jogs over to me, I meet him halfway and throw myself at him wrapping my arms around his neck and ignoring the pain that tears through me as I smash my lips to his. One arm locks around my waist to secure me to him while the other tangles in my hair as he deepens the kiss. I show him with this kiss that he means more to me then I want him to, I need him to know that I never meant to fall for him on my hunt for revenge but I'm not mad I got this taste of happiness with him before everything comes to an end.

He breaks the kiss when Havoc calls out to him, resting his forehead against mine he breathes me in as we just look at each other saying so much without words, he feels the same as I do and that scares the shit out of him.

"Be here when I get back and be ready to be owned." His words send a shiver down my spine, He places me on my feet and jogs back to the SUV. I stand here watching until the taillights disappear, I turn to head back inside but pause at the sight of Amelia leaning against the post on the porch. She stands there with her arms crossed over her chest and a smug look on her face that irks me.

"I've never seen him be gentle with a woman who wasn't his mother."

Frowning up at her I ask. "I don't follow."

She shakes her head and shoots me a deadpan look. "Royal Murdoch is a cold, heartless, killer with no moral compass." Anger bristles inside me at her description of him.

"You don't know shit."

"I know more than this family would like, trust me. I lied earlier."

"About?" She shrugs her shoulders and motions for me to follow her inside, I do as she says shocked to spot four men on the way inside patrolling the outside of the property, he left men behind to protect us. Amelia claims her seat from earlier and motions for me to take the other, once seated she begins to pull out what she needs from her bag and lines it all up on the counter. She begins to clean and disinfect each of my fingers ignoring my hiss of pain.

"My mom did tell me that Royal brought a girl home."

I snort. "That's not exactly how I would have put it." Amelia chuckles and applies bandages to my fingers.

"Well, from what I heard my cousin couldn't stand the sight or thought of you being hurt so he wouldn't watch any of the recordings from when they were.... Interrogating you." I jolt in shock, she shoots me a *told ya so* look. "Royal is worse than my uncle, unlike uncle Bishop my cousin thirsts for blood and loves to hurt, maim and end lives. The fact he couldn't watch some girl get the shit beaten out of her to extract the location of one of his cousins says more than you think."

I mull over her words trying to read between the lines but I'm scared to let myself think too hard on it because then that would mean Royal actually does care and I don't know if I could keep my word to Chanel if I knew there was a chance of him and I being together.

"Royal has never and I mean never allowed a woman to deter him or come between him, the twins and Chanel. It has always been the four of them against everyone else, even our parents. The four of them want this life, when he was denied taking over as Don, they created their own family."

"The Memento Mori?"

She nods. "Yes. Royal has amassed an army of his own behind Uncle Bishop's back. What my uncle doesn't know is that all the men under Royal's grandfather are all loyal to Royal, not him. My cousin isn't supposed to take over until he is twenty-one but that changed when he went to Miami."

"To kill Chance and get his family back, I know."

"No, Erika. Shit changed when my cousin started to realize he was falling in love with a woman and needed to do anything to keep her safe." My eyes widen as I recoil.

"No, Royal doesn't love me—."

"Don't be that girl who denies it when she knows it's true. Royal called on all the Bennett soldiers the day after you went to the airfield, everyone thinks he was fucking around and didn't care about Chaos. The truth is, he was waiting for his army to get into position to take Chance down. The Governor doesn't stand a chance against my cousins, they are going to murder him and there isn't anything anyone can do to stop him."

"Even if what you say is true, I'm marked by Chanel."

Amelia rolls her eyes and waves away my concern. "Chanel is a bitch." I snort out a laugh earning a smile from the doctor. "She wants you dead because you are a threat to what they have built. Unlike Royal, Havoc and Chaos, Chanel has had to work twice as hard to prove she is worthy because in this life, women aren't seen as equals. You taking Royal's attention scares her because she doesn't want him to forget the end goal."

"Which is?"

"To take over Miami and then when the time comes for Uncle Bishop to step down, they will take New York and continue to expand until they outdo their parents."

"How do I affect that plan?" She pulls the shirt down to expose the wound on my shoulder and gently removes the bandage to check the wound.

"She's scared Royal is going to grow content with just Miami and New York and not want to take over more places."

"Why does she want that?"

"She wants the four of them to take over the major cities, Miami, New York, LA, Chicago and so on. She wants to prove to the world and her father that she is good enough. Her and Royal both want to prove to their fathers that they are worthy, the twins are just along for the ride because they enjoy the thrill of it."

"I would never want to distract him from goals he has set or come between any of them, not that I think I could."

"You didn't need to try to come between them, his feelings

for you have already driven a wedge between him and them. If Chanel tries to honor her calling card, Royal will take her out. He hates being told he's like his father but the truth is, just like Uncle Bishop did, Royal will start a war for you whether you want him to or not because that is what being loved by a Murdoch is like."

Chapter Twenty-Four

ROYAL

We're a block away from Chance's house on the beach. Marco, Terry, Benny, Sin, Havoc and I all stand around the hood of the car where Terry has the blueprints of the house laid out. He points out the entry points and the best places to enter without detection. With how close his house is to the others we're all using silencers, taking out the Governor is going to cause problems but I don't care, I'll deal with that shit later.

"There's no basement so that means Chaos is being held in one of these rooms." I say point to the four bedrooms on the second level.

"We have a full tactical team ready to extract him while you three create the distraction." Benny says.

"Good, hang back until I give the signal." The three of them nod as they each leave to go inform their teams of the plan. Benny was the chief of staff for Grandpa, Terry ran all tactical teams and Marco and his team are the cleaners. Benny has been monitoring and scoping out this place for two days now. He told us Chance is antsy and has his men rotating every four hours to make sure they are fresh and alert for an attack. He knows we have funneled all the money he's laundered, the fucker is failing at being governor badly. He's missed meetings, press conferences, hospital wing openings and all that other shit so they shouldn't miss him too much when I kill the cunt.

The three of us climb in the car, I drive us to Chance's house, the minute I put the car in park men come out from all directions, I look beside me to Sin and nod. We exit the car leaving Havoc and Margaret in the back.

"Drop the fucking gun." Some pussy yells but I ignore the cunt and keep my gun at my side, Sin slides up next to me with her own gun in hand and knives strapped to her legs.

"Unless you want your boss's mother's throat slit, I suggest you go fetch him like a good little bitch." The fucker snarls at Sin, she doesn't cower. This cunt has another thing coming if he thinks he scares her, the girl is fucking crazy! She's already in a bad mood because I told her I wanted her by my side instead of being perched on a roof doing what she does best and being a sniper. He brings his wrist to his mouth and says to get Chance, we stand here relaxed and unbothered by the sheer number of men surrounding us, if they are all here then that means there would only be one or two men guarding Chaos.

"Kill them!" I dart my gaze to the front door where a disheveled looking Chance stands.

"Do that and your mother dies." I growl, the fucker couldn't play poker to save his life. He tries to hide the fear from his face but fails.

"You're lying, my mother left town."

I shake my head and tsk him, "I would have believed that but then my girl told me she locked mommy dearest in the attic before we all left for that meet. You know, the one where you called the fucking feds like a rat bitch."

"Your girl?" I stand taller and harden my stare as I scowl at the fucker.

"Yeah, *my* girl." His nostrils flare as he comes toward us but of course he makes sure to stand behind his men instead of facing me head on like a man.

"After we kill you three, I'm going to kill that bastard inside and then go retrieve my fiancée and show her how I treat disobedient pets. I'll make sure she knows how a real man fucks." Growling I step forward ready to beat the shit out of this bastard until Sin places a hand on my chest holding me in place.

"After I kill you, I'm going to fuck her right next to your rotting corpse so she knows she will never have to fear the thought of your pin-sized cock going near her." His face turns beat red, and he starts shouting but I ignore him as I hear Terry give me an update in my earpiece.

"Breaching the second floor now." Comes through the coms.

"Havoc, bring the bitch." Sin calls out knowing we will need to keep their attention on us after receiving the same update I did. Havoc slides from the car with a dark look on his face, being this close to his twin and not being able to barge in there and get him is killing him. Havoc needs Chaos, he can't function fully without his brother. Chaos is the only one who can keep Havoc in line, if he were to snap and go on a killing spree, Sin and I wouldn't be able to stop him. Havoc drags the bitch from the car and shoves her to her knees in front of him with his gun to the back of her head and the other tangled in her mattered hair.

"You bastard!" Chance roars.

"Unless you want to be scraping your cunt of a mother's brain matter off the ground, give me my fucking brother!" Havoc roars, guns begin to cock around us, music to my fucking ears. Chance pales at the sight of his mother at gunpoint, whilst these fucks have all been busy surrounding us, I took a leaf from my grandfather's playbook and had my men surround them and cage all these cunts in. The moment red lasers begin to appear on each of them they start to dart their gazes around.

"Package secured." Comes through the coms from Terry, I see Havoc visibly relax beside me knowing his brother is safe and out of harm's way.

"I'm the governor–."

I cut off Chance's tirade not bothered to hear what the fuck he has to say, I address his pathetic excuse for guards. "You have three seconds to lower your weapons and walk away, ignore this chance at mercy and you will die alongside the bitch you protect." It takes a second for fifteen men to drop their guns to the ground, raise their hands and back away. Marco and his guys come forward and collect the weapons and follow Chance's men out.

"You seem lonely there by yourself, governor." Sin taunts, the cunt shakes visibly as he looks around for an escape.

"You tried to kill my family, you went after my father. My fucking father!" I roar as I storm toward him and grip him by the scruff of his shirt, his bottom lip trembles as the pussy fights back tears. "You made the biggest mistake of your life when you went after my family, unlike my father I won't show mercy for your family because of what you did to mine. Shooting my uncles signed your mother's death warrant." His eyes widen in fear.

"No, no, no, please—." Lifting my arm I turn and peer over my shoulder, Havoc leaps out of the way as I pull the trigger and shoot Margaret right between the eyes. Chance screams like a bitch for his mommy, I drag the sack of shit around the other side of the car and shove him in the backseat, Chanel climbs in on the other side and keeps her gun on him as I stalk to the other side to check on Havoc. He stands there tense and staring at the house waiting for them to bring his brother out. The moment Terry steps out the door with his arm wrapped around Chaos to support him, Havoc takes off.

The moment Chaos spots his twin he stands tall and pushes away from Terry, Havoc grips the back of his brother's neck and places his forehead against his. They stand like that for a moment before Terry tells them we need to leave so Benny can clean the site. Havoc helps Chaos to the car, when he's within reach I pull the fucker in for a hug and hold him close.

"Missed me, did ya?" Smiling, I pull back and look him over, they beat him and by the looks of the dark circles under his eyes they haven't allowed him to sleep either.

"Yeah, yeah I fucking did asshole. Let's get you home and cleaned up."

He claps me on the shoulder. "That's the best thing you have ever said to me."

The four of us decide to crash in the Hamptons for the night and travel back to my house in Miami tomorrow. Marco and the others are driving back tonight with Chance, we'll deal with him tomorrow. After making sure Chaos was okay and Meelz was able to treat his injuries, I left him with his brother and Sin as I go in search of my girl. I find her asleep in one of the rooms upstairs, I drink in the sight of her. I had Benny buy her clothes and leave them here for her, I can't say I'm mad at the fact she chose to not wear any of them and remains in my shirt.

She lifts one of her legs drawing the shirt up, I spy yellow lace panties and my cock is instantly hard. I strip off and grip my cock in my hand, pumping it twice, gritting my teeth to remain quiet, my dick aches with the need to be inside her, I creep toward her and climb on the bed, she stirs rolling onto her back.

Just how I want you baby.

I force my way between her legs, she jerks and bolts upright but it's too late, my face is already pressed against her pussy inhaling her heady scent. "Royal." She breathes out.

Ignoring her, I dart my tongue out and lick her through the lace of her panties. A soft mewl comes from her as she slowly lays back down and leaves me to do as I please, she squirms as I blow against her clit. I grip her panties and push them to the side and growl my approval at the sight of her perfect pink cunt, my mouth waters with the need to taste her. I shift us so I'm on my knees on the ground while her legs are over my shoulders whilst she balances on the edge of the bed. She sits up and grips a handful of my hair as I plunge my tongue inside her tight wet hole.

"Fuck..." She cries out, I continue to feast on her like it's the last time I'll ever be able to taste her. This woman is becoming an addiction and I don't want to kick this habit. "Oh fuck, Royal, just like that." The way she says my name has my cock twitching and begging me to bury it inside her. "Oh fuck, I'm coming." She cries out as shudders begin to take over her body and she cries out louder as she comes all over my face, unlike the other times I bring her down slowly and bask in this moment. I push her legs off my shoulders and climb to my feet ready to force her flat on her back and fuck her until she shuffles off the bed, drops to her knees in front of me and grips my cock in her dainty little hand drawing a sharp groan from me.

"You gonna suck my cock, Sirena?" she darts her gaze up to mine, licks her lips and nods eagerly. Reaching down I run my fingers through her hair and then grip tight and yank it drawing a moan from her. "Open that pretty fucking mouth baby." She does as she's told, the moment I feel the warm wet heat of her mouth on my cock I drop my head back and groan, it's taking every ounce of my strength not to fuck her face hard like I want to but I also don't want to hurt her or split her lip further.

"Hmmmm." the vibration from her moan has my balls tightening, I yank free of her mouth not wanting to cum down her throat, she pouts up at me.

"You can swallow me later, right now I need to be balls deep inside that cunt."

"Promise?" My eyes darken as she darts her tongue out and licks my cock piercing.

"Get on the fucking bed or I'll be the only one coming tonight." I help her to her feet when I see her struggle, I can't wait till she's all healed so I can fuck her like a ragdoll and show her just how fucking rough I like to fuck, something tells me she'd love me throwing her around the bedroom and beg for more. I force my way between her legs and peer down at her, her eyes are hooded and her cheeks are rosy, nipples hard and ready for me to suck. I swipe a finger through her pussy and then push it inside her, loving how her back bows off the bed.

I pull my finger out and love how her eyes track my every move, I bring it to my mouth and suck it clean moaning at the taste of her on my tongue.

"Jesus Christ, I've never seen something so fucking hot." She rasps out. Grinning down at her, I grip my cock and line it up with her entrance, she keeps her gaze on mine as I slowly push inside her inch by inch loving how her greedy little cunt clamps down on my dick. "Royal." she moans when I bottom out inside her. Leaning down I capture her lips in a searing kiss as I continue to thrust in and out of her, I swallow her moans relishing in the way she goes from a lady to a freak in the sheets as she chases her orgasm. I pull back and hover my face over hers.

"Come with me, baby." She nods, I draw almost all the way out of her before slamming back in eliciting a cry from her and a groan from me, I continue to fuck her just like this until we're both coming with each other's names on our lips.

Panting and breathless from my release I stare down at her, that wasn't me just fucking her that was me staking my claim. Erika may be a Vargas but she is *my* fucking Vargas and Sin's mark isn't going to change that. If I have to fight my best friend for her life then so be it, I'm not letting her go, I can't.

Chapter Twenty-Five

ERIKA

Laying here naked with Royal's arms wrapped around me is like a dream, I never saw this coming, no, I never saw him coming. He's changed everything in the best possible way, it's nearly dawn and we're yet to go to sleep, it seems neither of us can keep our hands off each other. He's currently trying to catch his breath, I refused to allow him to fuck me again until he let's me taste him. Fuck, sucking a cock with a piercing is so freaking hot but tasting him is even hotter, God, he tastes so fucking good I'm craving another taste.

"Chanel won't hurt you." I lift my head from his chest and peer down at him, he runs his fingers through my hair.

"But, she gave me the card."

His eyes harden. "Fuck the card, I won't let her touch you. If anyone is going to murder your sexy ass, it's going to be me, got it?" His words shouldn't have me smiling and feeling all warm and shit inside but they do.

"So, you're gonna kill me huh?" The darkness in his eyes evaporates as a mischievous look enters his pale blue eyes.

"Death by orgasm overload sounds like a fucking good way to go if you ask me, Sirena." I giggle.

"Why do you call me that?"

He frowns. "Sirena?"

"Yeah."

"Because you're a siren."

I purse my lips. "You started calling me that before I spoke to you."

He nods. "Yes, because you didn't need to say a word and you already had me drawn to you like the call of a siren. I didn't need to hear the words out of your mouth, your eyes told me from the moment we met that you wanted me. Is that answer enough for you?"

"You say you can read me without needing me to say anything well, same goes for me, I knew you weren't who you said you were."

He closes his eyes and leans back into his pillow. "I know, you figuring that out is the reason you remained breathing." I balk at him.

"Seriously?" He opens one eye as he answers.

"Yes. No one has ever figured out who we are when we switched, you did. It intrigued me, you're still breathing aren't you so that has to mean something. Go to sleep Erika, we leave first thing and I plan to fuck you again before we leave." His words have me clenching my thighs, there is no way I am going to be able to sleep with the anticipation churning inside me.

The plane ride is quiet and filled with tension, Royal has been on the phone the whole time and I can see that he's stressed from how tightly he's wound. Havoc and Chaos sit opposite me, Havoc seems more at ease now that his twin is back,

Chaos on the other hand seems trapped in his own mind. All their phones have been ringing nonstop, I know that it must be one of their parents. Amelia sits beside me while Chanel sits with Royal across from us, when Havoc's phone begins to ring again, I pin him with a look.

"She's worried about you." He grabs his phone from the table between us and tosses it to me.

"You care so much, you tell her." He clips out.

I can feel everyone's gaze on me and I'm not one to back down from a challenge so I accept the call and bring it to my ear.

"Havoc, I have been trying to ring you for hours where the fuck are you?"

I clear my throat, I thought it was his mother calling, turns out, I was wrong, it's his dad.

"Uh, sorry but it's not Havoc." Both the twins are grinning at me like children.

"Chanel?"

"Uh, no, it's Erika."

A growl comes through the speaker. "Where the fuck is my son?" The anger in his tone is granted and I get it so I decide to try to ease some of that for him.

"Both of your son's are sitting right in front of me, sir." The moment the word *sir* leaves my mouth both the twins break out into hysterical laughter, I see both Royal and Chanel shaking with silent laughter, even Amelia is laughing at me.

"I'm the second fucking youngest in this family, I'm not a fucking Sir! You call Bishop and King that but not me."

"Okay." I squeak out causing the idiot twins to laugh harder.

"The fact I can hear those idiots laughing tells me they aren't your prisoner."

"No, they are not. If anything, I'm theirs."

He scoffs, "No, you're my nephew's not theirs." I remain

silent not wanting to answer. "Where are you all heading? Don't try to lie to me Erika because if my wife doesn't lay eyes on both her sons in the next twelve hours, she is going to start her killing spree with you being her first victim." I know I should ask Royal before I answer but I don't want him to deny his aunt the chance to see both her sons and deem for herself that Chaos is in fact alive and safe.

"We're heading back to Royal's house in Miami." Chaos snatches the phone from me and heads toward the back of the plane with Havoc hot on his heels, I rest my head back against the seat and take a deep breath.

"You'll get used to it." I lull my head to the side to look at Amelia.

"Used to what?"

She smiles kindly, she is the first person aside from Royal's mom to show me any real kindness. "How moody everyone in this family is, also just between us. You may think that you need to get the approval of the men and Uncle Bishop's blessing to be with his son but newsflash babe, it's the women." My eyes widen.

"You said women aren't treated equally."

"Outside of this family that is the case but, in this family, women are the Queens and the men are the heavy lifters. My mom and aunts are no weak defenseless women, Royal's mother was a cage fighter." My eyes nearly bulge out of my head. "Trust me, the ones you want to impress are the women, if you get in with them then the men have no choice but to obey, happy wife, happy life and all that."

"I'm not trying to do anything–."

"Remember what I said about girls and denying shit?" I clamp my mouth closed and slouch back into my chair and stare out the window. For the remainder of the flight I get lost in my thoughts thinking about how things might have turned out. When the plane lands and Royal comes to collect me I place my hand in his without a fight, the car ride back to his house I sit tucked into his side and remain silent as he and the other four Murdochs converse. How nice it must be to have a family that loves like theirs does, a wave of sadness washes over me. I'm an only child, with my parents and cousin gone I have no one else in this world except, Emilio, soon enough he will be gone and then it will be just me until Royal grows tired of me and then Chanel can finally get her wish and kill me.

As we turn down the street where his house is located I see numerous cars lined up out the front of his gate, Chanel, Royal and the twins all draw their guns.

"Of course the first thing you four do is go for your guns." Amelia snarks.

"Would you rather die?" Chanel snaps from her spot in the back.

"Look closely, wise ass, it's our parents." Sure enough as Havoc brings the car to a stop in front of the large gate, Bishop, Knight, King, Gage, Vincent, Rook and each of their wives stand with them, the women look relieved at the sight of our car while the men look pissed off.

"I'll deal with this shit." Royal growls as he opens his door and steps out, Havoc and Chaos roll the windows down so they can hear what is being said. Kiara pulls away from her husband to rush to her son, a smile tugs at my lips at the sight of him wrapping his arms around his mother and placing a kiss to the top of her head.

"Since when the fuck do you have a house in Miami?" Bishop growls. Koby and Knight ignore their bickering as they rush toward the car and yank the passenger door open to pull Chaos out of the car, Koby wraps her arms around her son and holds him close while Knight stands beside them, his hand on his son's shoulder.

"Grandpa left it to me, believe it or not you don't know everything." Royal grits out.

"Motherfucker is still fucking with me from the grave!" Bishop snaps as he turns away and stalks off toward his car, his brothers stand there shaking with silent laughter.

"He's just pissed because his big ass hand couldn't open the gate and the butler wouldn't grant him access even when he threatened to kill him." Gage says with amusement thick in his tone, King and Rook laugh.

"Come on, I'll let the grumpy bastard in." Royal answers.

"I fucking heard you!" Bishop shouts from his car and then honks his horn drawing laughter from everyone.

I feel like an outsider as I sit here in the living room with every Murdoch except for the three younger girls who I have just learned from overhearing Clare speak to Anya that they are being cared for by her brother Luka back in New York. This living area is large and easily fits the eighteen of us with chairs to spare but having so many alpha males and strong ass women in one room can be overwhelming. Bishop has been glaring at me since the moment I stepped out of the car and his son led me inside. I sit on one of the large leather sofas next to Amelia. Much like me she seems like she doesn't want to be here, she has barely said two words to her father and mother.

The moment Royal turns away from the conversation he was having with his mother and Gage and comes to occupy the empty seat next to me his father narrows his eyes. The second I try to shift away from him, he clamps his hand down on my thigh holding me in place, I glare up at him and try to convey without words that his father doesn't like me being near him but he ignores my look.

"Stay the fuck where you are." He warns.

"Royal Murdoch, watch your language!" He slams his eyes closed and takes a couple of deep breaths clearly praying for patience, I roll my lips over my teeth so I don't join in on his cousins laughing at him. When he opens his eyes and stares down at me I can't help it, laughter bursts out of me. I clamp my hand over my mouth to stop it but it's too late.

"Are you laughing at me?" I shake my head, the corners of his eyes crinkle and I can tell he's about to call me on my bullshit but Bishop cuts in before he can.

"We need to talk, get rid of your pet."

"Bishop!" Kiara scolds.

"What a dick." Comes from Gage but I ignore them as I watch the mirth in Royal's eyes disappear only to be replaced with rage, he slowly turns to face his father and everyone in the room quietens down as the tension ramps up between father and son. Bishop is an imposing force but so is his son. When Royal climbs to his feet, Bishop does the same and immediately Kiara and I are there standing in front of each of them trying to stop whatever the hell is happening.

"Royal, he's your father." I try to reason, I cut a glance to the side of the room where Chanel stands with the twins imploring her without words to help me stop this, she gives me a subtle shake of her head.

"You touch a single hair on my baby's head and I will shoot you myself," Kiara warns her husband, the fact she still scolds her son for cussing and calling him her baby when the man literally murders people and is set to take over the biggest mafia family in existence is comical as fuck.

"He needs to pop the fucking titty out of his mouth and stand on his own feet without you protecting him, the boy is begging for me to whoop his ass."

"Get to it old man, let's do it right here right now." Royal taunts his father, I peer over my shoulder and watch as Bishop shucks off his suit jacket and begins to unbutton his white shirt ignoring his wife's warnings. Royal grips the back of his shirt and yanks it over his head in that sexy way men do cracking his neck side to side. Bishop's entire body is covered in ink, but the one piece of ink that stands out is the name inscribed across his throat, *Royal.*

Fuck it.

I dart into the middle of them and hold my arms out pushing against both their chests, Bishop growls but I ignore him as I look at his son, all the others crowd us ready to intervene.

"He's your father, he is always going to push your buttons because it's his job to force you to become better than him." Royal continues to glare at his father but says nothing. "Jesus, your fucking name is tattooed across his throat! If you can't see that he is just lashing out at you because he doesn't know how else to tell you he's worried about you then you are fucking fool." That manages to get through to him, he frowns down at me before looking back to his dad. "He's just worried about you." I mumble quietly as I do the stupidest thing I have ever done in my life and drop my hands and turn my back to the Don of the mafia that I thought killed my family.

Royal keeps his gaze on mine as I slowly reach out and place my hands on either side of his waist, I can feel everyone's eyes on me but my only focus is getting Royal to back away from his dad. I gently push him hoping he'll take my hint and take a step back, relief floods through me when he takes two backward. I see it in his eyes, he isn't calm enough to deal with his father so I blurted out for him to take me for a walk. His face contorts for a minute before he nods stiffly, grips my hand, snags his shirt off the floor and drags me out of the room.

Chapter Twenty-Six

ROYAL

It's taken me close to an hour to calm the fuck down, if Erika didn't do what she did my dad and I would have thrown hands. We have argued before but not like that, I've never stepped to him with that sort of intent before. Something about the way he was looking at Erika and spoke to her snapped something inside me and the need to protect her was so strong I was willing to throw down with my old man.

"Royal?" I shake my head and peer down at the woman in question, I reach out and cup her face between my hands and lean in to kiss her but she yanks free of my hold and shakes her head.

"Get the fuck back here now!"

She shakes her head again and takes a step back so I move forward ready to grab her ass. "Not while your parents are there!" She screeches when I grip the front of her shirt and haul her toward me, I look to the back patio and sure enough, my mom and dad both stand there staring at us.

"Should we run and hide?"

Erika scoffs and laughs, she grabs my hand and leads me back toward the house but I plant my feet refusing to move. "Stop being a baby," I growl in warning, she throws her hands in the air in frustration. "They love you, they only want what is best for you and I don't blame them for hating me. You shouldn't either, be grateful you have parents to watch over you!" Gripping the back of her neck I drag her to me and force her to her tiptoes as I get right in her face not giving a fuck about my parents watching us.

"I don't give a fuck what he thinks, you're mine and no one, I do mean no one, not even the Don of the Murdoch mafia gets to disrespect you in my fucking presence." Her jaw unhinges. "Close your mouth Sirena or I'll fill it with my cock and give my parents a good show." She snaps her mouth closed and stares up at me with a dazed look, "I believe this is the part where you promise to worship the fuck out of me and agree to let me fuck your ass because I defended your honor?" That seems to snap her out of it.

"Even if I said no, you would find a way to make me agree anyway, plus that wasn't what had me shocked."

"Now you're getting it baby." She smacks me on the chest and pulls away walking toward the patio leaving me no choice but to fucking follow her sexy ass. The moment we step onto the porch I expect uncomfortable silence but Erika surprises the fuck out of me when she moves to stand in front of my dad with her head held high, my mom raises her brows as she looks to me, I shake my head having no idea what the fuck she is doing.

"I was wrong, sir. I had been given the wrong information and accused you of something heinous and I am really sorry for that. I know because of my last name I'm not welcome." I growl behind her, hating she thinks that. "But, I... I really like your son and–."

"If you're about to ask me for my son's hand in marriage

I'll shoot you." A light chuckle leaves my girl at my dad's taunt.

"God no sir, I like your son don't get me wrong, but I'm not putting a ring on anything for a hot minute."

"Is my son not good enough for you?" I bite my lip to keep from laughing knowing dad is just fucking with her but I remain silent to see what she does.

"To be honest with you sir, it's me that isn't worthy of him." That statement has my blood boiling. "I see how this looks from the outside, I'm the poor orphan who tried to fuck your family over only to fall into bed with your son. I know to most it looks like..." She looks at my mom. "I'm sorry for what I say next." Mom's brows raise but she says nothing as Erika looks back to my dad. "It looks like I'm fucking my way to the top to get the golden ticket but I'm not, I've busted my ass for everything I have and I have never been handed a godamn thing in my life."

Dad stares down at her with scrutiny. Not needing or wanting his opinion, I reach out and yank her back to me by her shirt. She huffs her annoyance when I anchor her to my front by wrapping an arm around her waist.

"So, are you here to say sorry?" I ask the big bastard, his face twitches telling me he wants to go the fuck off but then Mom clears her throat and he groans low in his throat.

"Sit the fuck down, you shithead." He forces out as he takes a seat on one of the wooden patio chairs, Mom perches on the arm of his seat while I drop into the other one and drag Erika onto my lap ignoring her protests.

"Quit fucking squirming." I snap at her, if she keeps wriggling her ass like that I'm going have to have this conversation with my parent's rock fucking hard.

"Your mother is sitting right there." She grits out through clenched teeth.

"So?"

"Royal, the girl is trying to be respectful." Mom cuts in and says, I frown up at Erika.

"Why?" I ask genuinely confused.

She stops wriggling and rolls her eyes. "Because no mother wants to see some girl perched on her son's lap. If I was her, I would have shot me by now!" My parents laugh while I sit here staring up at the craziest fucking woman I have ever met.

"Shut the fuck up and stay where you are."

"Such a gentleman." She mutters under her breath.

"Royal." My mom scolds but I ignore her as I look at my dad wanting to get this fucking chat over with, I have shit to do.

"If you're here to yell, scream or threaten me then save your breath. I'm not going back to UNLV, I'm staying in Miami. I've already taken control and have every exit blocked and locked down. Emilio is hiding somewhere around here and I'm going to find him."

"So you think you can just step up and run things?"

"I don't think so, I know because I've already done it. Miami is mine, you have New York. I'm not giving it up, dad. You raised me to stand on my own feet and be who I am, well this is me, I am who you created me to be. Even at UNLV we were already running shit there, we're all staying and taking everything on as a unit."

"You had a chance to be different, you didn't have to want this life." He argues.

"Why?"

"Because I wanted something different for my son!" He shouts. "I never got that choice, I was born to be who I am. I took over to save my siblings, I didn't have a choice but you do."

"No, I don't, this is who I am. I love this shit and I'm not giving it up, I'm a Murdoch and your son, I wasn't born to follow anyone I was born to lead so let me do that." Pride shines in his eyes, something tells me that this is a test and I just passed it.

"What happened earlier will never happen again." I nod my head, I never want to get to that point with him again. Regardless of how much he may piss me off, Erika is right, he's my father and I have no fucking right to ever lay my hands on him.

"I never want to see my son or husband come that close to hurting each other again, you will both learn to use your words, am I clear?"

"Yes, dear."

"Yes, mother." Dad and I say in unison then chuckle.

"Keep giving me lip and I'll make you both suffer." She warns, I shoot her a sheepish smile as Dad wraps his arms around her and pulls her onto his lap nuzzling his face into the side of her neck. I smile at the sight, growing up and seeing how much they love each other has always made me think that giving someone that type of power over you is a weakness. Now, I see I was wrong, it's a strength. Mom gives Dad the strength he needs to fight every day, I want Erika to be that strength for me. "Now, let's talk about what happens next because I refuse to dwell on the fact I nearly shot my husband for thinking he could harm my baby."

Dad scoffs while I laugh and shoot him a wink. "He's not a fucking baby." He grits out.

"Mommy, Daddy is being mean to me." I tease, Dad's eyes blaze while Mom shakes her head and waves me off then looks at Erika.

"I'm so sorry you have to witness my boys being such..."

"Children?" Erika supplies, I scowl at her and pinch her side causing her to laugh.

"I was going to say assholes." I balk at my mother while she and Erika laugh at our expense.

"What's your plan for, Emilio?" Both women go silent at Dad's question.

"I want him looking over his shoulder and going crazy trying to find a way out, he's trapped and can't get more of his men into the city, I made sure of that. If they even try, they will be taken out."

"And?" He pushes.

"When I catch him, I'm going to drag it out and make sure he feels everything I do to him so he will know he fucked with the wrong family."

"Royal–."

Dad cuts mom off. "You want me to hand over Miami to him but you treat him like a baby? Either you let the boy grow the fuck up and step up to run your father's empire or keep treating him like a child and I'll take it back from him and that shit will cause a rift, Kiara. He isn't wrong, he's stubborn and pigheaded like me and won't let go without a fight."

Mom pulls her gaze from Dad to look at me, I can see the war in her eyes. The mother in her wants to keep me safe and coddled and hidden from the world but then there's this other half of her, the side that makes her perfect to be the wife of a Don knows this is the right choice.

"How do I let you go?" I open my mouth to answer her but no words come out.

"You don't." The three of us look at Erika who shrugs her shoulders and continues. "He'll always be your baby and will always need his mother even when his stubborn ass thinks he won't. A mother's love is never not needed. He just needs you to let him be the man he is destined to be." A lone tear treks down my mom's cheek, I hate seeing her cry.

"He proved himself, baby. He took over and kept shit

going while I was away; the little shit even managed to snag Miami from right out under my nose." I smile at that, I knew that move would show him that I can do this. "We raised him to be ready for this." He looks directly at me as he finishes. "And, he's ready to lead." My breath hitches.

"Really?" I rasp out.

"You've been ready for a while now, I just didn't want to see it. You proved me wrong by doing what you did when I was taken; you kept our family safe and didn't take the money I left you all in the safety deposit boxes and run. You fought for what is yours, I would be a fool to not acknowledge that. Miami is yours son, New York will remain mine until I say otherwise." I open my mouth, but he pushes on. "I speak to you as a Don, not your father, you try to take New York from me, and I will treat you like I do everyone else."

"You have my word. I would never do that to you, I'll make you proud." I say with conviction, Erika places her hand on top of mine and gives it a gentle squeeze in silent support.

"I've been proud of you since the day you were born, Royal." Fuck, that shit has me choked up. I gently lift Erika off me and stand, Dad does the same and then I pull him to me for a hug. I never thought he would ever hand me Miami or stand by my side as I did it. This is the best fucking outcome I could have ever asked for. We pull apart and the old man smiles proudly, clapping me on the shoulder.

"You capture Emilio but I am ending the fucker, he tried to take my brothers from me. I'm not asking, Royal, I am telling you that I am going to end that mother fucker for that and what he said about your mother." Anger surges inside me.

"What did he say about her?" I grit out.

"Something that no man should ever say about a woman." Erika answers, drawing my father's attention to her once again.

"You gonna try save your last family member?" He asks.

"No. Emilio deserves what he is going to get." She answers without hesitation.

"With him gone, where does that leave you?" He pushes.

"Homeless and broke?" She answers.

"She stays with me." I say in a tone that leaves no room for argument.

Chapter Twenty-Seven

ERIKA

The past week has been crazy but in the best possible way. The Murdoch's aren't what I thought they would be. They are so humble and real, they don't try to be something they're not and honestly that's a breath of fresh air. King and Ally left the next day after we arrived here then Rook and Clare left four days ago with Gage and Anya to get back to their girls while the others remained. Bishop chose to remain here while King sorted everything back in New York to make sure everything went back to running smoothly. Bishop needed to be here so he could teach Royal and he may not see it but I can tell he's happy his dad is the one teaching him the ropes of everything.

Royal, Havoc, Chaos, Knight, Vincent and Bishop are in Royal's office trying to work out if the tip they got on a sighting of Emilio earlier is actually him or not. Kiara, Amelia, Chanel and Carlina are all in the living room working away on their laptops while I sit at the kitchen counter watching them.

"How's your shoulder?" I look to the side to see Koby

Murdoch enter the kitchen, her and I haven't spoken since the day she tortured my ass.

"Uh, it's good, thanks." She rests her forearms on the other side of the counter and looks toward the living at the others.

"Why don't you go join them?" I keep my gaze averted as I answer her.

"I don't want to intrude."

"Hmmm." I eye her out of the corner of my eye. "Take it from someone who came into this family in a similar position as you, they won't judge you. The only way to get them all to turn against you is to hurt one of them."

I swivel around and face her. "What do you mean by my position?"

"I'm not going to go into details but at the time I met Knight, I was married to the Pakhan of the Bratva that had kidnapped his brother." My mouth drops open in surprise. "Your last name means nothing, I love my nephew and would never hurt him." The threat is clear in her tone. "I have watched that boy grow and loved him from the moment he was born, hurt him and I'll make what happened in that shed look like child's play."

"You have my word." I answer honestly, she nods and walks off to join the others in the living room. Kiara looks to me and smiles motioning for me to join them, I want to deny her but I also don't want to piss off the mother of the guy I'm fucking numerous times a day. I take the seat between her and Carlina, I feel awkward as hell being in here. Royal and I may be sleeping together and he claims me as his but he's never actually told me what we are so I don't know how I fit into this dynamic.

"You're still here." Chanel snarks, I shoot her a snide look.

"Chanel, don't be rude." Her mother scolds but the girl doesn't listen.

"Why? It's not like she has much time left, as soon as Royal finds her uncle, she's dead." She says wagging her brows at me.

"God, why couldn't you like Barbies and dresses?" Carlina whines. Deciding to stick up for myself for a change I glare at Chanel.

"What did I ever do to you?" I ask.

"Not die when I shot you!" My nostrils flare, I can feel Amelia, Carlina, Koby and Kiara staring at the both of us.

"What a pity, you seem to be the only one pissed I survived."

"Bitch please. The only one that is happy you're alive is Royal and that's only because you are pussy on tap until your uncle is dead." Embarrassment has my cheeks heating and me dropping my gaze to my lap.

"If that was true then my son wouldn't be making sure that Erika gets a green card so she is able to remain in the US." I snap my gaze to Kiara in shock, she smiles at me.

"Are you kidding me?" Chanel snaps as she climbs to her feet and storms out of the room.

"Are you for real?" I ask, Kiara reaches over and grabs my uninjured hand clasping it in hers.

"I don't think you are just some girl to my son, Erika. I've never seen my boy touch a woman or even be infatuated by one until you, I see how he looks at you." I bite my lip to keep from smiling. "I also see the way you look at him." I drop my gaze feeling slightly exposed at this moment. "Erika?" I peek up at her through my lashes.

"Yes?"

"I know he cares for you and I dare say loves you." I gasp. "I can see the hearts in your eyes whenever he walks into a room, the same goes for him. From what I have seen of you and him together, you fit. As his mother it's my job to watch you and I have been, I think you are a clever girl with a bright future ahead of you. I will not stand in the way of my son's happiness but you need to understand this. His father may be the Don of this family and scary as fuck but if you ever hurt my son I'll make what Bishop does look like a bedtime story for children." I ignore the other three's laughter as I keep my focus on Kiara.

"I would never intentionally hurt your son but you also have to know that the outcome of my life is in limbo."

"My daughter marked you right?" Carlina asks, I nod.

"You leave my niece to me." Koby says but then Amelia stands and looks at me.

"I'll deal with Chanel, if killing you means hurting her best friend, she won't do shit. Your death would fucking shatter him and not even she can deny that."

"Do I get a say in any of this?" All our heads turn toward the far end of the room where Royal and the other men stand staring at all of us, the way his pale blue eyes bore into mine has me sitting up straighter and my breaths coming in short fast pants.

"No."

"Nope."

"Never." Kiara, Carlina and Koby all say in unison, Amelia shoots me a wink as she leaves to go in search of her cousin. Royal flicks his head motioning for me to follow him, I stand and follow him from the room silently feeling all eyes on us as we do. He says nothing when he places his hand on my lower back and leads me up the stairs to his bedroom. I've spent every night in here with him, every time I look at the bed heat unfurls inside me knowing what happens every time he and I are under those sheets together.

I stop in the center of the room and keep my back to him, nerves thrum through me when he closes the door and I hear the lock click into place. I feel him coming toward me, the second he presses up against me I melt into him. One arm goes around my waist while the other grips my chin and forces my head to the side so he can bend down and claim my lips in a kiss that has my toes curling into the plush carpet.

I reach up and wrap my arm around his neck holding him close, each time he kisses me like this I start to believe what Amelia said to me. I want to fall into bed with him and get lost in the euphoric feeling only he can give me but I need answers so I pull out of his hold and put a foot of space between us. His brows furrow but he says nothing as he stares at me.

"Am I going to die?"

"Yes." My eyes bulge.

"Oh."

He rolls his eyes. "From the moment we are born we begin to die, death is inevitable, you even said so yourself."

"You know what I'm asking you." I can't keep the annoyance out of my tone. I have always been good at reading people, when you remain silent in a room full of noise you hear more than anyone and notice more things but with him, I can never get a good read and it frustrates me.

"Ask me, don't be a pussy and ask what you want to know, baby."

"Fine. Am I going to die by the hands of your cousin or yours?" His eyes darken as he closes the space between us, grips my ponytail and yanks my head back so I'm forced to meet his gaze.

"Haven't I made it obvious? Have I not made shit clear? Want me to spell it out for ya, Sirena?"

I dart my tongue to moisten my lips. "Yes." I breathe out.

"You. Are. Mine." He pushes his free hand between us and cups my pussy drawing a gasp from me. "This. Is. Mine." I swallow loudly. "That clear enough for you baby?"

"No." His eyes narrow, he slips his hand inside my yoga pants and beneath the lace of my thong to slip a finger through my folds, the instant he feels how wet I am for him he growls.

"Ask your fucking question now so I can fuck you." A moan slips past my lips as he pushes a single digit inside my wet hole. I grip the front of his shirt in my hold to keep me steady as he pushes in and out of me. "Focus baby." He whispers against the shell of my ear.

"Are...Will." I clear my throat and try to form a coherent thought as he inflicts the most beautiful torture on my body. He knows exactly what he's doing to me and loves how easily he is able to distract me. "Are you going to let Chanel kill me?" He licks the shell of my ear and then shifts his face so his lips ghost over mine, he knows when he does this it drives me fucking crazy.

"No. I'll be the only one hurting you, and the thing I plan to hurt right now is this pussy, so are we done arguing?"

"Fuck." I rasp out when he presses the pad of thumb against my clit, if he thinks this is an argument he is sorely mistaken. Getting the answer I hoped for I press my lips to his when his tongue pushes past my lips drawing a strangled moan from me at the taste of him. I cup him through his jeans and relish in the hiss that escapes him, there is something empowering about being able to bring a powerful man like him to climax.

"Get this shit off now and get on the bed." He demands as he breaks the kiss, I strip for him loving the way his eyes drink in every inch of my skin sending shivers down my spine. Once I'm on the bed he grips his shirt from the back of his neck and yanks it over his head, I watch transfixed as he removes his jeans and moan at the sight of his cock hard and ready for me. He crawls up my body, peppering kisses all over me until he reaches my mouth, he sucks my bottom lip into his mouth and bites down on it lightly before releasing it. I push against his chest until he switches positions with me, I straddle him and grip his cock lining it up with my entrance. He cups my tits, flicking his thumbs over my nipples, I can't go slow I need him to make me come and mark me as his once again. I slam down onto him, we both cry out in unison.

"Fuck yes." I growl as I place my hands on his pecs for leverage as I begin to bounce up and down on his cock, he tries to grip my waist to slow me down but I knock his hands away needing this orgasm more than I need breath. "Fuck, Royal... please." I don't know what I'm begging for but I just need more. He wraps his arms around me and shuffles off the bed, he moves my legs so they are thrown over his shoulders and glides across the room until I'm pressed against the wall. He kisses me as he glides his cock in and out of me, I love it when he fucks me like this.

"I want you to come all over my cock." He orders.

"Yes, fuck me just like that." I cry out as he continues to rub his piercing against that sweet spot inside me. I grips his arms for support as I feel my orgasm building.

"Get there baby, I'm gonna cum." He grits out through clenched teeth, one more thrust and then I'm screaming his name loud enough for everyone in the house to hear, he follows me over the edge roaring my name. He gently shifts me so my legs are around his waist and grips my ass as I wrap my arms around his neck and kiss him. I feel his cock twitch inside me and smile against his mouth earning a swift slap to my ass.

"Royal." I screech. I love it when he looks at me like this, in this bedroom he isn't the Don of the Memento Mori or the heir to the Murdoch Mafia he's just... My Royal. "I love you." The moment the words are blurted out of my mouth he freezes, I tense and stare down at him in horror. Seconds pass with neither of us saying a word, I open my mouth to retract what I just said but nothing comes out.

Banging on the door has us both looking that way. "Royal,

we got a location." I can't tell if it's Havoc or Chaos that spoke.

"Give me a minute and I'll be out." He calls back, he places me on my feet and I race to the bathroom and slam the door closed behind me. I look at myself in the mirror and shake my head, I'm such a fucking fool! Those three stupid fucking words are going to ruin everything and I have no one else to blame but myself, why the fuck did I have to go and do something stupid like fall in love with the Don of Miami.

Chapter Twenty-Eight

ROYAL

I love you…

Those three words and the look on her face have been playing on repeat in my head for the past three hours. I've been distracted and that isn't a good fucking thing when my dad has agreed to let me take lead on this mission. Benny, Terry, Marco, Sin, Knight, Vin, dad and the twins are all in my office as we go over all the routes to block Emilio from escaping.

"Royal?" I snap my head up to face me dad, his eyes are narrowed and I can see he's pissed off. "Did you hear me?" I cut a glance to Chanel for a clue as to what he said but even she is looking at me with a worried frown on her face.

"Uh…" I rub the back of my neck not sure how to answer.

"All of you out now, I need a minute with my son." Sin shoots me an apologetic look as she follows the others out of the room, the second the door is closed he asks. "What the fuck is going on?"

"Nothing." I clip out.

"Bullshit, your head isn't in this and if I have to, I'll sit your ass out of this because you will be a liability to everyone." I slam my hands down on my desk.

"Like fuck! This is my team and my call, not yours." He leans over my desk to get right in my face.

"Then show me you can fucking lead and not have your head up your ass."

"Fuck." I snarl and drop back into my chair scrubbing a hand down my face.

"Where's your head at because it isn't on this mission, Royal?" I slump back in my chair and sigh, Dad drops into one of the seats in front of my desk and waits for me to answer.

I decide to confide in my old man for the first time in my life. "Erika told me she loved me." His brows raise as he leans back in his chair.

"You didn't say it back, did you?" I shoot him a deadpan look that has him laughing lightly and shaking his head.

"This shit isn't funny." I growl.

"Nothing to do with a woman is ever funny, son. I'm only laughing because something similar happened between me and your mother." That captures my attention and has me sitting up taller.

"Tell me." I push.

He sighs and reaches around to rub the back of his neck clearly uncomfortable, which only makes this situation so much sweeter. "You get the cliff notes, I'm not giving you any fucking ammo to use against me next time you throw a tantrum." He gives me the bird when I laugh and nod. "I told your mother I loved her and her reply was '*I've loved you since I was nine years old'*."

"She said it back!"

"The fuck she did, she never said the three fucking words directly and that shit pissed me off but she made up for it."

My face contorts in disgust. "That's fucking disgusting."

"And hearing Erika scream my sons name daily isn't fucking uncomfortable?" I bite the inside of my cheek to keep from laughing.

"Good point." I wheezed out still trying not to laugh.

"You get that stamina from your old man, not your mother."

I scrunch my eyes closed and shake my head. "Please stop, that is shit I don't need to hear." He laughs at my expense, the asshole, when he gets his laughter under control he asks.

"Why didn't you say it back?"

I mull over his words trying to think of a way to put into words why I froze. "I don't know. I mean I barely know the girl and here she is professing her love for me as I'm about to hunt down the last living member of her family and kill him. I mean, how do you even know you love someone? The only woman I have ever loved with every fiber of being and would burn the fucking world down for is my mother. Chanel is a close second."

"Time means nothing. If you look at her and see your future then that's love. When she walks into a room and you can't help but stare, or even without seeing her you can feel her presence, that's love. If she sets you on fire and has you wanting to tattoo your name on her just so every fucker knows she's yours, that's love. I'm gonna get straight with you, Royal. I may not think much of her or even trust her but I see the way you look at her, it's the same way I look at your mother. I've watched the girl and if I thought for a second, she was fucking playing you I would have put a bullet between her eyes. The only reason she is getting a free pass is because I can see you love her and I would never hurt you like that."

"But she drives me fucking crazy and doesn't listen, the girl defies me every chance she gets unless we're fucking." The bastard throws his head back and laughs earning a glare from me.

"That right there, is exactly how I feel about your mother. Kiara fights me every chance she gets but know this, that woman would be the first to stand by my side in battle. She is the only person who gets away with ordering me around and fighting back because I fucking love her and would murder any son of a bitch for hurting her. Your mother is the love of my life, Royal. If you don't feel half of that for Erika then get the fuck out of the way and stop blocking her from her true love finding her."

The thought of her screaming someone else's name, of looking at them with those big green eyes as they hold her close has a murderous rage burning inside me. I may not feel everything Dad does for my Mom but I have years to develop those feelings, I want Erika and there is no fucking way I'm going to let her go. If some cunt thinks for a second they have a shot with *my* girl I'll bury the cunt alive and fuck her on top of his grave.

"I guess you have your answer then, don't you?" I flick my gaze to him and nod slowly.

"I guess I do." I mutter.

"Oh, this is going to be fucking good."

Frowning, I ask. "What is?"

The bastard climbs to his feet and buttons his suit jackets as he smiles down at me. "Watching you grovel and beg for her forgiveness."

I scoff, "I'm not begging for shit!"

He quirks a condescending brow. "You stupid boy. Your girl is currently sitting out back drinking margaritas with your mother, aunts and Amelia." My face falls.

"Oh, no."

"Oh, yes." He taunts.

I shoot him a pleading look. "Can you get Mom away from her... Please?"

He scoffs. "Fuck off asshole, the first time you say *please* is because you're scared, you know she's going to have those four on her side and they are all going to make you work and not let you do it alone with Erika." I groan and scrub a hand down my face.

"Can we just go kill Emilio and then maybe that will make it up to her?" I plead.

"No. We have no clear route and the teams aren't in place, pick your fucking balls up and go face that pack of hungry lionesses."

I smile up at him. "Any chance you want to come with me?"

"Fuck no. Go deal with your *mommy* on your own you nutless prick, I'll watch from a safe distance."

Fucking pussy!

He stalks out of the room calling for all my uncles and Sin to meet him in the kitchen, the bastard is going to watch me beg from there. I'm not begging though, she's going to come crawling back, right?

I stand out on the back patio with five sets of eyes glaring at me. I even tried to put on the puppy dog eyes my mom always falls for but it didn't do shit. My Dad and the others are all watching me and I fucking hate that I have to do this shit in front of everyone. I tried asking Erika to take a walk with me but Amelia nixed that idea and said she wouldn't be going anywhere alone with me. They have formed a protective shield around my girl. Mom and Aunt Koby sit on one side of her while Aunt Carlina and Amelia sit on her other side. Killing is easier than this shit. Fuck, being shot is better than this.

I peer over my shoulder and lock eyes with Chanel, giving her a pleading look. The ruthless bitch just holds up her gun and raises her brows, gritting my teeth. I tear my gaze from her to look at Erika who refuses to meet my gaze and continues to twirl her glass in her hands.

"Jesus. Can't you all go inside and let me do this privately?" I ask, my aunts, cousin and mother scoff and begin to curse me out for even thinking they would leave me alone with her. "You tortured her and now you're buddies?" I ask aunt Koby.

"We came to an understanding." She answers.

"I'm your son!" My mom narrows her eyes at my tone of voice.

"And I raised you better than this, Royal."

"Fuck me sideways." I grit out, I shoot Amelia a scathing look when she laughs.

"Erika–." My mom clears her throat and shoots me a look telling me to change my tone. Clearing my throat and taking a deep breath, I try again "Erika, I'm... sorry."

"Oh, that was piss weak." Aunt Carlina abolishes.

"Pathetic." Amelia tacks on.

"I would have shot Knight if he did that." I glare at aunt Koby.

"Bishop would have been missing a nut sack." A shudder of disgust rolls through me.

"Mom!" I scold.

"What? You've seen your father and uncles grovel enough to know how to do better." Taking a calming breath, I decide to go all in or go out swinging. I close the space between me and my girl and drop to one knee in front of her, I gently grab the glass from her hold and pass it to my mom to hold. I grab her tiny hands and wrap mine around hers, she peeks up at me through her lashes.

"I'm sorry." Her eyes begin to fill with tears hearing me apologize for the first time. "I've never loved anyone aside from my family, the only woman to ever have a place in my heart is my Mom." I hear my aunts and Mom coo over that but ignore them. "When you told me you loved me, I froze because I had no idea what loving someone outside of my family felt like. All my life it's always been me, Sin and the twins, I never thought I needed anyone else until I met you. You called to me like a siren and I knew from the first moment I kissed you that I was fucked and in deeper than I should have been. If loving you means I can't bear the thought of not waking up next to you or wanting to commit mass murder over the thought of you with someone else. Then yes, I do. I love that you don't bow to me and fight me on shit, I don't want a pet to stroke my ego. I want a woman who is ballsy enough to tell me to pull my head out of my ass when I need it and that woman is you."

"Royal–."

She tries to cut in but I'm not done. "I want you with me, no, I need you with me Erika. So much of what I have done already is for you, I want a lifetime with you so I can fall in love with you more each fucking day. I'm not good with voicing my feelings, never have been, but if you need to hear me say the words then so be it, *I fucking love you*." Her eyes widen as tears slowly cascade down her cheeks. "Just know this, I have never given anyone that type of power over me. I've never let anyone get close enough to me because I never wanted a weakness, turns out you aren't my weakness you are my strength. Forgive me for being a dumbass and I'll prove to you I'm worthy of your love."

"Oh my God, Vincent needs to up his game." I hear my

aunt mutter, I pull my hand from hers and gently cup her cheek.

"I love you." I whisper as I lean my forehead against hers. She grips my face between her hands and leans in to ghost her lips over mine.

"Show me." I growl my approval, I smash my lips to hers, this right here is what I know. I don't do words but I sure as fuck do actions and now I'm showing her without words that I meant every fucking thing I just said.

"Okay, that's enough of that shit, some of us have to go to bed alone." Erika breaks the kiss giggling at Amelia's remark, I stare at my girl and for the first time I see it.

I see the life I'm going to have with her by side, we are going to rule Miami.

It's close to midnight by the time we have a plan formed for the takedown of the Vargas kingpin. We know that his lieutenant, Braga is running shit back in Columbia while he is cornered here. According to Erika, Braga has always been kind to her and all about the people, he wants the drugs out of Columbia rather than selling them there and getting his people hooked on them.

We know Emilio has at least a dozen hitmen that came in with him, what we don't know is how many more he has had join him from New York before we closed the borders. It's a risk we have to take going in blind but it's one I am more than willing to take if it means ending this son of a bitch. Everyone went to bed hours ago, I've stayed down here studying the map and blueprints trying to plan for every possible scenario that may arise. Just as I stand to head upstairs and get lost inside my girl's pussy until dawn the office door opens to reveal Chanel.

"Got a minute?" I motion for her to have a seat across from me and drop back into my own.

"What's on your mind, Sin?"

She looks away from me and gazes out the window at the night time sky. I can see from the strain on her face and how tense she is that something is bothering her so, I wait. Chanel isn't like most girls, she doesn't talk about feelings or go crazy about the latest sale at the mall, she's closed off and keeps her feelings locked down. She's a heartless bitch to most but not to me, I know her, because of how well I know her I know that once she loves you she will do anything for you. But, for the past two years something has been off with her, she no longer smiles freely or jokes around with me and the twins, she's serious all the time. She's even iced her parents out and no matter how many times I've asked what happened she won't tell me!

"I marked her." Those three words have me gripping the edge of my desk and grinding my teeth to the point they begin to ache.

"Don't do it, Chanel." I force out through clenched teeth.

She brings her gaze back to me, I expect to see anger or betrayal in her brown eyes but all I see is... understanding which baffles me. I know Chanel doesn't like Erika, honestly I don't fucking care what anyone thinks about her because she's mine and anyone who dares try to harm her will answer to me.

"I knew from the first moment I served her my card, I would never fulfill my vow to end her."

"Why?" I ask cautiously.

"Because you never backed me. You told me I could do what I wanted to her but I saw it in your eyes, from the moment you first saw her, you already started falling in love."

"Then why give her the card?" I push.

"I wanted to see if she meant enough to you for you to break our most sacred vow." My shoulders deflate, when we first started the Memento Mori, we all agreed to the rules.

Once marked, the kill is final or punishment will be inflicted.
A loved one can never be marked.
A royal flush is to be unanimous.
The caller is the one to kill.
If one shall fall their card will lay in rest.

"You want to inflict my punishment because I fell in love with your mark? Go for it Chanel, I won't stop you. But remember this, she is my loved one and you will never fucking mark her again."

She pushes her tongue into her cheek and eyes me like I'm a stranger and not her best friend. "We were equals, you, me and the twins. The moment we landed in Miami, you became the Don and changed. You no longer see us as equals, you see us as your subjects. Newsflash, cousin, I am your fucking equal and if I wanted her dead she would be."

"You had the shot that day, I know you fucking did because you never miss, Sin. Why didn't you kill her at the airstrip?" She grits her teeth and clenches her hands into fists.

"Just be grateful I saw a ghost or she would be dead."

"I have never viewed you as less than me, Chanel. You have always been by my side through everything and that won't change now. I want you to be the first to know that the Bennett Mafia is no longer in Miami, the Murdoch mafia will not be taking over either."

"What are you saying?"

I grin at my cousin. "The Memento Mori is taking over Miami and I want you by my side as my underboss. I can't do this shit without you, I need you with me, Sin." Her eyes are wide and mouth slightly ajar.

"You're serious?"

"Dead fucking serious. What do you say?"

"I'll always ride with you till the fucking wheels fall off, you know that. No matter how much you piss me off I will always be watching your six."

"And I'll always have your back, Chanel. No one believes in your abilities more than me. If you need to punish me for overturning your mark, then do it."

"I think you punished yourself enough by falling in love with her." I snort out a laugh, she wraps her knuckles on my desk as she stands. "One thing though."

"Name it."

"If there comes a time when I need you and the twins to drop your mark on someone, you do it without question, got it?" I search her gaze for a minute trying to get a read on what she is saying but come up blank, the girl is a fucking vault.

"You have my word."

She nods her thanks. "Good, remember you said that." I watch her walk out and know without a doubt there is a reason she asked me that, something big is going on with her and I plan to find out what the fuck it is as soon as I deal with Emilio but for now, I have a girl upstairs who needs to get fucked.

Chapter Twenty-Nine

ERIKA

"I said no!"

Placing my hands on my hips I glare up at this infuriating gorgeous asshole. "I heard you but I don't care, I'm coming and you can't stop me."

"Fucking try it and see what I do to you." He threatens.

"Oh, what are you going to do? Tie me to a chair and let your crazy ass cousin torture me again?" He tugs on the strands of his hair.

"I fucking said I was sorry about that shit!" He roars.

"And I'm still not over it! The bitch shot me and ripped my fucking fingernails off." I hold the hand in question up just to drive my point home, the shithead averts his gaze not wanting to see the damage. I'm not trying to throw this in his face but I need him to see that I'm not weak, I took everything they threw at me and I'm still standing here. "I want to be there, I have to know the truth, please," I beg. He stabs a hand through his hair and begins to pace the length of his bedroom. I know he only wants me to stay behind so I don't get hurt but what he doesn't know is, I can fight and shoot maybe not as well as him and the others but I'm no slouch!

"You stay the fuck in the car and don't move until I say or God fucking help you, Erika I will strangle you my-fucking-self." I throw myself at him, he catches me with ease as I lock my legs around his waist and pepper kisses all over his face. He growls out his annoyance but there is no heat to it, he wants me safe and I get that but I need to look my uncle in the eyes and find out why he lied. "We leave in ten minutes, be waiting out front." He says as he places me back on my feet.

"Where are you going?"

"I have to go get Chaos out of the basement."

I screw my face up. "Why is he in the basement?"

"Because that's where Chance is, we've left Chaos to deal with him for the time being. Now, get your shit, if you're not out front when we leave your ass is staying behind."

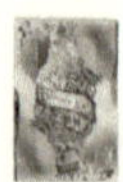

I'm standing out front waiting for Royal when the door behind me opens, peering over my shoulder to see it's Chanel, I fight the groan from breaking free at the sight of her. When she spots me the easy look on her face vanishes and is replaced by disgust, she pulls her sunglasses off the top of her head and puts them on. The sun isn't even out yet but I don't say anything as she comes to stand beside me. The awkwardness is suffocating, the tension is even worse. A dozen men mill about the front yard. I asked Royal why he didn't have all his men stationed here and his reply was, the less who know where he and the ones he loves live, the safer they are.

"If you do anything to distract him, I will fucking—." That's it, I spin around and pin her with a scathing look, tired of the shit she keeps doing to me and the shade she constantly throws my way.

"What? Torture me again? Kill me?" I shout. "I don't care what the hell you think of me, I have nothing to prove to you." She presses against me so we are chest to chest, she's close I feel her breath against my lips.

"Wrong. You have everything to prove to me, until I think you are worthy of him I'll never stop coming at you. He isn't some prize to be won or some sugar daddy you can use, he's my blood and I protect my own, don't ever forget that."

"Your loyalty is inspiring, Chanel, I mean that with respect. If you need me to prove to you that he isn't just some conquest then you clearly haven't been paying attention. Falling in love with him has cost me more than you know, loving him has cost me my family. I had the shit beaten out of me and shot because I saved him. Tell me again how I'm the one getting a free pass?" I scoff not giving her a chance to answer. "I haven't asked him to give shit up for me, I'm standing right here ready to stand by his side as he takes the life of my uncle, how the fuck else can I prove to you that I am not here to hurt him?"

"You can't." Chanel and I pull apart at the sound of her father's voice, he and Knight approach us with weapons strapped to every inch of their bodies. Vincent looks between the both of us as he answers. "Chanel is very protective of her cousin, all their lives it has always been her, Royal and the twins. You're a surprise none of them saw coming, it's going to take them all time to adjust to their new dynamic. Continue to prove your loyalty to their cousin and then you will gain their trust."

I don't respond to Vincent as the cars begin to pull around front of the house where we stand. Royal, Bishop and the twins round the side of the house, all of them dressed head to toe in black much like Knight and Vincent, I peek at Chanel and see she is even decked out in black. I'm so glad I have the forethought to dress in black, my greedy eyes drinking in the sight of my man. Fuck me, is it wrong that I want him to be covered in ink like his dad?

"I hope you're checking my nephew out and not my brother." I snap my head to the side to see Carlina standing beside Chanel with a grin on her face.

"Gucci, what the fuck are you doing?" Carlina glares up at her husband.

"Did you seriously think I was going to stay in bed while my daughter goes off to fight?" She scoffs and shakes her head as she brushes past us to hop into one of the waiting SUVs. Vincent turns his gaze to his daughter.

"You watch her six at all times, she stays stationed by your side. Any heat or if you're compromised you get the fuck out and drag her ass with you, do you understand?"

To my surprise Chanel doesn't fight him or argue about being ordered around. "Yes, sir." The pair head toward the same car that Carlina currently occupies, Knight smirks at me until the front door opens, the smile vanishes from his face.

"Get the fuck back inside now!" He growls at the sight of his wife and Kiara. Koby just ignores him as she passes by patting him on the chest, Kiara tries to do the same but at the sound of her husband and son's voices she freezes.

"Mom!"

"Kiara!" She turns toward them both and smiles, Knight shakes his head and motions for his son's to follow him to the car Koby is in, leaving the four of us standing here awkwardly, "Get your ass back in the fucking house now." I've never heard Bishop be so curt with her before and it kind of reminds me of Royal and how he bosses me around.

"You are out ya fucking mind if you think that I will be left behind while you and my only child go off to battle. Try and stop me and I'll break your fucking dick."

"Mom." Royal whines.

"Close your trap, Royal. I don't want to hear a word out of you either, get your asses in the car now." Both men open their mouths but she cuts them off. "Say one word, I dare you both." Their mouths snap closed in a second, I shake with silent laughter as they both bow their heads and stomp toward the car in the front like a couple of sulking toddlers. Kiara turns to me and winks with a smile on her face. "Never let my son think he has the upper hand, fight him at every turn and whatever you do, don't ever give into his demands."

I stare at her as she walks away with her head held high, the woman is a fucking queen. When I grow up I want to be Kiara Murdoch!

Not wanting to be left behind I chase after her and climb in the back row with Royal while his parents ride in the middle, the driver takes off like his ass on fire, as we hit the interstate I look out the back window to another eight blacked out SUVs join our convoy of six cars, between each car carrying Royal's family members is a car filled with guards. It's a clever tactic, if someone were to try to take them out they would think they are all congregated in the middle but in reality they are spread out. Two of the new cars joining our line cut in front of us. Chanel's car races by with four others following after her, frowning, I look up Royal and ask.

"Why are they racing ahead?" He wraps his arm around my shoulders and draws me into his side where I snuggle into him.

"Uncle Vin and Chanel are the best deadshots from a distance, they can hit a target as far as eighteen football fields away. They are going to be our eyes in the sky so to speak." Holy shit, I never realized how fucking good Chanel is until this moment.

"What about your Aunt Carlina?" Bishop snorts and peers around his seat to look at me.

"My sister is just as good, if you say otherwise she will poison your food and smile wide as she watches you eat it." I reel back, this whole family is fucking deadly.

"Bishop, stop exaggerating. She wouldn't do that." I relax at Kiara's words. "She would just shoot you and make Vin clean up her mess."

Jesus Christ!

I huddle into Royal's side further feeling kind of under-skilled compared to all these powerful people who can shoot, hack, run multi million dollar companies and still manage to have a semi normal life.

"What's that look for?" Royal asks quietly as his parents begin to bicker about Kiara needing to stay in the car, Royal really is so much like his father.

"I guess, I'm just wondering what I could possibly bring to the table, I can shoot and fight well enough but that's about it." He grips my chin and lifts my head, his gaze is hard and unrelenting as he peers down at me.

"What you bring is a skill set none of us have." I roll my eyes, he's just trying to make me feel better. "Roll your eyes again and your ass will pay the price." My eyes snap wide. "You're able to read people and blend in when we can't, I watched you, Rika from the first moment I met you. You watched and heard everything, you used the fact you didn't speak to your advantage and allowed everyone to underestimate you. Baby, you are an asset with a skill that non of my men or my family has, don't doubt yourself again because that shit pisses me the fuck off."

My heart skips a beat, I hear the truth in his words and can't keep the smile off my face. "Maybe I just needed someone to piss me off enough to speak again." His eyes narrow as his father begins to laugh at his expense.

"He seems to have a talent for doing that." Royal lifts his gaze to his father and smirks.

"Did Uncle King receive that shipment from Andreas yet?" Bishop's eye blaze, Kiara groans and smacks her head back against the headrest as I stare between the two men.

"You little fucker, if you rerouted my shipment again I am going to beat your ass!" Bishop growls, Royal just shrugs and beams at his father.

"I would *never*." The mocking tone of Royal's voice has Bishop gritting his teeth and looking at his wife.

"Deal with your fucking kid before I do." Royal shakes with silent laughter.

"You never learn." Just as the words leave his mouth, Kiara swivels in her seat to face her husband with the coldest look I have ever seen on her beautiful face.

"You are to deal with my son, huh?"

Bishop meets her angry look with one of his own. "The asshole continues to fuck with me daily, I've had enough of his pranks."

"What pranks?" I ask.

"Your stupid boyfriend thinks it's funny to freeze my accounts, reroute my shipments, dissolve my companies and donate money to charities that aren't his and make college funds for his cousins at my expense." My mouth drops open, Royal shrugs his father off and relaxes back into his seat.

"It's not my fault you can't take a joke." Royal quips.

"You cost me ten million dollars, you little shit!" Bishop roars, the moment Kiara begins to tear Bishop a new asshole Royal breaks out into uncontrollable laughter, this family is something else and I'm fucking happy I get to be a part of their craziness.

Chapter Thirty

ROYAL

No matter how much dad tried to convince mom to stay behind she refused and said she would follow us the moment we left, Erika agreed without a fuss to stay in the car knowing I would take her punishment out on her pussy. I really need my mom and dad to go home, I can already see some of my mom's bad habits are rubbing off on her. Don't get me wrong, I love that she is fitting in with my family, well except for Chanel but Sin doesn't like anyone who isn't related.

"Far warehouse." Havoc says pointing toward a large building at the far end of the lot from where we are huddled.

"There isn't coverage." Chaos says. I shake my head at both these idiots, I look at my Dad and nod. He pulls his phone from his pocket and dials the number before bringing it to his ear.

"Three minutes, we're coming from the west to take out the stragglers and sharpshooters." He orders then ends the call, I look back to the twins and explain.

"Sin, Aunt Carlina and Uncle Vin are our eyes, trust them to keep your asses alive and we'll be fine." I look down at my watch, two minutes and then we're on the move.

"The twins are with me." I clip out.

"Knight, Koby and your mother are with me. Spread your men out to draw the fire while we take the side and back." I do as my dad says and then hand everyone their ear pieces so we can keep in contact. I can't look at my mom and as I move with the twins to get in position, I know she's worried about me but I can't deal with that shit right now, which is why I didn't even look at Erika as I placed a kiss on her head and left.

"Ten seconds." Chaos whispers, nodding. I check my Heckler & Koch MP5 one last time before giving the signal to move in. Terry and Benny were already there when we arrived, they had the whole place surrounded making sure no one got in or out of this place. As we move as a unit I see Benny and Terry move toward the other side to draw fire so we can come in through the side. My Dad and the others are taking the back entrance to cut off any chance of this slippery fucker escaping, he's going to die today.

Our footsteps are light keeping the noise to a minimum, only a few of his men should be standing guard at this time. Just as we are twenty yards out a shot rings out, dropping to a crouch I peer through the scope on my gun to see a body on the ground to my far left, another shot rings out and another body drops near Terry's crew. I peer through my sight and sure enough, a block or so away I can just make Chanel's form out on the rooftop.

She's one bad bitch!

"Move, move, move." I shout, we all rush toward the warehouse. No point being quiet now, shots continue to ring out and bodies drop like shit, shouts can be heard from inside the warehouse. Uncle Vin and Chanel are taking out all the fuckers we can't see, I slam against the side of the warehouse next to the side door. Chaos and Havoc mimic my stance on the other side of the door, I look at Bronson and nod giving him the okay to kick the door in while we cover him. The second his foot connects with the door, gunfire sounds out all around us. We rush inside, I dive behind a stack of barrels and machine parts. I look around for the twins but in the fray of everything and rushing for cover I've lost sight of them.

"They scattered, no sign of the KP." Comes through the earpiece from Benny. Fuck, I shrink down further when a bullet whizzes past me. I look around and see all my guys firing back, I take a deep breath and close my eyes.

Lock it down, take out your mark and end this.

Snapping my eyes open, I swivel around the side of the barrel, flick my MP5 to semi auto and unload on these fuckers hitting as many as I can before dropping the mag and pulling another one that is strapped to my vest and slamming it in to shoot.

"Move in!" I roar as we push in as a solid unit to close in on the fuckers gaining ground and dropping down behind the numerous cars they have scattered throughout this warehouse, I spot Chaos crouched behind one of the cars checking his gun. "What's wrong?" I shout over the gunfire.

"I'm out, Havoc has the other mags." He calls back, I pull the Glock from my waistband and slide it across the ground to him then push over three mags. Once he's locked and loaded he nods, I look over the hood of the car and smirk at the sight of my dad and uncle leading their team in through the back. I give the old man that, he looks like a fucking beast and right in his element.

"Cover them!" I shout to my men, we all lean over the cars and take out as many cunts as we can to protect my dad, my heart leaps into my throat at the sight of my mom darting out from behind my dad to take out a fucker in my dad's blind spot. It surprises the fuck out of me when dad just nods at her and doesn't say anything. They fight and bicker but at this moment, there is no other that will have his back harder than my mother. I watched my mother break inside at the thought of losing my dad, I never want to see that look in her eyes ever again. I take out as many of those slimy fucks as I can as I creep in closer to my parents, the moment, Chaos, Havoc and me reach our parents we all form a circle with our backs to the each other and fire, it's like everything slows down.

Bullets fly through the air, we return fire and so do my men, I watch some of them fall and feel the loss of each of them. I may not know them all but I want to lead the right way, any soldiers that fall today I will make sure each of their families are taken care of and they will be honored. Dad taps me on the shoulder and motions for me to follow him, we position mom so she is in the middle of us. Only now after breaching the warehouse do we realize that they weren't just hiding out in one, the fuckers cut through the wall and have been using all three of the large buildings back here. As we enter the second I'm on high alert.

"Get down!" Dad roars as he spins and tackles both mom and me to the ground using his body as a shield to protect us from the grenade that was thrown. The bang rocks the foundation of the building and shrapnel from the cars it hits flies through the air, one of the cars explode. My ears ring, dad rolls to the side and looks over my mom and I quickly before rushing out into the fray and firing off round after round, Uncle Knight is right on his brother's ass watching his back. I shot a glance at the twins, both of them are on the ground, my aunt and uncle shielded them like my dad to us. Nodding to the twins we jump to our feet and follow after our dads. The three of us in a triangle formation with me at the front covering each other.

I fucked up, Emilio had more men stashed out here than I

thought, never once did it cross my mind that he would be using all three sheds to house men, I should have seen that coming but I didn't. I dive behind a large metal shelf when someone yells, grenade, the blast blows the large roller door open. More of the men stand out there shooting and fighting hand to hand as we all try to find the KP of this fucking crew.

I do a quick sweep of the room with my eyes and can't spot my dad or the twins anywhere, fuck! I jump to my feet and scurry along the wall of the warehouse watching my own ass as I search for my family, worry churns inside me. I hear the sound of two rifles coming from outside, Chanel and Uncle Vin have moved in closer to the fight. I know the sound of Chanel's gun, I knew there would be no way she would stay out of this when we're all pinned down in here.

"Royal?" I spin around to see my uncle standing a few feet away.

'Where the fuck is my dad?" I demand.

"Taking Kiara and Koby out the back way, he isn't here and there is a bomb rigged to blow in the last warehouse, we have three minutes, move out now!" Fuck.

"Where's the twins?" I'm not leaving without them.

"With Chanel and Vincent, move now!" He grips me by the vest and yanks me out through the roller door, the second we come out four shots ring out, Knight goes down and then gasping for air as I drop to my knees beside my uncle. Emilio Vargas and his men stand next to a Jeep with their assault rifles aimed at us. Emilio smiles at me, I look to Knight to see he's bleeding from his shoulder, the other bullet hit his vest. I look down at myself, both bullets hit me in the chest, if I wasn't wearing my Kevlar vest I'd be dead. Even with the vest on I find it hard to breath, the force of the shots knocked the wind out of me. I hear gunfire continue to ring out on the other side of the warehouse where we entered.

Clever fucker, he was never inside the warehouse he waited

out here for us to find the bomb and run this way to escape. His men rush forward to grab me and Knight, I fight each of the fuckers that try to grab me but the second one of them puts a gun to my uncles head, I stop and let the bastards drag me away.

Chapter Thirty-One

ERIKA

I startle when the car door is yanked open and Bishop pokes his head inside frowning when he notices it's only me inside the vehicle. "Where the fuck is Royal and Knight?"

Worry churns in my gut as I stare at him. "They're not here."

"Fuck." He shouts as he slams the door closed, I push the door open and just out the other side and rush around to find Bishop, Kiara, Koby and a at least a dozen of Royal's men, at the sound of foot falls I spin around to see, Chanel, Carlina, Vincent and the twins coming toward us but still no sign of Royal and Knight.

"Where is he?" I shout when Chanel stops a foot in front of me, she darts her gaze over my head to Bishop.

"Where the hell is Royal?" She demands.

"Where the fuck is my dad?" Havoc snaps.

"I don't know, wait here—." Before Bishop can finish, an explosion sounds out, the force of it throws me back into the car knocking the wind out of me and the others get thrown off their feet. Even breathless and aching from the impact all I can think about is getting to Royal and making sure he's okay. I push to my feet, ignoring the pain thrumming through me and the shouts for me to stop and come back as I run as fast as my feet will allow to get to him. Gun shots ring out in the distance but the fear of being shot doesn't compare to the fear of losing the man I love, I can feel the heat of the fire as I get close to the warehouse. I stifle the scream that wants to tear out of me when a man cries out in pain running from the wreck that was once a warehouse building on fire.

I dart my gaze at the bodies that lay slayed on the ground, I race through the bodies and ignore the men around crying out in pain as I hunt for my man. I race around the back of the warehouse spotting a break in the chain link fence not hesitating for a moment. I rush through the man-made cut and run through the thick grass. I hear people chasing me, I don't risk looking back to see if they are on my side or the Vargas cartel, I rush down a steep incline only to slam to a stop. Someone crashes into my back and knocks me off my feet, I fall to my knees with tears burning the backs of my eyes at the sight of my uncle with Royal in front of him and a gun to his head. Knight is in the position as his nephew with a gun trained on his head. Emilio may not have the number of men on his side that we do but right now he has the upper hand and he knows it.

"You pull that trigger, I'll not only murder you but I'll eradicate your entire fucking bloodline and make sure they each suffer, no woman or child will be safe, do you hear me? I'll kill each and everyone you hold fucking dear if you don't let my husband go." Koby's threat hangs heavy in the air, Knight even though he is bleeding from his shoulder and held at gunpoint puckers his lips and blows his wife a kiss. Royal's gaze collides with mine and the air rushes from my lungs, his brow is split and blood slowly leaks down the side of his face. My mouth dries as bile rises in my throat.

Memories of the night my parents were murdered surface and play on a reel inside my head, the sight of someone else I love being held at gunpoint has triggered these horrid memories. I was too weak and young to fight back then but now... I won't go down without a fight, I won't allow this fucking cartel to take someone else I love from me, I can't.

"Your problem is with me, release my son and take me in his place." Bishop tries to reason, Royal's gaze snaps to his father.

"No." That word holds so much strength and power, when will that silly boy learn that his father will never bow to him.

"Shut the fuck up." Emilio growls, he turns to me and smiles but it's cruel, I know that look it means I will be punished. "Monica, get up and come to me."

"Get fucked, you touch her and I'll fucking murder you!" Royal roars, Emilio kicks the back of his knees and he drops in front of him. The bastard pistol whips him over the back of the head but is smart enough to crouch down behind him so none of the Murdoch's have a clear shot at him.

"Don't touch my son!" Kiara screams, the men behind Emilio turn their guns on her, Bishop darts in front of his wife, Havoc, Chaos, Koby, Vincent and Carlina all have their guns aimed at the men. I frown when I notice Chanel is nowhere in sight, where the fuck is she?

"You don't hold the cards here. You ruined my family and killed my brother." At the mention of my father from Emilio's mouth I snap. I'm on my feet and rushing to the center of this little standoff, shouts ring out but I ignore them. Royal's angry glare doesn't deter me, if Emilio wanted me dead he would have done it by now.

"You killed him!" I scream as tears leak from my eyes.

"They lied to you, Monica. They know who you are, you're not safe with them, they are using you to get to me." Emilio pleads.

"I never lied to you, Sirena." Royal says as he looks me in the eyes, I know he isn't using me. If he was I would have been held at gunpoint and used at gunpoint to lure Emilio out of the warehouse.

Emilio's laughter has me turning back to him. "You stupid girl, you went and fell in love with the son of the man that raped your mother and killed your father." I fight back the mental images that flash through my mind of the masked men taking turns to rape my mother as my father and I were forced to watch.

I shake my head, denying his words. "Bishop never hurt my mom, you lied to me!" I scream. "Why the fuck did you lie to me? That night changed my whole life, I fucking changed everything about myself because of that night." I cry out. "I stopped talking because..." I cut myself off and clamp my mouth closed.

"Because the sight of those Murdoch scum hurting your mother scared you, I know." Shaking my head I deny what Emilio is trying to get me to believe.

"No. I stopped talking because what was the fucking point? No matter how much I begged, pleaded and screamed for them to stop hurting my parents they didn't, words didn't change the outcome so why bother with them?" I whisper the last part feeling utterly beaten. I flick my gaze to Royal and try to muster a smile for his benefit. "You woke me up. You brought me back, pulled me from the dark hole I was living in and for that I will always be grateful and love you–."

"Shut the fuck up, Rika." He growls but I ignore him and the distraught look on his face.

"You will be safe, I'll make sure of it." He tries to argue back but I look to my uncle and make a deal with the devil that will cost me not only my heart but my life. "Let them go and I swear to you I will do whatever you ask of me, I'll marry whoever you need me to and produce an heir that will carry the Vargas name."

"Like fuck you will, I'll hunt you down and kill any son of a cunt that touches you, do you fucking hear me, Erika? I'll kill them all!" Royal screams so fucking loud I stumble back a step.

"You may change your mind about going with him when you find out he's the one who ordered the hit on your parents." I spin around to face Havoc with wide eyes.

"You fucking maggot! How dare you–." I cut Emilio off.

"What?" Havoc steps forward and ignores the sound of guns cocking all around him as he comes to stand in front of me.

"Emilio Vargas ordered the hit on Estefan and Maria Vargas—."

"Shut your dirty fucking mouth!" Emilio roars.

"You don't speak to my son!" Knight roars, then a pained grunt comes from him, Koby steps forward but Chaos holds his mother back.

"Tell me!" I shout.

Havoc nods and continues. "Maria was promised to one brother but fell in love with the other." I reel back a step. "Maria was meant to marry your uncle but fell in love with your father." I turn sideways and look at my uncle, I see it in the way his face reddens and his jaw locks, Havoc is telling the truth. "Your father fled Columbia to get away from his tyrant brother and to keep you safe, he wanted you away from Emilio because—."

"Stop!" I order as I stare at the man who took me in after I was made an orphan, I swipe away the last remnants of my tears. I become numb the longer I stare at him, I see things I didn't notice before, he and I have the same cupid's bow, the same shaped eyes, oh my God, no this can't be.

I approach Emilio, he drags Royal to his feet and keeps him in front of himself as a shield. When I get to close he cocks his gun forcing me to stop just out of reach of my man.

"Did you order the murders of my mother and your brother?" I ask in a deadly calm tone. Emilio and I stand in a stare off, he won't be able to get a read on my thoughts, everything is locked down inside me. "Fucking answer me!" I scream.

"Estefan was weak, Maria needed a real man but she chose wrong. She was mine and he took her from me." Everything happens in the blink of an eye, a shot rings out and then the guard holding Knight at gunpoint drops, another shot whizzes past me, Royal cries out and then Emilio is on the ground. Royal rushes me and tackles me to the ground shielding me from the spray of bullets that fly over us. His eyes stay locked on mine the entire time, so many emotions swirl in his eyes but I'm too lost in my downward spiral to try to decipher what he's feeling.

"The truth changes nothing, you are who you are because of who raised you. Blood means nothing, your father loved you and gave his life for yours, hold onto that, Rika." Royal is yanked off me by Bishop, Chaos helps me to my feet before he follows his mother and brother over to their father, I leave Royal to be checked over by his parents as I stumble toward Emilio. He lays on his back staring up at the sky, at the sound of my approach he tilts his head to the side, a trickle of blood begins to form at the corner of his mouth. He reaches blindly for his gun as I crouch down beside him, before he can grab it I snatch it and push it against his head as he stares up at me with wide eyes.

"He fled Columbia to get away from you to keep me and my mother safe, didn't he?"

His eyes harden, I used to fear that look in his eyes knowing it would mean I would be punished. He loved to use his belt on the backs of my legs, he never hurt me or left a mark where others could see. He wanted to be known as the doting uncle that took in his orphan niece even though his brother dishonored the Vargas name by running.

"He was weak." He rasps out then begins to cough. "You're strong because you are mine."

Anger burns inside me. "My father wasn't weak, he was strong enough to turn his back on his family so he could protect the ones he loved most. She never wanted you, did she?" I grit out.

"She was mine until he stole her, so I stole her innocence and her womb." Disgust rolls through me, he raped my mother and got her pregnant.

"Even after you raped her, she still loved him. She didn't hate me even though I was a product of the rape committed, they both loved me. You took them from me and for that you will die like a dog but, before I send your disgusting ass to hell there is something you should know. I may hate you with every molecule inside my body and detest the name I share with a piece of shit like you, I am going to claim what you never intended to give me." It takes him a second to catch onto what I'm saying the moment he does anger and hatred fills his gaze. "You only wanted me back so no one could use me to claim what you built. I stupidly thought it was because you cared."

I press the barrel of the gun harder into his forehead as I feel Royal come up behind me. "You kept me being your daughter a secret so no one would ever use me to take over, hear me now when I tell you this. I will take the cartel from you."

"You are a woman..." He coughs and blood splatters my shoes. "My people won't follow a bitch."

I smile as I cock the trigger. "I won't be running it alone." His eyes blaze. "I'll marry him, I'll take Columbia and lead the cartel under a new name, my people will thrive under the new leadership of the Memento Mori." I pull the trigger, brain matter and blood sprays my face, chest and arms but I don't care, I pull the trigger again and again even when the magazine is empty I keep clicking the trigger. Royal crouches down behind me, he hisses as he reaches out and pulls the gun from my hold.

"We need to leave, Rika, this place will be crawling with cops soon. I only bought an hour's window." I say nothing as I allow him to help me to my feet and lead me away from my... from Emilio.

Chapter Thirty-Two

ROYAL

The whole ride back to the house Erika hasn't uttered a single word, she spent the time gazing out the window. I'm starting to worry that she'll retreat inside herself again and stop speaking, I wouldn't blame her after what she just learned. He used her, manipulated her for years. She spent her life hating my family for the death of her parents, the harsh reality of that is her own family was the one to kill her parents. The moment we get back to my house, I know everyone wants to deal with Chance and be rid of him once and for all but my focus is on my girl. I watch her walk inside with her shoulders hunched and her head down, I go to follow her but Chanel steps in front of me.

"She was going to take a bullet for you, wasn't she?" It's posed a question but she doesn't need me to answer, she already knows the answer.

"You saved my ass." I reply instead, Sin was the one who took the kill shot and took out the guard holding uncle Knight.

She shrugs. "I told you, I'll always have your back and never let you die, I kept my word." I wrap my good arm around her and pull her to me holding her close.

"Thank you, Sin." She pulls back and nods but I can see something else is on her mind. "Just say it."

"Fine. Your girlfriend may be... not as bad as I thought."

"How'd that taste coming out your mouth?" I tease.

The bitch punches me in my shoulder where my fucking dad shot me, I groan as she walks away smirking.

"We doing this now?" I look to the side to see my dad and the others standing there.

"Can I at least clean the bullet wound you gave me?" Dad rolls his lips over his teeth to keep from smiling.

"It's a flesh wound," he defends.

I balk at the bastard. "The fucking bullet went through my shoulder to hit that cunt!" The bastard laughs!

"You shouldn't have fucked with my shit." This mother fucker shot me on purpose! I knew it, He could have shot the fucker over my shoulder but nooooo, he had to teach me a lesson and shot me! I flick my gaze to my mom who stands there frowning looking between us.

"Mommy," I whine, Dad scoffs and throws his hands in the air as mom looks to me. "Dad shot me on purpose!" The bastard sputters and feigns hurt as he places his hand over his heart and looks to my mom with a fake look of shock.

"Baby, I would never shoot our baby boy." Now I scoff at the bastard, Mom turns a bright shade of red.

"Did you shoot my son on purpose?" At the angry tone of her voice Dad takes a step back.

"Baby, I didn't have a clear shot like I told you." He pleads.

"Yes, you did." Uncle Vin pipes up and says, Dad scowls at him. I walk away and leave him to face the wrath of my mother on his own, serves him right. I make my way upstairs to my bedroom, as I enter I hear the shower running. I pause in the doorway and stare at her through the glass screen, her back's to me and she stands directly under the spray letting the water cascade over her so it wash the sins of the day away. I kick my shoes off and without thinking, step into the shower with her fully clothed, she spins around in fright.

She stares up at me with a deer caught in the headlights look, I hate the pain filled look in her eyes. It has a murderous rage consuming me wanting to kill the cunt that made her hurt. I step into her relishing in the way her breath hitches and her eyes turn glassy, she needs to get out of her own head and the only way I know how to do that is by making her scream my name.

"Tell me to stop and I will," I say as I lean down and ghost my lips over hers, she doesn't respond with words. She presses her lips to mine, I wrap my uninjured arm around her waist and anchor her to me. I feel her hard nipples through my shirt, I fucking love how responsive she is to my touch. She pops the button on my pants and pushes them down my legs, freeing my cock without breaking the kiss. The instant her hand wraps around my length I groan into her mouth.

"Fuck me while his blood still lingers on my skin." She growls when she breaks the kiss and turns, pressing her chest flat against the glass screen and widening her legs. The sight of her ready and waiting for me has my cock twitching but it's the fact she spoke that has me pressing against her.

"You wet for me?"

She looks over her shoulder at me. "I'm dripping for you." Growling my approval I bend at the knees and line my cock up with her entrance, I want to drag this out but we both need this too much to tease. I slam inside her tight wet hole in one swift thrust, she screams out in pleasure. Gripping the back of her neck I press her harder against the glass as I bend back to get better leverage and slam inside her delicious little cunt over and over again until we're both crying out our release and shaking from the sheer magnitude of how fucking incredible we feel when we're joined together.

I wait till her breathing is under control before I pull out and step back, she spins around with a dark look in her eyes. I stand motionless as she cups her pussy, pushes a single finger inside it then brings her cum covered digit to her mouth and sucks it clean. My jaw slackens, she is fucking incredible and clearly has a blood kink. If I had more time and wasn't in fucking pain from the bullet wound I would cram my face in her pussy and suck my cum out just so I could spit it in her mouth and watch her swallow me.

Erika helps me undress and clean off as much of the blood as she can, I hiss the moment the spray hits my wound but she doesn't stop cleaning me. The dirty little minx takes her time cleaning my dick, the moment my cock is rock hard in her hand she releases me and steps out of the shower laughing under her breath. She's going to fucking pay for that stunt later. She helps me into a pair of sweats after she changes into a one piece jumpsuit looking thing that has an open back and shows she isn't wearing a fucking bra! I want to stomp my foot and demand she fucking change and cover up her perky tits but an idea occurs to me.

"When this is all over, you're getting my name tattooed." I growl possessively, she stares up at me unblinking for a minute as my words sink in. I expect her to rage and tell me I'm out of my mind but as per usual she shocks the fuck out of me when she grips my hand and leads me out of the room carry my shirt in her hand.

"I'm not getting your name but I'll get your calling card." I stare at the back of her head in wonder with a goofy grin on my face.

Marco had a doctor come to the house and patch me and Knight up, he tended to a couple of the others but I refused to have the rest of the men treated here and told Marco to take the doctor to them at my grandpa's house. I've allowed everyone to think that's where I live so I can keep this house off the books and private.

Dad has been a broody son of a bitch because mom won't speak to him, I don't even feel bad for the bastard, he shouldn't have shot me! Knight, the twins, Sin, Vin, dad and I all agreed that we would deal with Chance tonight. The news has been going crazy with the disappearance of the governor, we'll remove his teeth and fingers so if his body is discovered no one will be able to identify him. Erika is pissed I won't allow her to join us, but she's dealt with enough and needs to go over the cover story Sin and Chaos drafted for her, the fed's are going to come sniffing around and question her since she is still technically his fiance.

The seven of us stand in front of Chance who is chained to the wall of the basement, he's slumped in his chains and looks like a skinned pig. I flick my gaze to Chaos and raise a brow, the asshole just shrugs.

"The cunt deserved to be skinned, plus Havoc said I couldn't do it without killing him so I had to prove a point!" He defends.

"The fact I'm proud of you is so wrong." We all laugh at Knight's declaration, the sound of our laughter rouses Chance. Both his eyes are swollen and can open to tiny slits, when he registers who is here he slicks back against the wall and tries to cower but can't.

"You really thought you could take Miami from me?" I ask as I step closer to him, the pussy begins to tremble and his bottom wobbles, fucking pathetic. "You even thought you could try take my girl, newsflash cunt, she's mine."

"Y-yours." He stutters, he's a pathetic waste of space.

Without guards he is nothing but a little boy trying to play dress up. I step back when my dad and uncle's move forward, Sin, me and the twins stand off to the side and watch our fathers.

"You nearly succeeded in taking us out. You had the opportunity to end each of our lives but your need to gloat and show the world you were the one who could take out the Murdoch Mafia is the reason you failed. You threatened my brothers, our children and then you came for my fucking wife!" My dad roars, Chance whimpers and shakes his head. Dad lashes out and punches him repeatedly in the face until Uncle Vin pulls him back, dad breaks free of his hold. I see it now, I never understood why so many feared just my father's name but now I get it. He's a force, a ghost if you will. He looks like a dark spirit, his eyes look black and are void of all emotion, when he yanks his shirt over his head and displays all his tattoos it only adds to the fearsome look.

"Bullet?" Uncle Vin asks.

"Nah, I'm doing this with my bare hands. He came after my family for that, he'll die slowly." The coldness in my father's tone has pride swelling inside me, Bishop Murdoch truly is a bad mother fucker.

"You four." We turn to Uncle Knight. "You've done enough, we got this."

"Dad, we caught him though–."

Knight cuts his son off. "Now Chaos, you four can't be near this. Once he is dealt with we will be on the first plane home so they don't try and pin this shit on you all." He isn't wrong, once everyone learns about who we are they are going to try to pin this on us in the hopes of our fathers trading themselves for us which is why I lead the other three out of the basement so we can all get our story straight. The four of us walk silently around the back of the house at the sound of voice we all pause and stick the shadows to keep hidden,

Amelia, mom, aunt Koby and Erika all sit around the fire pit on the lawn with blankets wrapped around themselves.

"I didn't know if you would be able to convince me that you were a good fit for my son." The twins snicker beside me at my mom's comment, so I shoot them a glare.

"I knew from the moment she told Royal to go fuck himself that she was a perfect fit for my cousin." I chuckle lightly at Amelia's snarky ass retort.

"You raised an amazing man, Kiara." Pride swells inside me, I'm so fucking proud of her for not retreating inside herself after everything she went through today. "Royal, is a stubborn fool don't get me wrong." Annoyance radiates throughout me when everyone begins to laugh, I take a step froward ready to end this bullshit but Sin places a hand on my chest and holds me in place. "But that is one of the qualities I love about him, he fights for what he thinks is right and will never back down."

"Seems to me, you are the same way after what I saw today." Erika shrugs shyly at Aunt Koby's remark.

"What happened today?" Ameila asks.

"Erika was going to take a bullet for Royal, in this family that type of loyalty goes a long fucking way. I misjudged you, Erika. I'm sorry for what I did to you, as a mother my only focus was getting my son back."

"You don't need to apologize, Koby, I get it." Erika says.

"Look before we get all mushy and shit I just want to say, I think you are way too good for my cousin because he is an asshole and you could do so much better–." That's it, I stalk out of the shadows and glare at Amelia the moment her gaze connects with mine, the little shit just winks, she knew we were in the bushes the whole time. I press up against Erika's back, wrap my good arm around her waist and love how she melts into me. "As you can see he has stalker tendencies." Erika just laughs and shakes her head, she turns her head to the side and looks up at me with a smile.

"What's that look for?" I ask.

"Nothing, I just... Today was really hard and I honestly didn't know how to cope until you found me earlier." She whispers. Ignoring the pain in my arm I reach up and cup her cheek tenderly in my hand.

"I'll always find you baby, no matter where you hide or how fast you run I'll always be there to catch you." Her pupils dilate and her mouth forms a perfect O. "Close your mouth or I'll fill it." I growl.

"Please." Fuck, gripping her hand I drag her back toward the house with the others laughter following after us. I never thought I would ever blow off a night with my cousins for some girl but Erika isn't just some girl. She is the beginning to my story, my queen, my partner but most of all she is the light in my darkest hour and the keeper of my soul.

Chapter Thirty-Three

ERIKA

Two weeks later...

The feds have been sniffing around but no one has come to question me yet, I know it's only a matter of time though. Bishop, Vincent and Knight disposed of Chance's body and refused to tell Royal and the others where they dumped him. Royal and Chanel have been trying to regain order here in Miami, Chance had been involved in some shady shit. The moment Royal found out he was trying to get in with the Albanians and Sicilians to bring back sex trafficking he shut that shit down and now it's caused a divide between them and the Memento Mori. I know that shutting down the skin trade again is going to cause mass issues and no doubt spark a war, Bishop has agreed to back Royal and the others if that should happen.

Royal hasn't officially claimed publicly that he is the new don, with the heat surrounding Chance's death it's not ideal for him to own that shit. Many know about him but he's also refused to confirm it because the fact he can still hide in the shadows is an advantage for the Memento Mori. He's thinking smart and taking his time to deal with things instead of rushing and risking exposing himself, Bishop is sending Luka out here to help Royal but he isn't happy about that. He thinks Luka is coming to babysit him but I know that isn't the case, since Chaos wants to return to school and hopes to be drafted into the NFL he needs the extra help.

A week ago I spoke to Braga, Emilio's right hand man—well, he is now my right hand man and hearing the difficulties he is facing trying to keep the Vargas cartel alive sparked something inside me. I refused to allow my parents' deaths to be for nothing so, that night I told Royal I would be taking over the Vargas cartel and become Queen of the south. He said nothing for a good ten minutes and I began to worry until he said, '*marry me and it will all be yours, Sirena.*'

Looking down at the large black diamond engagement ring shaped like a club has a smile pulling the corners of my mouth, Royal can't leave Miami at the moment so I am flying back to Columbia tomorrow with Havoc to meet Braga and a few others, this union between Royal and me will bring peace between our countries and also provide a better distribution chain for the drugs and weapons.

I know it all seems so crazy that I'm going to marry Royal but in this life, there is no time like the present because tomorrow isn't promised. I love him and I know he loves me, he may not say it often but he shows me daily with his body how much he needs me. The man has me walking bow legged daily and honestly, I wouldn't have it any other way.

"Ready to see it?" I tear my gaze from my ring and look up at my sexy as fuck fiancée and groan internally. Him standing there shirtless with fresh ink on his skin, dear lord have mercy on my pussy. Royal was a fucking snack without tattoos but with them, the man is sexier than sin. My greedy eyes drink in the ink that covers his chest and the side of his neck, my mouth falls open to form a perfect O when I see the name inked across his chest. I slowly climb to my feet and cross the room to stand in front of him, tears burn the backs of my eyes. "Say something." He demands.

Lifting my gaze to his and smile, I've never felt so wanted or loved since my parents were murdered but with Royal, I not only feel it, I can see it in his eyes every time he looks at me. This man has been my rock, killing Emilio was hard and that day a part of me died with him. Not a part like you think, it was a part of me that clung to the past and thirsted for vengeance to avenge the deaths of my parents. I know Royal was scared I would retreat inside myself again but unlike last time where I had nobody to bring me back, I had him and there was no way I was going to risk losing the love of my life.

"That's my name." I whisper. Right there in the middle of his chest in the most stunning script writing is the name *Sirena*. He turns his head to the side to show me the tattoo on his neck, the one that matches the one on my ribs.

It's his calling card, the King of Clubs. The words *Memento Mori* are scripted beneath the image. The King has a skull face and wrapped in red robes, the king holds a dagger. Smoke rises up from the back of the King and the card looks like it's almost charred. There is smoke in the background but you can clearly see a pair of eyes and a mouth, it's a skull face made out of smoke. Havoc, Chaos and Sin are all getting their calling cards tattooed right now. Royal was pissed when I told him I wouldn't get his name tattooed but the moment he saw his card inked into my skin his eyes blazed. In his own way this is him stamping his ownership over me and I'm not even mad about it.

He reaches out and glides the tips of his fingertips over the ink on my ribs and growls his approval. He knows that the sugar skull on my back represents the celebration of my parents' lives and the two pit vipers on either side of my hips was my way of representing them and my vow for vengeance. Now, he gets to be represented on my body as well and this crazy overbearing man loves it.

"My card has never looked so fucking good baby."

Pride swells inside me. "Why did you get my name?" I ask hesitantly.

He reaches out and grips the back of my neck pulling me forward until our foreheads touch. "Because the artery that beats underneath this ink belongs to you so it seemed only right that I stamp the owner's name over it." I swoon, right here in the middle of the tattoo parlor. I seal my lips to his showing him without words that I am his as much as he is mine, Royal Murdoch is a force that can not be tamed but somehow, I managed to capture the beast.

"Stop that!" We both break a part and laugh at the disgusted look on Havoc's face, he and I have grown really close and I love that I have a friend in him. Chanel isn't as bitchy and she has warmed up to the idea of me sticking around. Chaos just goes with the flow and doesn't kick up a fuss, I know he doesn't like this life but lives it to stay loyal to the ones he loves most.

Havoc turns his head to the side to show me his tattoo on his neck in the same place Royal got his. "Wait, doesn't the Jack of Spades belong to Chaos?" I ask.

Havoc smirks and nods. "He got the Ace of Diamonds for me, so I got his." He says with a shrug, I close the space between us and wrap him in a hug, he sighs and returns my embrace ignoring Royal's growls from behind us.

"He is going to miss you just as much as you will miss him." I whisper low enough for only him to hear as I pull back. He nods solemnly, Chaos is going back to UNLV without Havoc and the thought of being away from his twin is twisting Havoc up inside. Going pro was Chaos's dream not his so he decided to remain here with us while his brother goes and chases his goal.

"I know. Just... promise you'll be there to pull me back from the brink if I need it." He murmurs, gripping his hands in mine. I give them a squeeze and nod.

"You have my word, I'll do whatever you need me to do." Our moment is shattered when Sin and Chaos announce they are finished, I pull away from my friend to see Chaos has his tattoo in the same place as Royal and Havoc, I look at Chanel and cock my head to the side when I don't see ink on her neck. She rolls her eyes and turns to the side to show me her tattoo, right there on her ribs in the same place I got my tattoo for Royal is the Queen of Hearts.

"Oh my God." I breathe out, Royal chuckles and wraps an arm around my waist drawing me back against his chest.

"I don't want to hear a fucking word about this, we're not sisters and going to have sleepovers and braid each other's hair. I liked the spot, that's it, nothing more." She grits out as she storms out of the shop in her sports bra. I bite my lip to keep from laughing, we so just got matching tattoos.

"I think the heartless bitch may actually have a caring bone in her body." Chaos says, we all laugh as we follow after Sin, she may not have said the words but her getting that tattoo in the same place as mine tells me she does care about me in her own weird, cold, toxic way.

I barely managed to get an hour's sleep last night thanks to Royals insatiable hunger for me. I know he's worried and scared that something will happen to me but much like him, no one back home knows who I am. Havoc and at least thirty of Royal's best men are coming with me, I'll be in Columbia for a max of twelve hours. He refused to allow me to spend the night. I could either agree to his timeframe or he refused to allow me to go and said he wasn't above chaining me to his bed and fucking me into submission, I'll admit I wanted to defy him just so he could keep true to his word but I thought better of it.

"Why don't you just wait a couple weeks and then I'll come with you?" He whines, I take a deep breath and pray for patience as I turn and face my man. Fuck he looks good in black jeans, Chucks and a white tee, the new ink just adds to his sex appeal. I cross into the living room where he stands with his hands stuffed in his pockets and a sad look on his face, I wrap my arms around his waist and peer up at him.

"Because I need to do this now, you have your family business and I have mine."

"When we get married you're still not going to hand over control of the cartel are you?" He quirks his brow, I bite my bottom lip and shake my head fighting back the smile that wants to break free.

"I want to fuck the defiance out of you." I clench my thighs together as memories of what he did to me last night flash through my mind. "But the truth is, it gets me fucking hard." I throw my head back and groan, he dips down and nips at the soft flesh between my neck and shoulder drawing a moan from me.

"Can you two not fuck right there?" I spin around and spot Chaos and Chanel standing in the entryway with bored looks on their faces.

"Jealous?" Royal teases.

"Yes!" Chaos shouts.

"Eww." Chanel snaps and shudders.

"Yo, incoming!" The four of us turn toward the front door where a panicked looking Havoc stands. Royal shoves me behind him while Chaos rushes to his brother, Chanel has her gun drawn.

"What is it?" Chaos asks.

"Feds are at the gate." Royal tenses in front of me.

"Fuck." Chanel clips out, I flick my gaze to her and frown at the pale look on her face. We all knew the feds would come looking for me, it was a matter of time so why the hell is she so shocked about this?

"Let them in." Royal snaps.

"No can do, you and Chaos need to disappear first." Havoc rushes to say.

"Why?" I ask.

"He was on Chance's payroll as a guard, remember? Chaos also pretended to be him, he was on surveillance so they need to leave." Havoc bites out.

"You're my fucking twin dick, so you need to come with us!" Chaos shouts, Havoc snorts out a laugh and nods. Royal spins around to face me and cups my face between his hands, his eyes search mine trying to find a hint of fear but he won't find it.

"You remember everything we discussed?" He whispers, I nod and reach up and grip his hands.

"I remember, you can hole up in your office and watch us on the cameras from there." I try to placate him knowing he hates that he is leaving me to deal with this on my own.

"Chanel will be with you the whole time."

"What?" She screeches, Royal pins her with a look of warning daring her to argue further but she clamps her mouth closed.

"You got this." I take a deep breath and nod as he presses his lips to mine before releasing me and ordering the twins to follow him out of the room.

It's been an hour, I'm late for my flight and that pisses me off. I have meetings to attend and the fact detectives, Rhodes and Muller don't seem to give a shit is pissing me off. Chanel sits beside me with a blank look on her face, she was wound tight until the agents stepped inside the house, the sight of them seemed to put her at ease which I found weird as fuck.

"Ms Martinez, your fiancee is missing and you don't seem like you want to help us locate him?" Rhodes says in a tone that tells me he knows I'm lying but he can't prove shit.

"Like I already told you both numerous times, I left Chance a week before he disappeared. That man was vile and beat me."

"You never filed a police report." Muller interjects.

I scoff. "Who would believe a nobody like me that the beloved governor was abusing me? Come on detectives, you both are smarter than this." They bristle at my underhanded insult. "Now, if there is nothing else I have a meeting I must get to." I say as I stand, Chanel follows my lead and does the same. The detectives share a look before climbing to their feet and shaking each of our hands and handing me a business card.

"We'll be in touch." Rhodes clips out as they leave, as soon as the door clicks shut I drop back into my seat and take a breath needing a second to decompress after dealing with them. Royal and the twins rush into the room, he gathers me in his arms and crushes me against his chest as I cling to him.

"You did good, Sirena." He says as he places a kiss to the top of my head.

"That was fucking tense." Havoc notes.

"They were fishing, they have nothing and are trying to get her to crack so they can get a lead off her." Chanel announces.

"They'll be back." I say dejectedly.

"Yeah they will, if we're going to Columbia, we need to go now." I nod knowing Havoc is right, it won't be long before they banned me from leaving the state. Suddenly the excitement of returning home is gone and now all I want to do is crawl into bed and get lost in Royal.

"You got this baby." He says as he places a kiss to my lips, I love how he has so much faith in me. "They can't prove shit, we just need to stick to our story and then we'll be fine." I wish I could say I believed him but there is this pit in my stomach that tells me our troubles are just beginning.

Chapter Thirty-Four

ROYAL

Two weeks later...

Shit is tense as fuck here.

The Albanians have been trying to push in their shit, those dumb fucks have no idea that we control the entry points to all the ports, I blew up one of their ships last week. 400 kilos of coke gone, I knew they would be game and try their luck to get one over on me but those dumb fucks have no idea who the fuck they are dealing with.

The feds have been lurking around and watching Erika's every move which has made me coming and going from the house harder, I've managed to slip back into the role of her bodyguard which has kept me off their radar but something isn't right with them either. I can't explain it but it's like they know something we don't. It's got me on edge and I don't like being in the fucking dark.

"Are you ready for tonight?" I look from my computer to see Havoc standing in the doorway, I groan at the sight of

London beside him. Who the fuck is London you ask? She is the nine year old demon spawn my fiancée brought back from Columbia two weeks ago! Why did she bring her back, you ask? Because the fucking devil told Erika she was hungry and her parents were dead so she plucked the little shit out of the slums and brought her home!

"He's going to die." The devil sing songs while I grit my teeth and refrain from losing my shit at a nine year old kid.

"Bellezza, what have I told you about taunting, Royal?" The little rat bats her lashes up at Havoc and pouts.

"I didn't mean to, maybe..." her bottom lip begins to tremble, I clench the edge of my desk in a vice like grip. "Maybe if he wasn't so mean to me I wouldn't do it." My eyes shoot wide and my mouth drops open, Havoc swings his angry stare to me.

"I haven't fucking done anything to Satan's Spawn!" I defend as I shove to my feet, the little shit whimpers and hides behind Havoc, the moment he turns his gaze back to me she winks and smiles. I'm going to hell, I'm going to kill a nine year old girl and get a first class ticket there.

"She is petrified of you." Havoc reprimands.

"Erika!" I roar, I'm so tired of her and Havoc's shit and how they always accuse me of targeting the little witch. She fucking slashed my tires, poured coffee all over my laptop, faked being drunk and told Erika I gave her shots so she would sleep and the fucking list goes on. Yes, I was pissed when she arrived here but I never fucking did anything to the little demon, to make matters worse the little rat has even bonded with Chanel and that is dangerous for me! Sin can kill you with a pencil so the fact she is teaching this little monster everything she knows scares the fuck out of me!

"What's up?" Erika asks as she squeezes past Havoc and London to come in, London attaches herself to my girl, Erika looks down at London and frowns. "What's wrong, Bellezza?"

"Would everyone stop calling her beauty! She is a fucking demon, I tell ya!" I shout, London gasps and turns on the water works, Havoc and Erika both shoot me a scathing look before turning around and kneeling down in front of London, Erika cuddles her and the fucking witch smiles at me over my girls shoulder.

I've met my match!

This is my karma for fucking with my dad for years, this little demon that didn't even come from my fucking balls is going to play me and my girl just like I do to my parents.

"Take the demon and get out, I'll meet you in two hours." I snap as I drop back into my chair.

"He won't make me drink that alcohol again will he?" I throw my head back and groan, Erika still doesn't believe me that I didn't get the shit head drunk.

"No, Bellezza. If he ever does that again I'll shoot him myself." Havoc growls.

"Get the fuck out!" I yell, Havoc leads the demon out and Erika shoots me a warning look, I throw my hands in the air. "What?"

She places her hands on her hips and gives me her best *watch your tone look*. "She is just a child–."

"I didn't ask for her! If I wanted a cum stain of my own I'd get you off birth control but I don't, she is evil baby, fucking evil and she is a master manipulator–."

She scoffs and rolls her eyes. "She is an innocent little girl–."

"She fucking slashed my tires, fucked my Macbook, flooded the bathroom and tried to electrocute me when I walked in there."

"You're being dramatic."

"Am not!"

"Royal, you are a grown ass man and she is a child–."

"I've seen the fucking *Orphan*, she is a grown ass woman

masking herself as an innocent child. Baby, call a priest and get her baptized and I swear she will burn in front of your eyes, she is a demon."

She shakes her head and laughs earning a glare from me. "Wow."

"What do you mean, *wow*?"

"The big bad, scary Don of the Memento Mori is scared of a little girl." I stare at her open mouthed as she winks at me and sashays out of my office, I swear to fucking Christ if I didn't love Erika as I much as I do I would wring her fucking neck and then throw that she devil off the nearest cliff. But, because I fucking love her I have no choice but to put up with the devil reincarnated. As fate has a sick sense of humor my phone begins to ring and I groan when I see my dad's name flash across the screen.

I stab the green button and bring it to my ear. "Now is not a good time, old man." I grit out.

"I'm not fucking old you asswipe." I pinch the bridge of my nose and try to calm my temper.

"I have shit to do–."

"Is someone still not bonding with their karma?" I grind my teeth so fucking hard I swear they are going to crack.

"Fuck. You." I grit out.

His laughter is loud and obnoxious and just pisses me off further. "I can't wait to meet this Angelic being."

I snap. "She isn't angelic, she's a fucking demon, dad. I can't do this shit, she has to go because she is going to kill me in my sleep. The little animal picked the locked on my bedroom door and I woke up to her standing over me, I reached for my gun but she fucking had it in her hand! Dad, you have to help me, please!" I beg, if he kills her Erika can't be mad at me and I'll play my part of being heart broken and comfort her through the loss but if I kill the devil she will hate me!

"Oh, fuck off, Royal. You never use your manners unless it involves me doing something for you that will wind up with your mother killing me!" I scoff.

"Liar."

"Fuck off, when do you ever say please?"

"Uh, I did that time when you did that thing."

"What thing?" he taunts.

"That thing!" I growl.

"I call bullshit."

Pissed off and over this conversation already I ask in a clipped tone. "What do you want?"

"Just to listen to Karma serve up sweet vengeance for all the shit you put me through and continue to put me through."

"Argh." I shout. "This shit isn't funny, she's ruining my life and she's a fucking cock block!" The bastard just laughs.

"Right, well that is not my problem and even if it was I would refuse to help you because you deserve it. Vincent and Luka land in an hour and will be with you for the raid on the port."

"I don't need a babysitter!"

"Never said you did but your uncle refused to stay back when he found out his daughter was going with you for the raid, Luka is there to help get the feds off your ass. He is the best fucking hacker contrary to what Knight and Koby think, listen to him and do as he says then you'll be free."

"Fine." I clip out. "Anything else?"

"Yeah, did you want to be buried or cremated when that angel kills you." I end the call muttering curses, I'm going to wind up begging the feds to arrest me just so I can escape the psycho that lives in my house.

"I love you." Erika whispers against my lips.

"Love you too, Sirena." I place a kiss to her lips, she tries to pull back but I grip the back of her head and deepen it relishing in the sound of the demon beside her gagging. Erika pushes against my chest, I hold on for a second longer before letting her go and shooting the glaring demon at her side a wink. "Watch out for the boogeyman under your bed." Erika gasps and smacks my arm but I just smirk.

"I hope your gun doesn't misfire." London snarks, the smile drops from my face as she shoots me a wink and skips back inside the house. I snap my gaze back to Erika who is biting her lip to keep from smiling.

"See, you heard that shit right?" She purses her lips and nods. "Well, what are you going to do about it?" I seethe.

"I want to adopt her." I splutter and choke on air, it takes me a minute to get myself under control. I shake my head and for good measure, tap each of my ears because I know I must have heard the love of my life wrong.

"Say what now?"

She huffs. "I want to adopt her after we get married so we can all be Murdochs." I throw my hands in the air and stalk toward the waiting SUVs.

"I fucking pray I get shot." I mumble.

"I heard that!" Erika shouts. I wave her off over my head and climb into the back of the car, Havoc and Sin are both shaking with silent laughter.

"Not a fucking word!" I yell, Uncle Vin and Luka snicker from their seats in the front, I glare at the backs of their heads. "Just fucking drive." I snarl.

"If it helps, you get to take out your frustrations on the Albanians in an hour." Sin supplies.

"I need to hurt some motherfuckers and then get drunk as fuck so I don't have to deal with the madness that awaits me at home." The four of them all burst out laughing, I want to tell them all to shut the fuck up but honestly, I can't fucking blame them.

I met some woman and fell in love, she made me feel and showed me that I could love someone who wasn't my family. The problem with that is, the woman has such a huge heart that she brought a stray home and fell in love with her as well.

"London looks up to you, Royal." I frown over at Havoc.

"Bullshit." He shakes his head denying my claim.

"She does, she pulls all these pranks on you so you see she is worthy to stay here with you and Erika." My brows draw in.

"Huh?"

"She knows what we do, she's hoping by showing you what she can do you will think she is useful and allow her to stay here. Can you honestly say that you would send her back to Columbia where she would be made to turn tricks on a corner and be okay with that?" My features harden and my jaw locks at that thought. "That's exactly what I thought, spend time with the kid and you might just change your mind." I thought Chaos leaving would see Havoc hide and not be as forward but it seems London being around has brought out this protective fatherly side of him, I think he may just be okay.

Epilogue

CHANEL

I'm nervous.

I never get nervous, that shit isn't in my makeup but tonight nerves thrum throughout my body. I can't even look Royal in the eye, when he finds out what I've done he's going to kill me and I'll be branded a *rat.* He never questioned me when I told him that the Albanians were planning a raid at the ports, some of the slippery fuckers were able to slip through our borders.

We took them down with ease, it was an easy kill but we made sure to wear masks so Terry could video us executing each of the scum so we can send the tape back to their boss with a King of Clubs attached and show him what happens when you try to fuck with the Memento Mori.

Rather than riding back with my dad and my cousins I chose to take one of the other cars telling them all I had a meet with a source, I lied.

I fucking hate lying to them, I detest it but if I don't do this then we're all fucked, he knows who I am and by default, he knows exactly who Royal and the twins are. I trusted him and betrayed that, he ruined me.

He is the only person in this world to ever break me and I will never allow anyone to have that type of power again. I fought against Royal and Erika because I never want her to do the same thing to him, he's my best friend and I would kill any bastard that ever hurt him.

Pulling to the abandoned warehouse, I see his black SUV, he stands in front of it with the headlights casting an eerie glow over him. I grit my teeth and leave my car idling as I climb out and make my way over, I stop in the middle not wanting to get any closer to the son of a bitch. Of course, being the self righteous bastard that he is he closes the space between us leaving, the moment I draw my gun he freezes a foot away and shakes his head.

"Seriously, Sin?" I close my eyes, I hate hearing that name come from him. My family thinks Royal was the one to give me that nickname but it wasn't, it was Connor.

"Just tell me what you want so I can get the fuck out of here." I snarl, his blue eyes have a look of hurt that flashes through them before he masks it. He runs his hand through his thick blonde hair and shakes his head.

"I never wanted it to be like this."

I scoff. "Then you shouldn't have fucking blackmailed me!" I shout.

"I had no fucking choice, Chanel. This is my job, I didn't know you were going to be there that day." The day he is referring to is the day at the airfield where Emilio took Chaos, Connor is the reason i missed the kill shot on Erika.

"You could have let me go." I whisper, a whoosh of air escapes him and he drops his gaze to the ground.

"I couldn't do that."

I push away all the hurt and latch onto my anger. "Just tell me what you want."

"I need to know where Chance is."

I keep my face blank as I answer. "I don't know where he is."

"Don't lie to me, Sin." He growls.

"Fuck you, I have no idea where that bastard is. I gave you the details of the raid tonight, you got the Albanians, that was the deal." A regretful look crosses his features, I shake my head as betrayal burns through my veins. "You're not letting me go, are you?" He tries to reach for me but I step back shaking my head. "You fucking lied to me. This is my life, Connor. If they find out what's happening, I'm dead. Blood or not they will kill me!"

His eyes darken. "I'll never let anyone hurt you, Chanel." He clips out.

I hold his gaze and drop my mask allowing him to see for the first time the pain he caused me, I wasn't always this heartless bitch. Connor made me who I am today.

"You already did." I whisper, a bang sounds out and then I spin around toward the way I came with our guns in the air, the second the person steps into the light my blood turns to ice.

"Hands up!" Connor shouts, I snap out of it and leap in front of Connor, his eyes widened. "What the fuck are you doing?" He yells.

"Put the fucking gun down." I plead.

"What? Do you know that guy?"

A whoosh of air escapes me as I nod. "Yes." I breathe out.

"Who the fuck is he?" Connor demands.

"His name is Vincent Murelo and he's, my father." Connor's eyes narrow as I feel my dad come up behind me, "Please." I plead, he hesitates for a second before lowering his gun.

"Chanel–."

"Just go, Connor." The look in my eyes tells him all he

needs to know, I have no idea if my dad is alone or if the others are with him, Connor grasps that concept and is smart enough to take my queue. He never turns his back to us as he makes his way back to his car, dad and I say nothing as we watch Connor drive away, when his taillights disappear dad grips my shoulders and spins me around to face him. I avert my gaze not wanting to see the look in his eyes.

"Chanel." The don't fuck with me tone of his voice has me slowly turning back to face him, the look in his brown eyes flays me. Disappointment, unease and worry shines stares back at me.

"I don't want to hear it." I growl as I pull out of his hold and try to head back to the car but he blocks my path.

"Who the fuck was that?"

"No one." I shout.

"Bullshit Chanel, he reeked like a fed, you know what will happen–."

"I didn't have a choice!" I scream in frustration.

"You always have a choice." He shouts just as loud.

"No, I didn't."

"Explain this to me now." The deathly calm tone of his voice has me tensing. "Now!"

The words spew out of me. "He has evidence against us, they found Chance's body four days ago and the feds are trying to pin it on us."

"Why, you?"

I don't pretend to misunderstand what he means. "He came to me because we knew each other."

"How?"

"I met him at UNLV when he was undercover investigating the Vargas heir but at the time, I didn't know he was a fed."

"And then what happened?"

Pain blooms inside my chest as I tell my dad the truth. "I fell in love with the enemy and he broke my heart."

"You let him live?" The disbelief in his tone is clear.

"I couldn't kill him, mom was the first shot you ever missed and Connor Ryker was mine." I know he is a fed and if the family finds out that I'm trading information to keep them all safe they are going to kill me, all I had to do was pull the trigger and keep my vow to my family but no matter how hard I tried, even when Connor told me to do it I couldn't because I was madly in love with the fucking enemy.

I'll figure out a way out of this and I'll make sure he gets Broken by Sin.

Also by Samantha Barrett

Paranormal Romance

The Dream Series

A Beautiful Dream

A Twisted Fate

A Beautiful Nightmare

Redemption

Anarchy

Brutal Savages

Savage Lies

Brutal Truth

Savage Beast

Brutal Beauty

Mafia Romance

Murdoch Mafia Series

Played By The Bishop

Tormented By The King

Tortured By The Knight

Tempted By The Queen

Turned By The Pawn

Ruined By The Rook

Murdoch Mafia Novella

Stalemate

Memento Mori Series

Reign Of Royal

Broken By Sin

In Havoc Lays Chaos

Fairytales With A Twist

Condemned Beast

Sports Romance

Playing For Keeps

Offside

Touchdown

End Game

Hail Mary

Blindside

RH Sports

Hate Us Like You Mean It

Love Me Like You Mean It

Acknowledgments

Firstly, I have to thank my team because without them I wouldn't be where I am today. You ladies read every book I write and love each of these men and women as much as I do. Thank you to my Army for always standing by my side and believing in me, you truly have no idea how much each of you mean to me!

My baby daddy! Booooy, I love you like a fat kid loves cake and that ain't ever gonna change. Thank you for coming up with the idea of the calling cards, it was genius baby. Thanks for always pushing me and supporting me through all of my crazy ass work times and my goal for releasing a book a month this year.

My gremlins, I love you both more than you will ever know! So much of you both are in each of these characters and I love that so freaking much honestly. Keep being you my babies.

My alphas, thank you so fucking much for always standing by me and dealing with my shit. I would not be here without you, I love you! Thank you all for planning this series with me and dealing with my meltdowns. Also, a special shout out to Keith for all your input, your sister wife appreciates you boo.

Jaye, thank you for sprinting with me and helping me through this series and holding my hand when I thought I would quit.

Leah, you bad bitch! I fucking love you Wednesday, no one can match your talent babe I am still so in awe of you and how you create these masterpiece book covers! Thank you for always being there babe I love you so fucking much xxx

Lizz, you the real MVP girl, thank you for always being ready and willing to edit these books and sticking with my crazy asf schedule, I appreciate you so much xxx

My readers, thank you so so so much for reading my books, I know you think this is just words but it's not, you mean the world to me and thanks to you, I get to live out my dream of being an author, thank you!

Sam xxx

About the Author

Samantha Barrett is a dark romance, PNR author who loves to write out-of-the-box stories. She is originally from the land of the long white cloud, New Zealand. She is totally fluking her way through this whole author gig, if she isn't writing you can find her kicking back with her kids and husband with a bag of chips and a glass of wine in her hand.

Sam loves Twilight and is a TWIHARD proudly.

www.ingramcontent.com/pod-product-compliance
Lightning Source LLC
Chambersburg PA
CBHW062011190726
48283CB00002BA/642

* 9 7 8 1 7 6 4 1 0 7 5 9 4 *